Reencounter

ANGELOS IOANNIS

Copyright © 2011 Angelos Ioannis
All rights reserved.
ISBN: 147525458X
ISBN-13: 978-1475254587

Oh Archangel Michael, may your Force guide us
when we are ready to open the door
with our hand trembling on the handle
May You show us the next room
in the labyrinth of life
when we are looking at the open door of opportunity with fear
May You use your sword to let our shell die
and free the butterfly that is sleeping inside it

Table of Contents

Table of Contents	**5**
Acknowledgements	**7**
Preface	**9**
Prologue	**11**
Part I: The early years 1687 - 1708	**13**
Part II: The spring	**35**
II.1 The meaning of travel	*37*
II.2 The art of finding	*44*
II.3 The balance of walking	*51*
II.4 The Other	*63*
II.5 The absence of time	*72*
Part III: The summer	**77**
III.1 I was normal	*79*
III.2 The encounter	*84*
III.3 The flow of energy	*90*
III.4 The vision of reality	*97*
III.5 Love and marriage	*106*
III.6 The moment of choice	*110*
III.7 The drama	*113*
III.8 The school of sorrow	*118*
III.9 The elephant	*125*
III.10 The path of pleasure	*130*
III.11 The choice comes back	*137*
III.12 The glass world	*140*
Part IV: The autumn	**145**
IV.1 The moment of the Lucifer	*147*
IV.2 The loss of the opportunity	*157*
IV.3 The path of confusion	*165*
IV.4 The return	*173*

IV.5 The parents	*177*
IV.6 The labyrinth of life	*180*
Part V: The winter	**189**
V.1 The Challenge	*191*
V.2 To be or to become	*198*
V.3 The beggar of love	*207*
V.4 Repeat and rewind	*214*
V.5 The Reencounter	*219*
V.6 The end of the winter	*229*
Part VI: The later years 1710 – 1720	**235**
VI.1 The awakening	*235*
VI.2 The voice of Truth	*246*
VI.3 The boomerang revealed	*253*
VI.4 The End	*258*

Acknowledgements

I would like to thank everybody who consciously or unconsciously contributed to the creation of this book: People who crossed my path during the one year that I was authoring the book and gave me the answers to the questions I had in my mind. Gifted humans like the Buddhist monk Venerable Bhikkhu Sanghasena, who lives in the Himalayan Range in the Indian state of Ladakh and whose words can be found in various places of this book. Or the words of the priest of the Orthodox monastery of Archangel Michael in Symi, who inspired me the parable of Jesus walking on the water, without knowing that at the time of his evening preaching he was contributing to this book. And of course I would like to thank people who consciously helped the enhancements in the final manuscript with their constructive critique, like Melissa Georgiou for her comments about grammar and wording and Manolis Manolessos together with Christos Karydis for their comments about history and culture. I would also like to thank Katrina Johanson for her inspiration creating the cover of this book.

Above all I feel honored to have had Jean Charity scrutinising my text for lingual mistakes. This work has been her final review before she was forced to retire due to health reasons and this strengthened my belief that she was meant to be part of this book and that her contributions were meant to be imprinted in the pages that follow

Finally, I would like to thank the Source of every inspiration on this planet, whose words and deeds come through the mouth and actions of humble humans, like the ones mentioned above and me, all of us expressing His will.

Preface

Mikhaela, a young girl in her twenties, lives in the beginning of the 18th century in the fortress of Malvasia. Located in the province of Morea in southern Greece, it is now known as the town of Monemvasia. During the years 1690 to 1715 Malvasia is again under Venetian ruling for the second time in its history.

Under the second Venetian ruling, Malvasia is flooded with new people and modern ideas that come from the leader of the Italian Renaissance. Along with these people Alessio, a young man from Venice, is appointed to work in the magistrate of Malvasia, which is under the direct commandment of the Doge of Venice.

Prologue

And there I was faced again with the Truth. Again the choice came back to me; again I realized I had thrown away the boomerang only to watch it return, hitting me with even greater force.

Always, the more power I would use to throw it into the air, the further away it would fly, the more time it would give me to breathe, to have a life again, to create my illusion and live in it. To get a little bit of happiness, joy, tranquility, like my parents were always telling me, like all normal people are supposed to be living. And suddenly, right when I would least expect it, this bent piece of wood would return, hitting me on the forehead with unbearable force, causing me to bleed and to hurt, using the same force I gave it when I threw it out in the air.

Alessio used to say: "It is your own karma. What is put around in the wheel of life, comes around. Your actions always return."

And here I was again, holding the same bent piece of wood, seeing again the same old story, bleeding again, in ever greater pain, again faced with the choice, this painful decision that forces me to be the killer, the assassinator of the non-chosen. And again I would be tempted from the same option: To throw this boomerang away, with all my force, so far, hoping that it would never return or that it would return so late that I would be dead, already lost into the eternal, where choice does not exist, where the coach moves by itself and you are the passenger enjoying the scenery.

The choice not to choose, the right to have some more time, the hope that something would happen, someone would help and the decision would not be mine anymore, something or someone else would choose for me. Alessio was telling me: "The wrong decision is better than the non-decision. Ultimately, the river will flow into the sea; there is no other destination. You can only delay it. The only way to be sure for the correct decision is to take the wrong one". But no matter what he said, I was always throwing away the boomerang with all my force, in an illusion that I was safe.

But now I know: It shall always return, wound me with the force I gave it, now I know, the decision shall be made.

Deep inside Mikhaela knew what was right for her. But if only there were no other factors. If only there was one decision simply right, and one simply wrong. But there was not. She knew that the one defining right and wrong was only herself. Or better put: The feelings she would get after her decision was made final. The feelings of an assassinator standing in front of a dead body, knowing that there is no way of undoing the act.

She cried. No she didn't want to be the killer. Once again, she didn't want to decide. With the boomerang in her hand she felt once again weak.

Part I: The early years 1687 - 1708

I was once a simple person. Like everyone else, I too had a routine. First it was school then it was work. Important was that something had to occupy my day and this something should bring joy and should be approved by the others, the people I respected, my family and my friends. People hearing my life story would think that I was a simple person too, somebody normal that was trying for her best and the best of society. Days would pass, months would go and I would be looking at my life, astonished by how fast time goes by, bringing both beautiful and tough moments.

Like most of my friends, I would rarely use exclamations, such as "amazing" or "fabulous", neither would I use negative expressions, like "depressing" or "devastating". Mediocrity would rule my feelings and expressions. "No" was not part of my dictionary. I would prefer a temporary dissatisfaction of myself, maybe a little suppression of my emotions, in order to see others and especially my family to be happy. I was not selfish.

Even if my life was happy, I would say, I could feel that something was missing. Thus I started combining this "something" with needs. I first needed to grow up, but when I grew up I found out that this was not it. I then needed to go to school and meet new friends, but when I went to school and met them I realized that this was not it. Then I needed to finish school, then to find a partner, then to occupy myself with work, then to become independent and plan to get married. Once a need would vanish, a new one would appear. Even if I had to wait a lot – or at least this is how I was judging it – life was generous enough with me and my wish would generally realize, even if sometimes not fully – or at least this is what I would say. But still I could feel that something was missing.

Then I started complaining about my surroundings. If life would not bring what was missing, I would easily accuse somebody else. Sometimes my boyfriend would not understand me, so I would wish to change him. Sometimes my daily tasks were too boring, so I would look for something more sparkling. Sometimes my house, my old furniture, sometimes my friends would cheat, sometimes my father was too strict, sometimes my town was too small. Always in the moments of silence, when I could feel that something was missing, I was trying to attach it to something else in order to explain it. But this something else was steadily shifting as I would advance through life and take actions on my complaints.

The most satisfactory, and at the same time deceiving solution I found was doing. Doing my homework, doing my work, doing a change in my room, doing the daily house cleaning at home, a continuous doing in order to fill in the gap and keep myself busy. I found out that by doing something I was getting satisfaction, and by not doing I was thinking that I was losing my time, feeling that something was missing. The others would praise my doing. They would say that doing is productive, it makes us better, it brings money, it keeps us going forward. Thus I developed hobbies. I learned how to knit, how to cook, I began to dry and collect flowers, and if I still had free time, I would share it with a lot of friends, just to be occupied, just to avoid being on my own, bored by myself, realize that in the silence something was always missing, realize that in the silence myself was absent.

Until one day my self came to find me.

He came in the form of a boy. He came uninvited, like a storm in my calm waters, throwing lightning in my darkness. And there I saw what was missing: a whole new world, a hidden paradise that was unveiled by the flash of the lightning and vanished in darkness right after it. Like an illusion, like a dream that I was sure I had lived, a dream that I knew was reality itself. The storm passed and after it, everything looked normal again. But I was not normal any more. That innocent little girl, always seeking and always dissatisfied was washed away too. A whole new life began, a life devoted not to spending it, but to gaining it. I would empty the full and in emptiness I would find fulfillment. Having seen the light I devoted my life to find the light again. But this time I knew where to look for it. During the storm I had seen that the darkness resided inside myself, along with him, along with what was missing, along with the fallen paradise, the universe and at the end: God.

Born just two days before the end of 1687 in Sparta, once a city famous for its brave warriors, I spent the most important years of my early childhood living alone with my grandmother. Although I missed my parents, I had developed some kind of anesthesia that allowed me to play happily together with the other children without thinking too much of the family I was longing. My parents had left Sparta at my age of three, together with my two elder sisters in search of a better fortune in the nearby town of Malvasia. However, their financial situation did not allow them to take the youngest member of the family to Malvasia. So, I was left in the caring company of my grandmother with a promise that I would join them once I grew older.

Even though my grandmother was old, she was taking good care of me in Sparta; she was cooking for me, collecting vegetables from the fields, working hard to ensure that there would be enough food for both of us. I developed very warm feelings for her. In her heart, I was the only child. It was as if she existed only in order to take care of me. Even if I missed my parents and my two sisters who followed them, I loved my grandmother; she was the only person who was really close to me.

From time to time I wondered how life would be in Malvasia. Although I had never seen it, I was always hearing glorious stories. People said that the Malvasians were as brave as the ancient Spartans. Although Sparta had lost many wars in its recent history, Malvasia's impressive natural fortress stood proudly for centuries and no enemy was able to conquer it without significant losses.

During my early childhood years my family survived through fierce wars in Sparta and the entire peninsula of Morea between the Venetians and the Ottomans. In 1685 the Venetian general Francisco Morosini set his foot on the peninsula and within less than a year he managed to outfight the Ottomans from all the cities of the peninsula, including

Sparta. When the Ottomans left Sparta, the Greeks accepted a new ruler: The Empire of Venice. Even though freedom of speech and language returned to our small city, the war brought to the region scarcity of food and poverty. In 1687, just months before I was born, Morosini crossed the short passage of Corinth towards the city of Athens and in a short operation he managed to conquer the once most important city of Greece, sacrificing its most important monument: The Parthenon. With a bomb that he directed against the holy temple, the two thousand year old monument was left in ruins.

Only one town withstood the wrath of this ferocious warrior: Malvasia.

Malvasia was a legend in the Mediterranean. It was a huge rock formation jutting proudly from the sea with its elevated plateau surrounded by stiff cliffs. Only one small passage of land connected the rock with the mainland. And only one small path could lead any visitor to the plateau of the upper town and the castle. The Greeks called this rock Monemvasia: Translated, the single passage.

Placed strategically in the southeastern tip of Morea, it oversaw the sea traffic of the Aegean Sea. After an almost three year siege, the Venetians realized that it was practically impossible to conquer this elevated peninsular plateau. Therefore they convinced the inhabitants to open the sealed gates of their castle by offering religious and financial independence, if Malvasia joined the republic of Venice. Thus, for the second time in its history, Malvasia agreed to be governed by the Doge of Venice: Francisco Morosini.

Venice had been growing ever since its birth in the tenth century. The production of salt, a resource abundant in its shallow waters, had driven growth and capital inflow to the recently founded city. The "white gold" was an invaluable asset, as it was the only material that allowed the preservation of meat and fish during transport. The trade of salt provided so much money to the city that Venice quickly became an empire, overpowering cities with long history like Rome, Florence and Milan.

Soon after Malvasia agreed to join the Venetian Empire, it became an important node of trade between the Eastern and the Western world. Trading convoys from the East would moor to the harbor of Malvasia before continuing their journey to Venice. The art movement started growing again in the city with many artists visiting Malvasia to paint its imposing elevated plateau, its small alleys and the mansions standing on its top with their flags flattering on their colossal towers.

The shift of power from the Islamic Ottoman Empire to the leader of the Renaissance had opened the way from suppression to love and from protectionism to freedom of expression. Travel emerged with art and trade and Malvasia quickly became the home of independent thinking and religious tolerance. People along with products of the entire civilized world were passing through its busy port on their way between the West and the East. Also, the short one-day route between Sparta and Malvasia had led many Spartans to migrate to the flourishing fort of Malvasia and between them, my parents.

Even though Malvasia was not far away from Sparta, my parents rarely visited us. They had their peace of mind, knowing that I was in good hands. And I was. My grandmother had fully taken the role of my parents. In my heart she was like my mother. But I also kept an empty space for my parents. A placeholder that would be filled in once I would migrate to Malvasia too, keeping my grandmother unmoved at her position in my heart and my parents next to her, but never replacing her.

I did not know if migrating to Malvasia would be better for me or not. I missed both my parents and my sisters, but I had also managed not to think about them too much. I was wondering: Would it better to miss them or miss my grandmother? Choice was not made for me, it was a painful experience to select, to leave one option and go for the other. In my innocent mind I concluded that a life of choices would be a life of pain. I preferred not to choose, I preferred to accept. Subconsciously this led to my first important choice in life: The choice to accept.

Even if we know that one day an ending will come to everything, our mind has the habit of ignoring it, as if that day doesn't exist. Even if it could well be the next day, the mind cannot perceive it, unless a number is attached to it. A vague, unknown date always appears further than a certain and set date even if in reality it could as well be the next day. I figured out that the mind can only work with numbers.

And so was my mind functioning until my age of seven, when my parents appeared one day at our home in Sparta with a bright smile on their face. I would move to Malvasia! Finally conditions were appropriate and I could also join them, along with my two elder sisters and my younger sister who was born while they were there. I could go with them, or better put, I had to go with them. Nobody asked me if I wanted, of course I was a small child, so I was asked to accept rather than to choose.

It was exciting! Finally I would reside with my family, I would have a mother and a father; finally I would be able to play with my sisters. My house would be full of people. The forgotten member of the family finally remembered.

I thought about my grandmother staying alone back in Sparta. Loneliness; that is what she would feel after I would leave. My feelings were mixed. On the one hand I missed my parents and my family, but on the other I loved my grandmother deeply and I didn't want to leave. Even if I would be happy in Malvasia, she would have lost her only partner: me. I felt that by leaving I would be the one guilty for her loneliness and depression.

My parents stayed for two days in our house, until I would gather my few belongings in a small bag. This time the future had a number. In two days I would leave. These two days I didn't sleep.

I still remember the day we left. I cried a lot. I didn't want to leave the hug of my grandmother. Couldn't I take her with me? Fold her in my travel bag? But in a strange way this day felt better than the two days before. Waiting to be executed must be a lot more torturing than walking towards the fire of the Inquisition. That day my feelings were numb, time stood still and the only persons in the picture were me and my grandmother. My senses were gone. I was moving in slow motion.

Maybe because of that day, in the future I would not only detest choosing, but I would also refuse to say goodbye. Even for small events, I would rather say "see you soon" or "talk to you later" than saying "goodbye". Separating by expressing a promise for the termination of the very action. What kind of a goodbye is this? Instead of closing a door I would prefer to just go and leave it open with a promise to step through it again. My life would be full of open doors and promises.

As I was walking away towards the carriage coach I kept my head turned towards the back watching my grandmother waving me off. I adopted one more style of living: To move forth with my head turned towards the back. To avoid looking towards an unfamiliar future. I developed attachment.

During the entire trip to Malvasia I kept on repeating this moment. Me, holding the hand of my father, walking away from Sparta, looking over my left shoulder and my grandmother at the door, just looking at me going away. She was standing still, moving her lips as if she was trying to say something, or better put, as if she was whispering something to herself. She was more than a grandmother to me. She was my best friend; even if we didn't talk so much, we were keeping company to each other. At the moment of separation, I was watching her getting lost in the distance.

The trip from Sparta to Malvasia was a short one-day trip by carriage coach. Since Sparta did not have access to the sea, carriage coaches were frequently transporting goods and passengers from the ports of Morea, among them Malvasia.

But even with the trip lasting one day only, it seemed tiring and long to me. An entire day that had to be lived in order to make my first significant change in life. A tasteless time between the past and the future that was passing by slowly. A lake after the waterfall that I had to cross before the river could resume its flow at the end of it. If only I could sleep now and wake up at the end of this trip. Patience was not my childhood gift.

In the early morning we woke up inside the coach that had stopped near the shore to overnight. Malvasia closed its entrance after dark to prevent pirates and thieves from entering the city and so we had to stay outside and enter in the morning.

Hearing the waves of the sea, I stepped outside of the coach. The view was stunning. For the first time in my life I was seeing such a magnificent creation of God. A huge rock formation rising from inside the sea, just a few hundred meters from the flat mainland. I stood and gazed at the view. The sea was tranquil. Small waves were cruising on its surface approaching the coast. Having lived through all my childhood in Sparta it was the first time I could watch the sea. I felt as if these small waves continued their journey beyond the coast inside my heart, cleansing me to an inner serenity. Such a wonderful and calm feeling!

My father thanked the driver, packed our belongings fast and we got prepared for the short walk up the hill. My father was a handsome young man. Being in craftsmanship, he was very muscular, capable of protecting all his five women in his life: my mother, my three sisters and me. He was a wonderful man, sometimes very direct and commanding, but always right and aiming to our well-being. In fact he had devoted his life to our well-being. Even if I missed him so much time apart, now that I was standing next to him I was feeling protected; it was this security that I was missing during my stay in Sparta. Walking next to him, it felt as if everything went back to normal, as if we had always been living together.

Soon we started climbing up the road leading to the main entrance. As I was walking up I gazed at the cliff over my head. This fortress should have been immune from any threat. Nobody would be able to climb this stiff cliff and enter the city without using its one and only walkable path, the path to the main entrance. I thought that God was unfair. The Spartans had to develop the most efficient war machine of the ancient world to defend themselves, whereas Malvasians only needed to enjoy the natural gift of God.

When we entered the main gate I felt a smooth breeze of Venetian air. Some people were smiling, some singing, some walking in pairs. Everyone seemed to enjoy life and work in an unusual, relaxed way. In this city I would live through adolescence, in its narrow streets I would discover love and with love I would discover myself.

Standing in front of my house I welcomed a new life. Although my grandmother was still standing at her door in my mind, this already belonged to the past. I missed her. I had just made a huge change in my life and if changes were like this, I preferred not to have them. Even if I could see a new era in my life, I would prefer a safe and familiar world. The image of my grandmother standing at the door was already imprinted in my mind. Right outside my new house, my head instinctively turned over my left shoulder. She was not there anymore.

The days in Malvasia flowed like a gentle stream. The city seemed to reside in a world of its own, like an island in the ocean, where nothing else exists outside of its narrow borders. Boats were entering and leaving its busy port, appearing and disappearing in the horizon as if they were sailing towards a distant nowhere. My life and my thoughts were residing in this small piece of land. I rarely thought about my life in Sparta anymore, neither did I feel that I wanted to. This island had become my new world and I was content that this world included my sisters, my parents and my new friends. I was spending my days free of worries, playing around the main cathedral on the central square of the lower town.

The rock of Malvasia hosted two towns and two different worlds, the upper and the lower town. The upper town was the home of the noble community of Malvasia, which was not small. A lot of wealthy merchants and landowners had chosen this fortress for their home, since it was the safest place against the pirates. Never had the pirates managed to cross its single passage to the upper town, which would remain closed and well guarded during the night.

The upper town looked magnificent from the sea. Its western side hosted the castle and on the eastern side stood the mansions of the rich with their tall towers extending into the sky, looking like palaces on their own. On the eastern brink of the upper town, on the edge of the cliff, the church of Madonna del Carmine was overlooking the Mediterranean. This was the church that the rich people would visit. It was my favorite spot of the upper town too. Sitting on the outer yard of the church, I was contemplating the entire Aegean Sea, imagining its countless islands. Sometimes I would wake up early and go there to see the sunrise and the boats leaving in the morning as soon as the first rays of sun appeared.

Like most common people, I too lived in the lower town of Malvasia. Its busy harbor hosted boats from all over the Mediterranean that docked either to overnight or to sell their merchandise in the market. Sometimes I was going there to look at all these different people, trying to recognize where they were coming from and what language they were speaking. Travelers from Venice and Naples, merchants from Alexandria and Tripoli, sailors from Constantinople, and traders from Damascus and Jerusalem, all would mix into this harbor somehow managing to communicate, sell their goods, and enjoy some local food and wine before going back to the sea.

In the heart of the lower town the central square was the meeting point of Malvasians, dressed formally to take their morning walk and visit the market of the busy commercial street that was extending from the central square to the main entrance of the town. The main cathedral of Jesus standing on the one side of the central square was visited by the majority of the inhabitants of the lower town during the Sunday mass. Next to it the chapel of St. John served mainly for smaller ceremonies. In the evenings we would sit with my girlfriends at the southern edge of the square, which had a magnificent elevated view to the Aegean Sea. Sitting there we were mostly discussing about the young boys sometimes looking at us out of the corner of their eyes, as if we would not be able to notice their interest.

Boys were the central topic of discussion with my friends. I had many wishes and dreams in my head and a handsome boy would always accompany me inside them. I would never build a dream where I was the only participant and even though my dreams would remain roughly the same, the companions would change as often as the seasons. But everything was created and lived inside my mind, sometimes leaving its borders to be shared with my close friends, but never with my parents and sisters.

Even if the upper town was always overlooking us, we would rarely visit it. It seemed as if we were not welcome there, even if that was not verbally expressed. I was a girl of the lower town and I was proud of it. I was playing only with children of the lower town, not because of preference, but because the children of the upper town seemed so distant, even being really very close. Also the boys of the upper town would not attract me so much. To my eyes they were too closed into themselves and I would not even try to approach them. To me they were distant, but maybe to them I was distant too.

Even if in reality I was from Sparta, I felt Malvasia as my home. The vibrant commercial street of the town had merchandise from all around the world. Rugs from Persia, shishas from Egypt, paintings from Italy, even tea from China and incense from India could be found in the countless stores of this street. Walking around the commercial street, I was trying to imagine the culture of all those countries and the life in their cities. And then, in the afternoon, I would go to the lighthouse, on the eastern edge of our island, to stare at the vast sea and travel with its waves to the world. Just sitting there I would drink tea in China served by thin eyed dark-haired ladies, I would stand in front of the pyramids of Giza feeling the dryness of the desert, I would cruise around Venice on long gondolas listening to the songs of handsome gondoliers.

I had heard a lot of stories about Venice. The sailors were always talking about its well-designed system of canals that served as streets. Venetians were living in houses built literally inside the water. For me it was difficult to imagine how people could move around in those water canals. Instead of horses and donkeys they would have gondolas and gondoliers driving these long and narrow boats to transport goods and passengers. They said that the gondoliers were always singing songs in Italian, greeting the ladies that appeared out of the windows to hang their clothes.

The ladies in Venice had a distinct position in the society. They were treated equally to men both in the society and in the law. There were many cases of women seeking justice in the pien collegio, the appeals court of Venice, and in the majority of the cases the court decided based on testimonies of both men and women. Even more impressive were the cases where the patriarchal court of Venice decided in favor of women asking for a divorce from their husbands due to various reasons such as adultery or violence. In the Ottoman Empire not even was divorce not allowed, but also the men were legally married to more than one woman and were praised for being violent to their wives. What a different world.

Women in Venice were also treated equally in education and work. The virgin unmarried ladies, the nubile, were sent to school since it was considered that the educated girls were more capable of finding the right man for a successful marriage. Especially in noble families the private teachers were educating both the brothers and the sisters inside the house. Work was also important for women without children. In a city where ninety five percent of the homes were rented both the man and the woman had to work for the couple to be financially independent and able to get married. Before marriage women were usually helpers in homes, or in some cases even running their own businesses, such as tailors, bakers, jewelers, painters and fruit sellers. More educated women could work for the government as scribes and secretaries. After marriage most of the women worked at home knitting, spinning, sewing, selling clothes and furs, preparing and selling bread and cheese in order to support their family income.

Though the parents would generally not approve a marriage if the couple was not financially independent, there were numerous cases of unmarried couples that were meeting in the night. The gondolas played a significant role for these secret encounters. Most of the gondolas had a wooden chamber where the couple could hide during a romantic ride across the canals. The gondoliers were secret witnesses of many love stories between single or even married mates. Married women were more frequently seduced by single men, since the nubile had to prove their virginity on their wedding night.

The masks were playing a key role for these secret encounters. Even if the Ducal Palace had legislatively banned the usage of masks on the streets outside the period of the Carnival, nobody seemed to fear the tortures imposed by these laws. In a city where the Carnival lasted for half of the year, such legislation was useless. Masks were still used all year round by the majority of the women when they participated in public events or even meeting their friends at night. No wonder that even gondoliers would not be able to name the culprits of adultery.

But who was able to impose legislation in this independent republic? The Doge, who was the elected governor of Venice, was controlled by the council of ten, which was in turn controlled by the Great Council of all noble people of Venice, numbering more than two thousand members. The Doge was only officially representing the state, in practice however the state was governed by the noble merchants who had the financial power, living in the palazzi along the Canal Grande. The Doge could not even leave the Ducal Palace without the permission of the council.

Even if Malvasia was part of this independent republic, it was just a small town compared to the rich and prosperous Venice. However, as part of the Venetian Empire we were following the republic's legislation and the ducal orders. After the shift of power all the patriarchic regulations of Islam were abandoned and the role of the woman in the house and the society was upgraded. Even the feminist movement of Venice came to be known in our town and the books of the feminists Lucrezia Marinella, Moderatta Fonte and Arcangela Tarabotti were available in the public library. Teachers from Venice came to staff the schools and Latin became part of the curriculum. Malvasia was vibrating in the pulse of Venice, luckily without masks.

My father had not received formal education, however he encouraged all of us to go to school. And so we did. In school we learned to read and write both the Greek and the Latin alphabet. We learned about the sciences of ancient Greece, philosophy, astronomy, mathematics and geometry. As part of the peace treaty signed with Venice we were allowed to learn and practice our own religion, so we all chose the Christian Orthodox teachings. We also learned about democracy and the republic political system of Venice, which impressed me with its complexity and the level of freedom it provided to the citizens.

The more I would learn about Venice, the more intense would my desire grow to escape from our small fortress and merge into the extravagance of the empire's capital. I knew of several examples of family friends that had a member of their family sent to Venice either to work or study at the university. I too promised myself that one day, when I would find the love of my life, I would live together with him in Venice.

It was at the end of my school days that I met Elias. He was a tall, handsome and sporty young man. His straight look combined with his captivating smile was enough to make any girl think about him for the rest of the day. Originally from the nearby town of Mystras he had a dark complexion that gave him the appearance of a man, even if he was still only a boy.

All the girls in my class liked Elias. When he was passing by on the street many girls would discuss with each other about him, but he was never talking to us, like other boys tried to do. Since our class was the only female class of Malvasia we were the center of attention quite frequently. But not for Elias; when he was passing by he would never turn his attention to us. From the start I noticed that he was different.

It was in a swimming competition that I finally managed to talk to him for the first time. My sisters and I always liked to attend swimming competitions not only to participate in the public events of Malvasia, but also to observe the handsome boys that were competing. I always wished for Elias to win, however I never expressed it to my sisters. There was a certain amount of competition in the family and they'd better not know. It was my secret; even before talking to him, I had fallen in love.

It takes time for two shy people to meet and such was the case for us too. Just before the end of my school days I realized that there was not so much time left for to act. I could sense that he was interested, but also I could sense that he was reluctant. And so I found the opportunity to talk to him and take the first innocent step. However it only took little time for our relationship to become intimate and before the school year ended, my dream had come true. We had both fallen in love.

Soon I started to come home later and spend less time with my family and my sisters. My father started questioning me but I always had an excuse. I knew that he would not like Elias. He was not from a wealthy family neither was he from Sparta. His family had migrated to Malvasia from Mystras seeking for a better future, which is just what our family had done too. His father was neither rich nor educated, working in the fields of the nobles to cultivate vegetables and grapes. But my father was not a noble either; he was a mason working in the excavation and construction of stones. I did not understand the logic of my father. He always wanted something better for us, as if we could not determine ourselves what was better.

But on the other side I could give right to my father. I was a tall, thin girl, already a woman, with sharp dark eyes and straight dark hair. I was the tallest of my sisters and my father was always proud of me. Whenever my family traveled to Sparta a lot of noble people were picking me among my sisters, asking for my hand. My father was then arranging a dinner with the ones that he judged trustworthy, so that they could come into our house and I could meet them. However, to my disappointment, they were all old and ugly. I figured out that to be noble and rich should go together with having a fat belly and suffering from hair loss. I preferred to die poor with Elias than to be enslaved to a rich monkey. No, I did not want to become noble.

Soon I started looking for work. It did not take long for my family to find out about my relationship with Elias and prevent me from returning late at home. We either needed to find a new home together and get married or we could not maintain our relationship any more. My father was concerned about my virginity. A used woman was considered worthless. But I had already decided that my future was with Elias. And thus I did not mind sacrificing my virginity for him. He was my first and only love.

It was at my age of twenty that luck came to our side and my dreams came true. The government office of Venice in Malvasia announced that they were looking for a scribe to copy government documents and official correspondence. The woman working there got pregnant and she decided to leave the position in order to dedicate herself to her family. Young, educated women were always preferred for this position, since they were considered more diligent and careful than men and also they were more eager to perform a work that men would describe as repetitive and boring. I figured out that this was a gift of God for me and I immediately applied. This was my chance to become independent, stay with Elias and create my family.

Elias was already working at the harbor, but his income was not enough to support a household. Since I had no house as a dowry and I was one out of four sisters, getting married and living together with Elias meant being able to pay for the rent. And even a small house inside the walls of Malvasia would cost at least seven golden ducats per year, an amount higher than the annual income of an unskilled worker.

However, luck was at my side and in October of 1708 I was informed by the magistrate of Malvasia that I was selected for the position. It was the happiest day of my life! Even my family was excited with my achievement. My father suddenly changed his behavior towards me and started to even approve Elias and my plans with him. My salary would be five lire per month, amounting to over ten golden ducats per year. Together with the income of Elias that amount would suffice for us to start a household. My father starting approving my plans as feasible.

At my twenty first birthday in December of 1708 I invited Elias to my house and we finally blew the candles on my birthday cake together. My life with him could finally start! Everything was planned and foreseen, or at least this is what I would think in a life full of changes.

Part II: The spring

Blessed are the patient and the wise. The fields look empty and clear, but really something wonderful is happening inside. In this fertile soil of Malvasia, may the seeds break, may the water penetrate their hard exterior, join their interior, may they surrender to their mother, earth. For the mother is aware of her holy task: To break the seed and let the flower inside free to bloom. Because the seed is not born to remain a seed.

The time has come, the winter has gone. And even if mother earth appears dormant, she is not. May the citizens of this fortress allow their seeds to die, allow the time for the mother to bear and create. May they forget the past, because the past is in the seed. May they live the present, may they look at this soil and say: The time has come and the earth shall flourish. May they spread the seeds and only wait. Because the earth is a female. And as a female she lives in cycles. As much as we wanted her to feed us in the cold winter, that was not the time. But now the time is coming and looking over the empty fields we know that they won't remain empty for long.

II.1 The meaning of travel

Even if it sounds absurd, I do believe in the female ability to feel important changes in life. My own feeling is like the feeling of expectation even if there seems nothing to be expected.

Most of the times I hated this feeling. I did not feel comfortable with big changes in my life. I never liked the uncertainty that accompanied them. For me no news was good news and many times I would attribute this feeling to other reasons, such as my last night sleep or someone that had irritated me.

But life never proved my feelings wrong. Just as I was entering my office in the morning, I saw a new person sitting at the long table inside the velvet room that was used for temporary guests. Even though I only took a quick look in the room, I recognized that this person was not local.

The government office of Malvasia was often visited by Venetian people. A lot of times Venetian officers would come to perform a temporary assignment and then leave. Venetians were easily distinguished. Their clothing would always be colorful and distinct, as if in Venice the clothes were all unique, as if no two clothes were made the same. I figured out he too must have been Italian. His nose was straight and thin and his hair was fair. Northern Italians always had a fair complexion compared to local Malvasians. With his image in my mind I sat at my desk.

The days that followed I was taking a quick look into that room as I walked by to my desk. Surprisingly I found that he continued to be there. Venetians would usually leave after a month at the most, but he continued to come there long after one month had passed. Curiosity grew inside me.

Until one day of the spring I met him inside the small pantry room. He was quite busy preparing a drink that looked promising, but didn't remind me of anything I had seen. It must be an Italian specialty, I thought. I wondered if he had noticed my presence. He seemed quite devoted to the procedure. That day the office was almost empty. It was a public holiday for the Orthodox. The kitchen was occupied only by the two of us.

- Coffee, he said interrupting my thoughts. This is what this herbal drink is called. It helps you to stay awake, even if your body needs to rest. It is made out of a bean that recently reached the shops of Venice, coming from the Muslim world.

Venice was the first city to receive many of the items of trade. Its central location and its busy port made Venice the entrance of many products of the eastern world to the west. I had heard about coffee from the elder people in Malvasia. They said that during the times of the Ottoman Empire it was available in selected shops. As it was an expensive herb, coffee could only be bought by a handful of people and it was the favorite drink of the sultan.

- It looks quite promising, I said looking at the dark drink inside his cup. And its smell is indulging!

- It is indeed. I bought it from Venice from the single coffee shop that exists in the city. It is imported from Africa. Do you want to try it?

I felt very special. This handsome man in front of me definitely knew how to make a woman feel special.

I accepted the drink. His name was Alessio.

The days that followed were interesting. We greeted each other every morning and we met in the pantry room very frequently. Even if we hadn't made an appointment, somehow our schedule would coincide and we would randomly go to the pantry room at the same time. He was always offering me that coffee drink, which I always accepted. Initially I found it bitter but soon I got used to its taste, as it was keeping me awake through my busy day a lot more effectively than the usual herbal drinks I was drinking. Also it was a very good excuse to meet with Alessio and discuss.

My days began to be pleasant. I started to develop more energy at work and somehow the daily tasks would not tire me out any more. I had even found work to be a getaway from my increasing fights with Elias. After four years of relationship we were fighting every day more and more, usually over small issues. It felt as if everything that happened when we were together was a good reason for a fight. This was devastating for me and many times I would even cry. But I knew that on the next day I would go to work, I would meet Alessio and he would prepare for me this dark herbal drink from Venice. Then we would talk over new and interesting topics coming from a different world.

I quickly noticed that Alessio liked to talk a lot and that with him I was a good listener. If only I could be a listener when I talked with Elias, then fights would never occur. Alessio was seamlessly shifting from one topic to another like the posture changes of an experienced dancer and I would follow this dance, lost inside his words, as if I was dreaming and yet awake at the same time, as if I was watching doors to be opening inside myself, doors that led me to journeys that I had never experienced.

We started going out during the lunch break and talk. To be precise he would be the one usually talking and I would be the one listening. Strangely enough, he seemed to be grabbing my thoughts, stealing my questions and ideas and leading me through a different path, an interesting alternative that would open a new perspective inside me. I was his favorite topic and even if he did not know me at all, he seemed to know perfectly my way of thinking, my ideas and my feelings.

His favorite tavern was opposite the main cathedral on the central square. It was serving local food. Even if in the town there were some choices of Italian food, he preferred to taste the local food. For him travel was a choice and he had chosen to go out of Venice in order to experience.

- The world is full of experiences, Mikhaela, he once said to me. Life is so unique and interesting that it is a pity for us to constrain it to a small shell of surroundings.

» Tasting the different makes you compare and comparison is a war; a war between opposites. The different keeps you in motion, it keeps you in a swing. You are swinging between the one opposite and the other, like the dancer that moves smoothly on the dance floor, never standing in one place. The different prevents you from getting stagnant. When you get stagnant you start feeling too weak to make a change, even when a change is needed in your life. You start hating changes but what you really hate is yourself not having the power to perform them and sustain them. This is the result of getting stagnant.

I hated changes, but how could he know that? Indeed I felt weak in front of any significant change. I felt weak both to perform it or to avoid it. I hated changes because I was overpowered by them.

He continued.

- The motion, the travel, the war between the opposites keeps you in shape, it trains your force. When you keep traveling you feel powerful enough to make changes in your life that otherwise would be difficult even to imagine! By traveling you gain the force to change even the foundations. You are a nomad. You change your house, your friends, your food, your work, everything, and then no change can make you fear or feel weak.

» Most important of all, what you change is your own identity. In fact this is what changes: Yourself. You become somebody else. And you see your world with somebody else's eyes. When you get angry with your partner the most difficult task is to see the world though his eyes. And since your position is the only place you have been, you try to explain his proper world with your own eyes.

» This is wrong, Mikhaela. In order to be able to change position you must be able to dance, you must be a good dancer. And if you are not, how do you expect somebody else to be?

» Soon you will find that this is a flow. Everything and everyone around you remains fixed. In your world you are the only one that can change. Even if you completely switch the people surrounding you, the new people tend to be quite similar to the people you were interacting before. You keep on attracting the same kind of people. This is because the only one who can change is you, Mikhaela. In your world there is nobody else than you and you have to be able to change instead of expecting a change from the others. Travel is your partner in this effort. It keeps you in shape and able to shift seamlessly from your point to the other's.

I had never thought myself that travel has such an important role in our lives. My mind went again to Elias. Yes, I wanted him to change. Not totally, but certainly I didn't like him to be stubborn.

- By traveling the one who changes is you. And since the only one that can change in your world is you, you will then notice that the other people are miraculously changing as well. That may seem irrational but it is not. You will stop attracting the same kind of people and you will start attracting different persons. But even the people who will continue to be part of your world will have changed. This is because the ones staying stubborn at their place cannot accept your change and they sooner or later go. When you observe a change in the people surrounding you, you will know that you have managed to change yourself. Even if you lose yourself in this process, this is the only way to really find you. And even if you lose your partner in this process, this is also the only way to really find him. Through the dark tunnel comes the light. With distance you come closer.

This seemed absurd but somehow it made sense. I understood that finding yourself must involve missing yourself a lot. And also I understood that this was the path to finding your partner too. Life should be painful that way. To find him through losing him, was it the only way?

- Mikhaela, we are always unsatisfied with what we have and we always want to have what is distant. And soon we understand that it is very difficult to change what we have, even if we strive. Then we look towards what is distant and that provokes travel. Travel is far more than the change of location. In fact travel can happen even without moving at all. While traveling we lose what we have and what was near becomes suddenly distant. What we wanted gets what we have and what we had gets what we want. The swing changes dynamic but what swings is our self and the dynamic is in fact our desire. And since desire moves the world, the world is swinging too. Back and forth like our travel, everything remains impermanent, obliging us to travel too, bringing frustration when we want to remain stagnant. In the Far East this swing of the world is called the Circle of Life. It is the result of our travel, our swing in desire.

I had heard before of the Circle of Life. Eastern sailors would point towards the upper town and say as if talking to the nobles: "What goes around comes around". In a swing, I thought. Traveling back and forth like the movement of a boomerang.

- Human relationships are like that. The more you swing, the more they swing too. The more you change, the more you see your partner changing too and the more you remain stubborn, the more you observe it in your partner too.

I had not told Alessio about Elias. Even if I did not admit it, I tried to avoid mentioning this topic on purpose. Generally, instead of acting, I had the habit of delaying things. That was always dragging my life situation and at the end it would make it too difficult for me to change anything.

- And one last thing, Mikhaela: Travel requires decisiveness and action. If you are unable to decide and act, you are unable to change and thus you are unable to travel. The ability to decide is an ability to kill, and if you are not able to kill yourself, you will not be able to change yourself either.

Soon I discovered that he was able to guess my thoughts without me speaking them aloud and that he was defining my personality better than I was doing it myself. Our conversations were always interesting. And I could feel that the time with him was bringing me forward. Lunch became my favorite time of the day, including my life at work.

II.2 The art of finding

Although we would not go every day for lunch with Alessio, we would often meet at the tavern. I too liked local food and the tavern on the central square was my regular choice as well. In fact, I did not want to go too frequently to the tavern alone with Alessio. The town was small and I was already receiving annoying questions from my colleagues, especially from the men. Anna was more discreet and never questioned my devotion to Elias. Of course I liked to talk with Alessio, of course I liked to hear new ideas coming from a progressive part of the world, but that was the limit. I did not intend, nor did I want to destroy my dignity. And although I admitted that he was behaving in an attractive way, there was nothing more than this.

Less than one month after my introduction to Alessio, I went to the same tavern with my colleague, Anna. Anna was a happily married woman in her late twenties. She was born in Crete, the southernmost island of the Aegean Sea, and migrated to Malvasia with her parents right after her birth, when Malvasia was still under Ottoman ruling. Her brownish, sunburned color easily revealed her southern origin.

When we entered the tavern, there he was, waiting to receive his food. Alessio's tranquil appearance was always attracting me. Even his clothes, usually in white, were completing an image of a well-rounded, peaceful person. With a gentle gesture he invited us to his table.

Anna seemed worried. Something was obviously occupying her mind.

- Is everything right? I asked her
- I am looking for a new house, she finally said. We are expecting a baby in a few months and our house just can't fit so many people. But no matter how hard I tried it seems there are no decent houses in the town.

- Indeed, I nodded in agreement. After the war with the Ottomans many houses of the lower town were ruined. Only the upper town mansions remained intact. Our father had a difficulty rebuilding our own house too.

I was also looking at the house market. Since I started working and we had enough money to support a rent, we decided with Elias to live together. However, after my father changed his opinion about Elias, I was allowed to meet him and return home late at night. Thus we decided to wait until we would find a suitable home, since the lower town of Malvasia was still being rebuilt.

- I am also looking for a small house you know. When you move out of your house maybe you can notify me, since I also have difficulty in finding one.

Of course I did not mention that I wanted to find a house together with Elias. Did I do that because I did not want to expose my personal life or because I was hiding the existence of Elias from Alessio?

Our discussion continued on to the difficulty of finding necessary things or people in life when looking for specific qualities. Especially when the time is running out, it almost seems impossible to find anything worthwhile.

Alessio observed us carefully. His eyes always started shining when he was about to start speaking. I observed these brown islands on a white sea. I could easily get drunk in these waters. It was true that Italian men were attractive.

- Seeking is what we usually do in our lives, he finally said. We seek for a partner, then for a house, then for proper furniture, then for a better house. And this goes on. We live a life of endless crave and seek, and even when we do find, we still crave for something more.

» The procedure of seeking though is a ceremony itself. In this ceremony you don't only identify what is available, but you also identify your own needs and desires by watching, imagining and trying out. If you are open, it is your blessing since you may find what you never guessed you wanted. If you are closed, it is your curse, because it stands in between you and your object of desire. When you are determined about what you want, you decide not to participate in the ceremony of seeking, you wish to skip the procedure as a whole, instead of enjoying it, you suffer. You rush through the market wishing to terminate what you are just doing and to finally find it in order to move on. And when you don't find it, God comes in opposition.

» Tired of the procedure, you sit to rest. You are exhausted, one step before quitting, you need a break. And there your eyes focus on the small table of the merchant opposite to you. It can't be true. It's there! One last piece. You found it! In fact it has always been there. What was absent was you. In your rush, you were running beyond it. Whenever you are seeking for too long, it is because you are rushing. Whenever you are not finding, it is because you don't want to seek.

He was obsessed. His eyes were shining more than before. Anna and I were tuned in. In fact this was true. I even did not want to search. I wanted to find. The only purpose behind searching was to terminate searching, thus to find.

Then he fixed his eyes at mine. I felt as if I could see myself inside them.

What you have always been looking for, your greatest desire, is right in front of you. Right now.

My mind stopped. He sounded like a bell vibrating me from the inside. Right now in front of me it was him. He was right.

- You need to look no further. You just need to stop and concentrate. In fact while rushing you passed by the same spot several times. And you oversaw it. Finding comes through the acceptance of seeking.

We both stayed in silence looking at him. Anna was thinking about the house. Maybe he was right, maybe she was not willing to seek either, she knew exactly what she wanted, she only needed to find it. And I was thinking about him. Maybe he was right, maybe what I had always been looking for was right in front of me. I looked at his shiny eyes. Was he the one? Anna interrupted the silence:

- You are right Alessio. I don't want to search. When I began searching I was not prepared for it, I wished it to end soon; I wished to find quickly a house like my current one, but just one room bigger. I had this in mind and I would not accept anything similar. In fact I did not wish to find another house. I wished my current house to have one more room.

Alessio smiled in agreement.

- Anna you need to know that finding follows the mastery of four virtues that are gained during the ceremony of seeking. Seeking will continue until you prove that you possess them.

» The first virtue you gain is wisdom. It extends your knowledge of what you want, to why you want it. What you are seeking is sometimes a means to a greater goal you are trying to reach. What you perceive as a goal is sometimes just an intermediary step, a battle that is just part of a war.

» Wisdom is gained while seeking when you are open to all options, when you consider them and imagine them in your life. While you are trying them out, even mentally, you gain knowledge of what you really want. God always gives you the right to fulfill your ultimate wish, but He reserves the right to give you a different means from what you expected. When you perceive that you lost the war, in fact you need to see that you just lost a battle. A battle sometimes needs to be lost, in order to win the war.

Did I need to experience in order to get wisdom? Was this virtue gained only through trial and error? I was not allowed to experience. I only had one option in this life. My religion said that getting married happens once and for life. And how could I get wisdom from this? How could I find the love? My religion did not allow it.

- The second virtue you gain in this ceremony is concentration, he continued. Without concentration you can't find. Sometimes you walk through the market, but your mind is not there. Your mind is traveling in your wishes and desires, you are not concentrated.

» In these moments you need to close your eyes, take a deep breath and sync it with your heartbeat. By concentrating only on what is in front of you, you leave the dreams of your mind behind. They can only distract you. Keep in mind that God wants us to reach our goal and move on and for that He readily gives us the means. Since the means are in front of us we need to concentrate on what is there, not in our dreams. Becoming attentive is the only way to observe your surroundings, listen to the signs of the universe and feel what is there for you.

Was he there for me? Was Elias the one for me? They were both there. Yes, I was dreaming about love, security and a family. I did not want to be alone. But I was also dreaming about Venice. Even if I was looking for a house in Malvasia, I was still dreaming about a life in Venice and Elias was not at all fascinated with my dream. So many conflicting dreams, how could they all realize? I needed to concentrate. Was Alessio sent by a distant God listening to my conflicting desires? I wanted to flee.

- The third virtue is faith. If there is one single, most difficult, most important, most rare piece of the puzzle, this is it. Faith is the knowledge that something is happening, before it really happens. Faith is not expectation. Faith is knowledge. If you expect that God will give you a message, you will keep on expecting. If you know that God is already giving you a message, but you are just not ready, not yet capable of hearing it, then this is faith. Faith lies in the extension of your mind's perception, beyond the six senses. Faith is a force of creation. Faith gives you the knowledge that a mountain has a tip, even if you don't see it, even if it is covered by the clouds.

Something is really happening before it happens. That was interesting. Very interesting.

» Patience, finally, compensates your lack of faith. Those with absolute faith do not need to be patient. It is lack of faith, lack of the knowledge that you are already on the path of receiving your wish, which calls for the necessity of patience. Once dreamt, your dream is immediately put on the path of fulfillment. Minute by minute, day by day, year by year, when you are patient, you are building up your faith. And out of nowhere, once ready, you receive. This is the fourth virtue gained in the ceremony of seeking.

I stayed in silence. It was the first time that I was observing myself, my true feelings, and I did not have the will or even the power to stop it. In a way, I was meditating. It was one of these rare moments, like after culmination, when silence says everything. Yes, I was in love. Although I loved Elias, although he was my childhood love, although I selected him to accompany me in my dreams, it was the first time in my life that I was feeling an inner silence. All my inner voices, the ones usually mixing up my mind and my life, were silent. With this silence I felt as if I was already receiving my dream. I felt that I was already there. Faith was there. Patience comes with faith.

- I can see many human beings in this small wonderful peninsular island, seeking for something. Some people seek gold, some people a child, some people work. But it is the mastery of the four virtues that has not yet converted the seekers into finders.

I could not lift my eyes from his mouth. Inside it, I was lost in the seven seas. This horizontal line between his lips, this small part of his attractive face, resulted in forming my world. I could live inside it. The clock stopped ticking.

I had not finished my lunch, I had barely eaten. But I didn't feel hungry any more. The inner feeling of completeness had penetrated my entire body.

-"Won't you eat?" he asked me.

- No thanks. I need to get back to work.

- Thanks, Alessio, said Anna. Now I realize I was too closed in my search. I will start all over again. And now I somehow know that I will find.

This talk had carved my mind. I would refer to it for the rest of my life, always when I was seeking for my dream without being able to find it. I would refer to it later, when I was seeking for him. I had fallen in love. But I was not feeling guilty. It was my little, well-kept secret. Although the wise said that thought triggers the word, and word triggers the action, I did not pay attention to it. I was full, I was experiencing a new feeling and I would not give it up. I sat at my desk and started again my daily work. From now on, and for the rest of my days, my thoughts would follow him.

II.3 The balance of walking

Life is a collection of moments. And if we add up those moments for an entire lifetime, we might not even end up to a year. But I was sure. This spring was full of those moments. The moments when we would meet in the kitchen, the moments when we would meet in the tavern, even the moments when I would think about him. All these moments provided a silence in my day. It was exactly this silence that I was missing when I was with Elias, it was exactly these special moments that I had long lost from my life with him. Maybe I was too used to him. Maybe love is deemed to fade away. But I had to admit that my life was now refreshed. Did I have to feel guilty about it? Not in my innocent mind.

I began feeling happy when going to work. After my introduction with Alessio, I was giving him short thoughts while working. Although these thoughts barely lasted for some seconds, they were enough to give a breeze of fresh air to a tiring day. They were like the short naps that give energy to the body within the day, the moments of breath intake that provide oxygen to the blood. I was more energetic, it was like working while waiting for lunch time, the time I would meet him. And this gave the meaning to the day.

- Do you see the bells, he asked. It was again lunch time.
- Yes, I can see them, I replied.

The bell tower was directly opposite our usual tavern on the central square. I was seeing this bell tower every day I passed by that church to go to work.

- I know you are passing by every day around this corner, he replied. But how many times have you made a short stop in front of them, contemplated them for a moment, then continued?

Not a single time. They were always there, even tomorrow they would be there, I knew them so well, why should I stop?

- So, how many bells are inside the bell tower?

I stopped to think for a while. How many? I felt ashamed. I didn't know it. Neither did I know the tower's history. Neither the name of the priest ringing them every morning. I was seeing this bell tower every single day, but I knew nothing about it.

- I don't know, I finally said in a soft voice.
- It is because you are used to walking fast. In fact most people are like this. Whenever we walk, we are walking fast. We are even used to eating fast, drinking fast, thinking fast; our life, we live it fast. We tend to minimize each present moment to such an extent that we make it non-existent. However, life is only the present. There is really nothing else in life. Thus, minimizing the present, in reality we minimize life.

» Tomorrow when you go to work, wake up half an hour earlier and walk to your office very slowly, one step at a time. So slowly that from the moment you lift up your foot from the ground until you move it forward and step it on earth you will let at least one second pass by.

So there I was, the next morning on my usual path, one hour earlier, to compensate for the extra time I needed and to ensure that people would still be in their homes, so that I would avoid being seen walking like a ghost. I didn't want them to make comments about me. I wanted to be ordinary. I valued the opinion of the others so much, that I tended to lose my own self and desires.

My experience that morning was unexpected. I didn't imagine that it would be so difficult to walk slowly, standing on one foot while moving the other in the air, waiting for the eternal second to pass by in order to place it on earth again. I couldn't find my equilibrium on one foot. "I can't walk like that!" I thought. I was almost always about to collapse on one side. This was a torturing exercise. Sometimes I hated him for making me deviate.

After much effort, I reached St. John church. I stood by and stared at the bell tower. Amazing! I realized: The bell tower didn't have a clock. I went around the tower to find the clock on the other side. "It can't be true! Where is the clock? Did they forget it?" I thought.

I felt like crying. For the first time in my life I was really seeing this bell tower. It was a stunning building! For the first time in my life I was using this word: Stunning! My life was so blunt. It was the first time I was using an exclamation mark in my thoughts. Did all this happen only because I walked slowly?

I could not continue this exercise. I left, walking at a normal pace, and I arrived at work early.

- You know why you couldn't find your equilibrium, Mikhaela? Alessio asked when he met me in the office.

How did he know? Was he watching me? I remained silent staring at his expressive pair of eyes, as if I was waiting for them to talk. If I could keep one part of his body, it would be his eyes.

- You are used to a two-paced walk: The previous step and the next. You walk as fast as you can, suppressing the step in between. This step is called balance. Between the past and the future step, there lies the balance, the present and suppressing it, you suppress life. To live the present, to just be, to balance in the step in between is a lesson you need to learn. Right now you don't live in balance. You are either on a previous or on a next step while living. Balance is not part of your life. You live a life of imbalance.

I felt like crying. If I were his girlfriend, I would be out of tears. Tears of happiness. Indeed this was me. I was constantly swinging between the future and the past and that led me to imbalance. I was always switching from one thought to the other, back and forth, but I was never able to stay in equilibrium. I figured out: That was not only me. I was not the only one unable to balance myself in the present, to make a firm decision now.

- In order to stay in balance you just need to focus. The reason you can't stay in balance while walking is the same as the reason you can't be in the present while living. You are always looking around but never at something. You don't focus your eyes on any object. Try one thing: In tomorrow's slow walking exercise add one component: Maintain your eyes fixed at a certain object in front of you and at a certain distance. This object is called the goal. Don't deviate your eyesight from this object until you reach it or until you take a turn and it is no longer in front of you. The object can be anything, the cross of a church, a hole in the wall, a branch of a tree. But it will help a lot if the object is outstanding, impressive and special in your eyes. Your goal ahead will drive your journey in the present.

And so on the next day I managed to really walk slowly for the first time in my life. Only one day after I gained my ability to truly see the bell tower, that tall structure that stood twice per day in front of me, only that next day was I able to walk for the first time in my life. I was able to focus and stand in balance, even for more than one second. How fascinating was my everyday path! Full of flowers, olive trees, passages, curves! Everything was beautiful, both God made and manmade.

- Mikhaela, once you learn to walk, you learn to live as well, as life is indeed a walk, a journey. When you stay unfocused, when you suppress the present step, then you become imbalanced. If you fear that you will fall, if you fear that you will fail, then you bias your next step, you rush your lifted foot to the earth, you avoid equilibrium, you avoid the present. But every step, even the next step needs balance. When you carry on making next steps, your life gets a life of futures that turn to pasts. You don't focus on the beauty of the current moment, on the real risks in it. You focus on the challenges of the future and the sorrows of the past and because you can't really see the risks of the present, you fear of everything in it. Learning to walk encompasses learning to focus on your goal, the goal right in front of your eyes, not the goal of your entire trip.

» When you realize that you have lost the joy in your path, that there is no meaning in it, that memories don't stay, that time is passing by too fast and that you are not able to understand it or stop it, then in fact you need to realize that you are walking too fast. No matter how many steps you take in this path, you will be walking even faster, in an ever-increasing effort to avoid the present, until you reach a point where you will see a dead end, when you will understand that there is no further step in the path that you have chosen. Having still not learned to balance, this time there is no next step, you hit yourself on the wall, you can't go forward any more. And this time you fall, and most of the times you hurt yourself too.

Indeed. Sometimes I would walk so fast through life that I was led to decisions without really taking them. Sometimes I wondered why I had taken a certain path and most of the times I would find that I had naturally flown into it without thinking too much, without selecting it, it was just a next step in a series of steps that were leading me towards a dead end that I could not foresee.

- You need to learn to walk, you need to learn to balance, Mikhaela. It is not your choice. It is your obligation, your mission; you are losing life without it. You cannot walk forever at a fast pace, there will not always be a next step, you cannot continue ignoring the fact that there is only one step in life, the current one. And in order to balance you need to focus. And in order to focus you need to find something impressive, outstanding, special, fascinating in your eyes, your goal. And after finding it, you need to discard the rest of the picture, you need to focus only on it. This is called the state of Being. And if you need to change your object of focus, you can. But remember to focus again. You cannot keep your eyes on two points simultaneously. It will certainly make you fall. You don't have to find something that looks perfect, not every path has perfect objects in it. Just the most impressive one will do.

» But if this object is not impressive any more in your eyes, look around, seek and then switch it. Until you focus on another object, you will feel the imbalance and this is natural. After all, the decision to switch was yours and as such, it was wise. This is the only way, Mikhaela. It is the way of Being. Only in this way you will be able to walk slowly and be in balance, really be in the current step, enjoy your ability to see the bell tower.

» In the state of Being you focus on the present, measuring the current step and not the previous or next one, being and not wanting to be, neither hating to have been. The state of Being is an exclamation mark by itself. When you feel it, you feel its joy, you become careless about the future, forgiveful about the past. And the only component you missed until now in order to feel it, was to focus.

Indeed. While he was speaking these words I was totally in focus. And I could feel the balance inside, I could feel the state of just being. I interpreted it as: Being in love. With him?

- I have written a small note to accompany you in the rest of your walking experience. I wrote it in Venice but I will give it to you and I will devote it to you, Mikhaela, he said.

He was always devoting something to me. In fact I felt that he had devoted his entire life to me. Why? I felt I did not deserve it. The note was titled: "Learn to walk".

Learn how to walk.
Learn it again.
Do it by forgetting what you already know.

Begin your walk at your favorite place.
Choose it by intuition.
Begin only after you come to a full stop.

Look around you.
Some paths are calling for you,
some leave you indifferent.

Follow your heart.
Be faithful to your feelings.
Examine.

A small unnoticeable path may lead you to a beautiful garden.
Make a wish.
Wait until it is fulfilled.
Never doubt that it will get fulfilled.
'Cos then, it won't.
Walk slowly.

Whenever you need to stop, stop.
Whenever you walk too fast, also stop.
Then take a deep breath.
Look around you.
Then walk again.
Do not start if you don't remain first in silence.
Silence improves your ability to hear.
Avoid the noise and…
Walk slowly.

Watch the people.
Find and stare into the true faces.
They might stare back at you because you are true too.
But most probably they won't notice you.
Because they look into themselves.
And this is why they are true.
They are a few.

Ignore the lost souls.
They will look at you but soon,
they will look away.
Because they are only looking around.
They are many.
Walk slowly.

Go through the market.

Observe the goods.
Stop at the ones that draw your attention.
Try to find their value.
Buy them at par, knowing their par value.

When you like something try to acquire it.
Many times the cost of it is high.
But the higher cost of not paying for it
is to think about it for the rest of your journey.

The worst thing you can do is to acquire something similar.
This similar will never be it,
and this will give you a reason to think about it
as long as you hold this.
If you did so, discard this.
If you missed the opportunity to get it then think away.
As long as you think about it,
your walk will be miserable,
you will try to walk fast
and you will oversee other very interesting goods.
Once not acquired it can only hurt you.

Trying to forget it will only keep your thought attached to it.
Stop and take a deep breath.
Cry if you feel like it.
Scream.
Walk slowly and look around.
Then you will forget it.

Never fear when walking.
Negative things can only happen to you
if you fear them or
if you feel miserable.
Once you spoil yourself with miserable thoughts stop.
Cleanse yourself, then continue.
Never walk dirty.
Walk clean, and…

Walk slowly.

Never think of what you have to do next.
It will only make you walk faster.
If you are under time pressure,
terminate your walk,
even if you have not reached somewhere.

Know one thing:
There is no time.
Time is an invention of man.
It serves very well for people to communicate and meet.
But once you put time to guide your walk,
it destroys it.

Never estimate when you will reach your destination.
Your destination will be reached only after a series of events,
not after a certain time.
Constraining your destination with time
can only make you not reach it.
Walk slowly.

Don't ever choose a similar goal.
This will never replace your destination.
If you haven't reached your destination then this could mean that
you walked fast and skipped the events.
If so, then you have to go back.
If not, then maybe your destination is not it.
You cannot know your true destination in advance.
You will only know it once you reach it.
Your destination is your destiny and you will reach it
if you don't impede it.
Don't get frustrated, it will only delay your walk.
Always pay the cost and most important:
Don't acquire substitutes.
Walk slowly.

*If your walk becomes unpleasant,
don't try to walk away from it.
You have to go through it.
Don't walk faster.
But look away.
There is something there in the background that looks pleasant.
Focus on it and head there but always..
Walk slowly.*

*Don't be afraid to walk into paths that you don't know
or you are not supposed to trespass.
Unless you are told otherwise, you are supposed to.
But respect your obstacles.
If you are prohibited to enter a path, then this path is not for you.
And thus it does not lead you to your True Destination.
Even if it does, then this is not the only one.
Whatever is there for you is open and welcome.
Whatever is not for you is full of obstacles.
Do not follow it.
Then keep in silence.
And listen to the signs.
They are there to help you.
And continue to…
Walk slowly.*

*And if the time comes to rain,
let it rain.
Stop your walk, you can resume later.
Now try to protect yourself.
You can walk both in the storm and in the sunshine.
Depending on how brave you are, it is your decision.
If you know your power, you know what to do.
Respect yourself and respect the power of God.
And when the rain stops, continue to…
Walk slowly.*

Dream.

You only need to know what makes you happy.
And be patient for it.
And pay the cost of it.
And do not accept substitutes.
And so, walking slowly, you will find that your dream is there,
waiting for you, and staring at you, waiting for you to acquire it.
In fact it was always there waiting for you.
You were just not noticing it or
you were not brave enough to ask for it.
Sometimes man is brave enough to go through the storm,
but not brave enough to go for their dream.
And man accepts substitutes.
And man walks faster.
Never accept substitutes, and…
Walk slowly.

And when your walk reaches its end,
realize it and accept it.
Be grateful if you liked it, be thoughtful if not.
Sometimes you reach your destination, sometimes not.
In case you reach it, don't feel disappointed
if it doesn't meet your expectations.
This destination led you to a wonderful walk
and this was its purpose.
In case you don't reach it, don't feel disappointed either.
Because with every walk you reach somewhere.
And this somewhere is indeed a destination.
A destination that has moved you forward.
Closer to your dream.
Closer to your True Destination.
Closer to your destiny.
And this will lead you to your next walk.

Because every walk
is part of the walk of life.

I folded the note into my chest. I promised myself that I would keep this note with me all the time. Even now, in my most critical moments in life I read it. And the answer comes to my mind.

It was already night. I went home. My lunch times with Alessio were extending to my home, they were penetrating my life. Alessio had become part of my life. Subconsciously I was falling in love with him. I started to neglect Elias. I didn't want to, but I admit I did. Alessio was talking right from inside myself. Sometimes I wondered if Alessio was indeed residing inside me.

Blowing off the lamp, I whispered my night prayer and fell asleep.

II.4 The Other

- Mikhaela, look at this group of people talking at the next table.

It was lunch time again and we had met in the usual tavern. Even on days full of work my mind was still getting distracted around the moment when we would go for lunch with Alessio. Initially I was not paying attention to it, but soon it started affecting my work and even my relationship with Elias. Soon I found out that I was thinking about Alessio even when I was with him.

Alessio always liked to observe the people surrounding him. He was telling me that all people deep inside were the same, male or female, younger or older, belonging to a higher class or a lower class. I was always struggling to believe this. For me all people were so different!

- Observing the others is a great way to observe yourself. You have once been there, behaving in the same manner, just remember and you will find that moment. Even if not, you might be there in the future. What makes people different is their different experiences in life. Behavior is usually only the reaction of millions of different actions experienced throughout the entire life.

» I call all these received actions during life, "experience". Our experience forms our own world, our own version of truth. What the experience in fact forms is the Other. The Other is a personality living within our body and using it to react to our experience. For the Other the entire experience, both past and present, is judged equally, combined in present terms as if everything was happening right now. The Other sometimes is just playing back a reaction to a similar past experience in present terms. I call this "projection". The Other is a plain reaction mechanism. It is not based on reason. And sometimes, indeed, our actions are unreasonable. And many times we regret them wondering why we performed them.

The group at the opposite table was having a loud discussion. They must have been talking about the present political situation. The story was always the same. These discussions were like groups of monologues. Each party was throwing something in the air. Somebody else would interrupt and throw his own something in the air. The sentence would usually begin with "Yes, but" or "I agree, but". I was always wondering why people claimed agreement when the whole sentence after "but" was a disagreement.

- Mikhaela, remember, the Other inside us is just a reaction mechanism, not an intelligence based on reason. The first part of the sentence, the "Yes", only affirms that the action was received and combined with all previous experience and that the Other is ready for reaction. The Other does not wait for the sentence to be completed because the Other does not need to comprehend in order to react. It just needs to combine.

» In fact the Other does not have the ability to comprehend. The Other has a predetermined number of reactions, ready for attack, just as the cannons of this fortress that surrounds us have the ammunition ready by their side to shoot immediately once an enemy-like boat appears. The word that is expressed as agreement, "Yes", is not actually an agreement. It confirms the matching of the current experience with a past experience, which triggers reaction.

» Everything that comes after the "but" is the reaction, usually a playback that refers to all experiences, not only the current one, but the entire one. Thus the reaction is not necessarily relevant to the present situation or the present person and sometimes this is hard to understand and even harder to accept. However, this is how the Other behaves.

I remembered my fights with Elias. I loved him but still we were fighting often and our fights indeed seemed like parallel monologues, as if we were freeing unexpressed energies that were boiling inside ourselves, like the lava inside earth waiting for a small hole on the top of a mountain to erupt.

Indeed our fights never referred entirely to the present situation. They were always starting with a present problem, but they were always spreading through issues we had during the entire four years of our relationship. We were playing back the same things, again and again, only dressed in different clothes in order to look different. This was the way to believe that after every fight the problem was "solved", and thus it should not appear again. Not in the same clothes.

- Mikhaela, the Other is not able to solve problems. Its only ability is to match them and repeat a certain reaction. How many times in your life are you really acting and not reacting? Once you understand that the Other is not reacting to the present experience but to the entire experience, you will see why the Other is unable to solve problems. Likewise, the Other is not reacting to the present person but to the entire group of persons that have behaved similarly, even said a similar sentence, moved their hands in a similar way, even as far as only wearing similar clothes, having a similar odor of their body or having the same mark on their face. For the Other everything and everybody is the same, the Other works based on degree of similarity and not on degree of relevance. The Other's reaction is triggered from the present, but the reaction itself refers to the entire experience. For the Other everything similar is equal and for this reason we sometimes behave irrationally.

Indeed. Sometimes I would look back to my reactions with Elias and indeed they were exaggerated. But it was also his fault. He too exaggerated most of the time. Our relationship had started as love and it had ended up being a constant fight.

- The Other is fighting with its past experiences. The Other was not always strong enough to fight and win. So now it is replaying previous reactions, irrelevant, impersonal, a race to win against whom? The Other is fighting with itself. Look at these people. Their Other selves are fighting with the Other selves of the rest.

The discussion at the next table had become louder. Now they were not even saying "Yes, but", they were directly going to their playback, constantly changing its clothes. They were not even listening to what the others had to say. They were pretending to listen to the others while in reality they were just using this time to assemble their thoughts in order to throw their own attack. They would not even wait for the other party to finish. As soon as they had put together their thought, they would interrupt in order to throw it in a bilateral monologue. Or sometimes they were only waiting for a magic phrase of their counterpart that would trigger the attack, already prepared in their minds. In a louder voice, they would interrupt and begin their attack basing it only on the magic phrase, disregarding tenths of other sentences and thoughts of their counterparts. Of course. They had not even paid attention to what the others had to say.

Of course. I would not even pay attention to what Elias had to say when we were fighting. Why was he saying that? What did I do wrong, or better said what experience of his had I triggered? What did he truly want to say? To whom was he speaking? Was he the one saying that or his Other self? Nothing. I would wait in the corner for the magic moment just like the cat is observing the rat before it attacks it, waiting for the most adequate moment to jump on it. Why does the cat always want to attack a rat? What did this little grey animal do wrong? Nothing. Even if I would take a piece of rope and move it on the ground, the cat would still attack. It is not the rat; the cat reacts to the moving tail. The tail and the moving rope, they all look similar. Everything that looks similar is the same.

The cat was me.

The discussion at the next table had nearly finished. People would have to go to work. The lunch was over. But I knew: Even if they would sit there for hours, days or weeks, the result would be the same: They would never reach anywhere, they would never agree. They would go back and resume in their next gathering with the same playback, singing the same song.

-Mikhaela, the Other is not meant to agree. In fact the Other cannot agree.

» The Other is alone.

Alone. The Other is alone. Yes I felt very lonely after fighting with my boyfriend. Then I would seek refugee to Alessio. With him I never felt lonely. I would stand still, he would grab my thoughts and begin talking, I would lose myself in his words and forget everything else, all past worries and future thoughts, I would lose myself in the present. Instantaneously I would merge myself into him, I would enter his warm mouth and dive into his expressive eyes, I would not feel a lonely unit any more, I would feel again whole.

- Mikhaela, I want to talk to you about this loneliness.

Once again he grabbed my thoughts. I realized I had not spoken a word since we sat at this table. But a stream of thoughts was coming into my mind, like a flowing river of fresh and cooling water. It was the opposite of what I felt with Elias. There I would not think. I would only observe the rat, waiting for its tail to move, waiting for the magic moment and then attack. Yes. This was the Other me. The Other cannot think, it can only match. The tail equals the rope.

- These people, Mikhaela, feel very lonely. I have observed them, every day they are eating in groups, they try to never have lunch alone. Even if one day they eat alone they feel very strange. They are looking at the others, they think that the others are watching them, noticing the fact that they are eating alone. If you go around the tables you will notice that these people will always look at you if you point your eyes at them. Inside themselves they are scared that you observe their loneliness, the fact that they are eating alone, when everybody else is eating in groups. Being different, not like the others, triggers their loneliness. Therefore they only want to be ordinary, normal, like the other people, they never want to stand out alone, because for them alone means lonely and this is their true nature. When they are talking they are leading monologues, thus even when they communicate with others they are still alone. They are trying to hide the fact of their loneliness behind the others and this is why they are lonely.

Was he talking about me? I realized that I never went to lunch alone. I would never like to sit alone at a table facing three other empty chairs. I was facing my emptiness. I was feeling weird. I would rather take the food with me and eat it at my desk than eating it alone in the tavern.

- Loneliness is the constant state of the Other. The Other tries to cover this cold state with thick blankets, by doing things. It tries to occupy itself, to fill its constant emptiness with the material. The Other is a big mouth eating and drinking to fill an always empty stomach. Have you heard about the gluttony in the Roman Empire?

- No, I guess this story has not yet crossed the Adriatic Sea.

It was the first time I spoke that afternoon. My food was already cold, but the conversation was interesting. I realized why I kept on losing weight.

- Well in the Roman parties of the knights they were having entire days of eating and drinking. They would sit the entire day at a long table in the dining hall eating meat and drinking wine. When their stomachs were full they would sit up from the table to go to the vomitory. They continued this process for the entire day, eating, vomiting, eating. Eating for eating. Working for working. Having sex to have sex. Talking for talking. A life of pointless actions with one sole point:

» To act. To do. To perform. An empty action in order to fill in the emptiness. The avoidance of the lonely. A covering with a blanket. The thicker the blanket the more it will cover the loneliness. The more blankets the better. A satisfaction in quantity. A material society. The emptiness expressed. The Other in its point of culmination.

By that time Alessio was obsessed. His eyes were shining again.

- Mikhaela, the Other is lonely. Understand it.

Tears came to my eyes. It was true.

- You know what the biggest fear of the human is?

- Fear of death? The fear that everything we create will one day cease to exist?

- Great! But what lies behind the fear of death?

Why did he always search for what is behind things? Behind always has a behind. This is endless. For me sometimes behind there is a wall.

- The greatest fear of the human race, the source of all fears, is loneliness.

- Loneliness?

- What you fear in death is the fact that you will die alone, that you will leave everything and everybody behind and enter a state when you can only exist without them.

» Would you mind dying, if you could die with me?

I would die right away if I knew I could be with him. I would never feel lonely. I would always feel full. An eternity with Alessio; that was a dream rather than a fear.

- I would die with you right away, Alessio!

Why did I say that? How about Elias? I was exposing myself. I figured out, it was better for me to keep my mouth shut.

- Exactly, Mikhaela! The whole energy of the fear of death is powered by the fear of loneliness.

Silence followed. It was true. I did not want to be lonely. I avoided being alone. I always tried to do something. To act on the denial of my state. To deny the state of loneliness. I was so afraid of facing the truth and I would do anything to avoid it.

- And this is the pointless doing. Doing only in order to do. Only covering the empty. Until it gets exposed again. Walking in order to walk, stepping forward and backward but never stop, never stay in balance, never focus. Acting in order to avoid the most obvious and shining truth on earth:

» The fact that the Other is lonely.

The Other is lonely. I was the Other. Alone I felt lonely. Yes, this would all match now in my mind.

- The Other is not only feeling lonely. The Other is loneliness itself.

» Remember that God is a state, not a third party. A state of Being. And as such, it cannot be reached by a pointless doing. God, Love and Truth is the same state of the Being. You can only be in this state and by being any of these, you are all of them together. God equals Love equals Truth. This is the holy trinity.

I got the feeling of understanding.

- In this state you can never feel lonely. God is alone, for He is the only Being that exists. But He is never lonely. He is the Creator. He is the mother looking at her newborn baby. He has no gender, in Him duality does not exist. He is a Trinity. The Trinity of One.

» Everything that is not God is the Other. And since God is everything that exists, the Other is empty, lonely and non-existent. And since it is non-existent, the Other is constantly craving to be something. It is fighting through its illusionary duality, always living in separation. "I do, therefore I exist". This is the philosophy of the Other.

» The Other is fear, the Other is loneliness, the Other is incomplete. The Truth is Completeness. Whatever is not complete is not True. And vice versa: Whatever is not True is not complete. Completeness is only found in Truth. And Truth only in Completeness. Completeness is the Truth itself.

Indeed. I was incomplete. I was blaming Elias because our relationship was incomplete. I would see even my friends moving on to the next level with their partners, getting engaged, getting married, having children, wanting grandchildren, in their endless craving to complete. In their craving to fill in their emptiness, in a necessity to move away from the loneliness, the loneliness of the untrue, the loneliness inside the relationship, in a necessity to do something, to act. The whole world is turning around craving for completeness, the resistance of loneliness, the subconscious understanding of the incomplete. Only to find the vanity of doing. Only to discover that their actions are empty. And blame the others in an attempt to blame the Other. And then separate.

I realized that I was on this same track with Elias. The track towards emptiness. The track of separation. I realized: The final destination of this path was loneliness itself. I realized. The destination is also the beginning. In a vicious circle, thus in a vanity of action. The loneliness inside emptiness. Empty relationships. Temporary blankets to warm up the constant cold. I had seen so many people getting old in this track. Their reward: They always ended up dying alone. They were realizing and living their greatest fear, the greatest fear of the human race.

Alessio was saying: "Your greatest fear shall be realized". It was true. I was seeing it in them. The only way to ensure fear will not manifest itself is not to fear.

And I realized what was going wrong in my relationship with Elias. It was me. I was fear. I was not Truth. I was incomplete. My Other was relating to his Other in a mutual effort to cover the empty. By doing. That relationship could only end. I needed to change something.

Myself.

II.5 The absence of time

It was obvious. There was no question about it. The game had started, and yes, I was playing along. Why was I fooling myself? My friends were increasingly asking if something was going on with Alessio. I always denied it. In a way it was true. Nothing was going on. On the ground in front of me the fields were empty, not even a sprout stood out of the empty soil. It was spring.

Alessio was talking about the procedure of birth:

- A seed is bound to be a flower once found on fertile ground. What is important is really the ground, not the seed. With time, a seed is brought. The birds, the bees, the ants, the entire nature is there to ensure that a fertile ground will indeed be fertilized. The farmers know it well. If they agitate the surface of the soil, move it with their hoe, prepare the ground, plants will always grow. And even if a plant does not grow in a year, it will grow in two, or in three. And for the long run the farmers know: It is impossible for the fertile ground to remain empty.

» In a world where time does not exist, what is important is the ground, not the seed. Once the ground is ready, the seed will appear.

For me this was weird. In fact he was weird, but his words made sense. What did he mean saying that time does not exist? A day has twenty four hours. A week has seven days. I need to work six of them. Time was in my life, I was bound to it. And it was running fast.

- Mikhaela, what you need to observe is that you are the ruler of your time. You define yourself how much time you want to live.

That was too much. He was becoming irrational.

- What are you usually doing at work?

- I mainly copy the government correspondence, I replied.

- So, imagine that I give you one thousand pages to be copied within a week only. You need to write each page manually, one by one with your pen, observing that the text matches exactly the original without mistakes. Even writing constantly with your hand attached to the pen for the entire week, you might not have it ready. You need to rush, there is no time to come to lunch with me, there is no time for coffee, the time for sleep is limited. You need to finish. How much is a week?

- Nothing, I replied. An instant. In fact I am copying documents every day, every day I have to copy tenths of pages, a day is never enough in my work. Sometimes a month will pass and I wonder, was this yesterday? Imagine a week with so much work. This week will pass in an instant.

- Now imagine that I lock you in an empty room. In this room there is nothing, except four white walls and the closed door. How much is a week?

His examples resembled the religious tortures of the Inquisition.

- Endless! In one week I will go crazy in that room. Even a day inside there would seem eternal. I prefer to copy the thousand pages!

- You see, Mikhaela, the week has no sense. It can range from a small fragment of time to eternity. Time has no sense either. It shrinks and expands, it never remains. Time is non-existent, it is not a fixed measure, not a reference. There is no time. Time exists only in your mind, time cannot measure the chronic sequence. Your life might proceed fast or slow, but time is an irrelevant measure of this speed. Time is needed for your mind. Cut off time and you have managed to cut off your mind as well.

He was right. How much time is a week? I can remember weeks going in a flash and weeks staying forever. I can still remember the day I was migrating with my parents from Sparta to Malvasia. It was only one day, but I still remember it passing like one week. What is the value of time if it can't be used as a measure?

- Nothing, he responded interrupting my thoughts.

I was used to this. I remained silent.

- Time is a measure of doing. When you do much, time flies, when you do less, time stops. And when you don't do at all, then you are. And if you manage to accept this state then you experience the state of Being. Then you can observe time flowing without you, you can observe that time is an illusion, that time does not exist. In the absolute state of Being, the state of God, time vanishes and with it vanishes the mind. The material gets lost and the spirit reveals its qualities. You can reach this state through observation of your breathing. In this state you refrain from doing, you only are. In this state you can see the holy Trinity: Truth equaling Love equaling God. In the state of Being you can experience all of them as one. It is the state where you are that you can experience.

» I will remind you an excerpt from The Exodus in the Old Testament:

"And Moses said to God: Suppose I go to the people of Israel and say to them: The God of our fathers has sent me to you. And suppose they ask me: What is His name? What shall I answer to them?"

"And God said to Moses: I am the Being, this shall you say to the people of Israel, the Being has sent me to you."

» God has named himself "Being". And God is the Being, the state of being. In this state you shall experience Him.

I had also heard about a technique called "meditation". In this technique I would observe something repetitive inside, such as my breath or my heart. This way I would refrain from doing, come in the state of just being. In this state time should vanish. Alessio was saying that it was not easy to reach this experience. The mind would fear the seizure of its existence, the effort to stop its continuous operation, and it would resist. It would then bring up thoughts to the observer. The observer would react, trying to abolish the thoughts and maintain the state of being. Right at the moment of reaction, action would occur and the state of being would be lost, time would return. The observer would stop being and start doing again, doing something to abolish the thoughts. Right at that time meditation would stop and the meditator would return to the material world.

Alessio described meditation as the absence of doing. Even if the thoughts would come, the trained meditator would just observe them, just like observing the breath. He said that thoughts were repetitive too. He would not try to abolish them, neither would he develop sentiments arising from them. In this way he would not lose the state of being, he would not return to the state of doing.

- In the state of Being, Mikhaela, you can observe the material and also observe time. And once you manage to really observe it and not be dragged from it, then you will realize that what is constant in time is not speed but repetition. It is an ever-moving quartz, the constant state of the Being, the producer of the entire energy of this Universe. Everything repeats in a circle of life and time is not there; what is there instead is sequence and repetition. Like the seasons of the year. The summer will always follow the spring, it will never come directly after the winter. The sequence is constant. But who knows exactly when summer will come or exactly how much time it will last? In sequence lies the most important truth of the material world: That everything is first coming and then going, the ebb and the flow, that nothing stays permanent. And in repetition lies the second truth of the material world. That whatever comes, will come again. And if you are ready for it, you will be able to grab it. There is nothing to lose without the opportunity to regain.

All these words were circulating in my mind. Yes, there was no time, I had understood this. I had no illusions. And since time was not there, the seed was not important. On a fertile ground, the seed would come. I knew what he meant. I was already fighting with Elias, I needed a change in my life, I needed a breeze of fresh air. And in my mind, I had found a meaning in my routine: Our daily encounter. And what was behind it: His word. And what was behind his word: My thoughts. Me. Me, encountering myself, waking up, hearing what I always silently thought and suppressed; hearing myself from his mouth, in fact, me, reencountering myself through him.

Indeed I was fertile ground. And by now I knew the role of sequence. I should only wait. Do nothing and wait for the seed to come, for it to break, for the roots to grow slowly out of it, along with the branches, the leaves and the flowers. It was spring. I only needed to wait for the summer.

I decided to be very careful with Alessio and remain loyal to Elias. But how could I cover the fertile ground? How could I prevent the flowers from growing? How could I stop the summer and remain in the spring, keeping the flirt while abolishing the very act of love?

Indeed. I realized that in a timeless world, the spring had already ended.

Part III: The summer

Open your heart, look at the sun and fill your lungs with the breeze of the fresh air. Enjoy the chanting of nature, look at the beauty of the flowers. Everything is now at your favor, the birds are singing for you. Let wisdom guide your path. The summer is a season and as such it shall not last forever. Under the sun nothing is to be left for tomorrow, since tomorrow clouds might cover the sky. Enjoy.

May the citizens of this fortress understand that this is not the time to strive. May they take off their uniforms, leave their horses in the barn, tie their boats to the docks. There are enough vegetables in the baskets, enough meat in the cellars, enough wine in the jars. May they understand that it is time to enjoy what is already there. May they understand that what is there is indeed enough. May the Force free the people from greed and lust. And may you enjoy the summer, knowing that the summer too will cease and the energy that it brings will be needed for the rest of the year.

III.1 I was normal

In God I believe and I shall not commit sin. The wise in our village were speaking of the law of karma. The action performed by you defines the reaction performed upon you. They said that even if it doesn't happen immediately, it might happen after some time and from a totally different source. It might even happen in another life, some said, whereas the Christian priests were speaking about it happening in an after-death environment, which they called Paradise or Hell.

All agreed though that the universe remains in a long-term equilibrium. Once you create a wave, the wave will cruise to the opposite coast, bounce on the rocks and return back to you.

I had one rule: If I didn't like an action as a receiver, I should not be the performer. My encounter with Alessio was indeed challenging my rules. I wanted to be with him but at the same time I knew that I didn't want to hurt Elias. I would be breaking my own rule.

In fact I had a lot of rules, several interpretations of the rules, contradictions among them. Sometimes I would get confused as to which rule should apply in each situation. I was feeling like a firefly trapped in the web of a spider that was observing me every time I stood still and was approaching me every time that I tried to escape out of its complex web of rules. I was afraid. One day the spider would be too close and I would be too weak to escape.

The spider was me.

Or better put: The Other me. Alessio used to tell me:

"You are the joint of two persons, the You and the Other."

"The Other has been formed in your body after years of socialization, following much advice from parents, teachers, friends, elders, the wise; all of those people adored by you, perceived as being better than you, more mature, but none of them you."

"The Other is not You. The Other is a personality created by the others inside your body. What is loved by them, what participates in their society, what makes the money and brings food home, what acts and performs is the Other. You are silent and depressed. And you let them form the Other inside you in your endless crave to receive love."

I was trapped in the web. I had tried to escape in the past. I did crazy things too. But all with negative results. The spider would then get closer. I would lose strength and worst of all: The spider would not return back to its initial position. In its new position it would wait for my next move to approach even closer. This would create fear inside me. And immediately I would repent my "malicious" actions and I would stop them. But the negative results were already there. The karma was watching me closely.

Alessio was saying:

"When you leave the revolutionary plan of You and return back to the normal plan of the Other, then the Other wins and your revolution is considered as negative. As an immediate result it creates bad karma, bad action, for you. Look at all the revolutions in history: The suppressed revolutions created torturing results for revolutionaries. The action and reaction. But the persisted and finally performed revolutions have brought humanity into a new era. Even your religion, Christianity, was established through a long-persisted revolution. In fact, rapid and significant changes require revolution. And in the magic instant of its completion, the revolution performed is not bad karma any more. This happens also with your personal revolutions. They need to go through to their final point. Otherwise the wave will return back to you, you will be compensated with sorrow, fear and reaction; the Other will become even stronger."

It was true. The spider would get even closer; it would look even bigger in my eyes. And then I would fear even more, I would feel even weaker to make the same revolution or another one. Being myself would look even more distant.

In a triumph of the Other and a punishment of myself, it would require a lot of time for me to recuperate and get used to the new position of the spider.

"What people love is not You. They love their creations. Mikhaela, it is very dangerous to be loved for what you are not. For the immediate result inside you is fear. Fear that they will discover one day who you really are. Fear that you will not be able to satisfy their image of what you are not."

He was right. I was looking at the spider. I feared. I feared the gates of Paradise would never open for me. I feared the wrath of God. I feared that something bad would happen to me, some negative karma, maybe repaid in my next life.

"God is Love. And this is You. You are Love. What God is not is fear. And this is not You. This is the Other. God rules through love, not through fear."

By that time I had felt the presence of the Other inside me. In fact, I had been substituted by the Other. In a free society, I was nothing more than a slave.

"God will challenge you as long as it is needed for you to understand who you really are. He created you to realize yourself as a means towards consciousness, a holy purpose for you to become Him, for God to realize Himself. You are a seed put in fertile ground, bound to become a flower. You are not a seed. You are a flower, yet in the form of a seed. You – are – God."

I was not. I was just a small bug inside the web of a spider, full of fear. Or maybe not? I did not know what love was. But I knew I loved him. Or maybe not? But I didn't want to commit sin, I was already about to get married, have children. Or was that the Other? I was already on a fixed path, a path that all normal people follow. My parents were happy. Everybody was smiling. I was also smiling! Was I smiling? Everybody was happy! And I was happy too! Was I happy? My destiny was normal. Everybody was like that. I was normal. What is normal?

I didn't know. My head would break. After crossing my way with Alessio, my life had been filled with questions. At least before I had some answers. Where would all these questions lead me? I feared. But of one thing I was sure: I once lived in stability and now I lived in instability. I wanted to return to the good old me.

"Be sure of one thing, Mikhaela: God will always give you the choice. The first choice is to be Him. To embrace love and abolish your fear. This choice is full of challenge. Because love always needs to be challenged and you, only by feeling love, can withstand any challenge. In this choice you will realize that everything is unstable and ever-changing except one thing: Love."

"The second choice is not to be Him. To embrace the fear and abolish your love. This is the way of the mortal. The impermanent stability, such a fake stability that even you know that one day it will cease to exist. In this track you are bound to evidence the end of it, suffer in the fear of the certainty that it will come, try to hide your suffering and replace it with a smile. You will even believe that everything is stable, but deep inside you will not be able to hide the absolute truth, that the only thing stable and unchangeable in this path is death itself, the end of your perceived stability. You will be governed by the law of anicca, the law of transformation of everything around you, through endless deaths and births. You shall experience dukha, the state of suffering from your non-acceptance of mortality, from trying to create a fake stability, from not accepting that everything is ending and transforming around you, both good and bad. Embracing this way you shall fear death. And at the end, you shall experience it."

I knew I would die. I had no illusions. One day I should be resting beneath the earth, but I was young, that day was far away. Or wasn't it? There is no fixed contract with God.

Once again I felt insecure. Fear had found a warm home in this body. I could feel it and suppress it at the same time. It was my hidden secret, hidden even from myself. That was me. My life was Ok. I was the spider and the bug at the same time. Inside a web created by me, I was both me and the Other, two conflicting personalities that acted interchangeably and always incomplete, fearing and then experiencing punishment either from society or from my own emotions.

I was normal.

III.2 The encounter

I had decided not to act improperly. Until the day Alessio got sick. That day I went to the office and I noticed that Alessio was not there. I thought he was late. Maybe his director had sent him for some inspection to the harbor? The day passed by until lunchtime. I went by his desk to see if he was there and ask him to go out to eat. He was still not there. Then I asked his director: Indeed he was not feeling well, he could not come in that day. After work, I decided to pay him a visit.

I did care about him. He had become a part of my life. Sometimes I would catch myself thinking about him during the day. I was feeling weird because I noticed that I was thinking more about him than about Elias. I really shouldn't do that. My mother was saying that approaching too close to a man could produce negative results that I would regret. She was saying that men always want something, they always have an intention behind their seemingly innocent moves. Sometimes I would try not to come too close to Alessio but this would not last long. Something inside me was eager to be with him, have lunch with him, maybe take a walk to the upper town or just discuss, just listen to him and become hypnotized by his word.

Today was one of these times. I wanted to visit him, I wanted to see how he was doing but I feared the thought of going to his house. I had only visited his house once, accompanied by a friend, but I had never been there alone. What would people say about this? Everybody knew that I was with Elias. Even Alessio knew it by now, I had already told him, secrets cannot be kept for long. But I felt sorry for him. He was alone in this city, far away from his family, he had nobody to take care of him. I was his good friend, I did want to take care of him.

Knowing that he would be in his house alone, I decided to go. In the afternoon, people were taking their midday nap and so not many people were walking on the streets. Taking care that nobody would see me, I knocked on his door. He opened it.

- I heard you were sick and I decided to drop by. I thought that you would not have food and I brought you some soup.

- That is so nice of you, Mikhaela! Come inside. In fact I have not eaten anything all day, I feel too weak to cook. You are so kind!

I felt very good! All these nice words. That man really knew how to make a woman feel special. I stepped inside and watched him eating the soup. I felt like his mother, taking care of him. Somehow I liked that role, this was strange. I wondered if this was a sign that I had feelings for him. After he finished, I boiled for him mountain tea and washed the dishes. I figured out that I had never washed the dishes for Elias. Anyway he was still living with his family, he didn't need my help on this. After washing the dishes I sat next to him. He was always ready for conversation.

- Thank you for all this, Mikhaela. My words cannot be enough to thank you. I feel already better. Let's pour some Malvasian wine to celebrate that you are here, I seldom have such kind guests in my house.

My mother was right. Men always have an intention. But I didn't mind. He was attractive and I felt warm with him. I wanted to let myself free, my mind was a sinner already. But I managed to keep myself tied up. I should behave.

- In ancient Greece wine was the drink of the Gods. Wine was deemed to be a revealer. It was said that it reveals the truth, what people truly think, what people truly desire, what people truly are. Even if the mortals sometimes say that wine makes them behave in an absurd manner, the Gods knew that wine does not bring up the absurd. It brings up the truth. It breaks the barrier of society, it is a lethal weapon against the Other. And although wine puts the Other asleep, it is certain that the Other will wake up again, therefore wine cannot be used for the real You to dominate, but it can be used for the real You to appear.

I had heard a lot of stories about men getting drunk and then beating their wives and children. Many men were driven to the margin of society by overconsumption of wine and some were even imprisoned for their actions while they were drunk.

- Mikhaela, you will be astonished if you see how much people suppress their real personality. It seems that their real self does not get accepted. The more normal a person appears, the more aggressive will wine make this person. The more open, extrovert is a person, the least will wine affect him. Mikhaela, the solution to wine is not to avoid it. It is to observe what you are doing during its influence and question yourself: "What brings up this behavior? What is lying behind? What do I suppress? What do I really want? What am I in reality?"

» Of course, Mikhaela, you cannot do whatever you want. But certainly you can admit that you want it and you can find what brings you to want it.

I could admit that I wanted him. I could admit that I wanted to hug him tight, to kiss him, even to make love to him. But I couldn't tell it, I didn't want to cheat on Elias, this was not right at all. I didn't know why I wanted it, maybe because my relationship with Elias was fading away, maybe because I liked the idea of being with a stranger, a foreigner, somebody different, who could take me to distant places and tell me stories; stories about gondolas, about coffee, about houses built on the sea. I craved for the new, I wanted to taste a new experience, I wanted to know the unknown, I liked the adventure and maybe that was me.

Drinking wine I was laughing more and more. I could see a shy little girl disappearing and an extrovert, strong and happy young lady taking its place. I was feeling attractive. I was feeling potent. Little by little, the small little girl got lost. I was somebody else.

- If you want to be wise, Mikhaela, if you want to say you know and to really know, then you should first really know yourself. Not only think that you know yourself. Not consider that you are what you seem to be in society.

» You are what you feel when you are alone, not what you show in society. You are all your thoughts, all your feelings, all this mixing bowl that contains everything and all of it different. If you consider that you are simple, you know nothing about you. And if you say that you know then you are one of these people who think that they know. These are people to be avoided. They always say that they know; what they are is simple, what they want is simple, and the entire world is simple too. They are using tags to understand themselves and everything around them. Anything that matches a set of characteristics is tagged and this categorizes it as good or bad, as wanted or not wanted. In their silly mind there are thieves, kings, monks, fishermen and nobles. A thief is never to be trusted. A king never talks to common people. A monk has never made love. A fisherman never reads books. A scholar does not get drunk. When they meet you, the first thing they do is try to tag you. Sometimes they have already tagged you before meeting you.

» Avoid these people, Mikhaela. They are the ones who think they know, there is nothing you can either get from them or give to them. They are useless. And as a rule, they try not to get drunk, because once they get drunk, they cannot stay in control. They have been substituted by their Other selves and what is brought up after drinking is totally unknown.

- You are right, Alessio, but under the influence of wine you can do things that you will later regret. My parents are always advising me not to drink wine at all. My mother is telling us that too much wine unveils the evil.

- There is nothing good or evil, Mikhaela. What I do believe is that wine in fact helps you fight the Other. You should be very skeptic of your actions when you have drunk wine. Behind these actions lies somebody else. Somebody who does not know the social rules. And in these actions the thoughts are hiding. The real thoughts, the real feelings. If these differ from what you think and feel when you are sober, then you should really be skeptic. Are you suppressing yourself? Are you suppressing what you really want? Are you the Other? Are you following your path or the path of the mortal?

» Wine should not be the means for you to see yourself. A mature person has access to her real self without using alcohol. A mature person respects both herself and the others. This is why a mature person is never in need of alcohol. And this is why a mature person, even having drunk wine, does not change her behavior. Your seemingly mature scholars, those who think that they know, are just façades. Pour a little wine into their mouth and you will see somebody else governing that silly body. That somebody else is always a child. And this is the real self of everybody who has decided to stay with the Other. Immature and childish.

I sat back for a while. I never knew that wine had such qualities. Everybody was considering wine dangerous.

- For your real self, Mikhaela, there is no danger. There is nothing to fear and of course there is nothing to fear about alcohol. Your real self knows that she does not need alcohol to appear. Mikhaela, I value more the drunkards than the scholars.

That was a tough hit. But it was true. The drunkards were not all the same. Not all of them were aggressive. Some were depressive, some were lonely, some were social. But they were telling the truth. If they were to see a fat man on the street they would scream: "Fat pig!" If they were to see a young lady on the street they would whistle. Even if they had no manners at all, I could recognize that what they were saying was always true. But that was not the case with the scholars. I had heard these old ladies after the church telling to each other: "You look so young!" They were looking like vampires, just one step before the grave.

I had drunk enough for today. I didn't want to drink more and I stopped. I was in total control of my actions, I was fully conscious. However I was not a little girl any more. I felt that I was a dynamic woman who had the world in her hands. If that was the real me, I really liked that person. She was and felt attractive, she could speak, she could laugh and smile. My thoughts were flowing freely. And yes, I did feel attracted to him. It was not weird, he was attractive, that was the reality, there was nothing to hide about it. And I was attractive too, that was for sure. I was tall, sharp-eyed and dark haired, many men would look at me when I was walking on the street. We were two young attractive people close to each other.

I wanted to kiss him. And I did. In a world without barriers I was free and now I was freer than ever. He was talking too much. A man is not valued only in the talks. Looking him straight in the eyes I told him:

- Alessio, I want to make love to you.

III.3 The flow of energy

The morning of the following day was awkward. I woke up at my home. A mix of intense feelings was penetrating me. I opened my eyes and I immediately closed them. I did not want to see the outside world yet, or to be more precise, I did not want to be seen. I stayed for a while under my blanket to gather my feelings. Inside me I felt a series of abrupt changes from excitement to embarrassment, as if there was a force inside my body that was furiously shifting me back and forth without my control. Force. I understood that force was nothing more than the cause and the result of flow. The flow of my feelings, the flow of the water that causes the tide, the flow of the air that causes the wind. The flow happening between the two polar opposites that lie far away from each other. The greater the difference, the more intense the flow, the air, the tide, my feelings. The flow from excitement to embarrassment.

And then I understood: Feeling is the force that people are trying to tame ever since they are born. It seems as if this was the omnipresent wish of society, of the entire humanity. The search for stability. The desire to control the flow. The desire to control the emotion. But who managed to stop the wind in the past of the centuries?

Today I had a far more personal question: What had happened? To me it was like a dream. But I knew it was real: I had made love with Alessio. And this was not reversible. Neither did I want it to be. Continuously shifting from right to wrong, desire to regret, from Alessio to Elias, from the past to the future, from absurd to reasonable I was clearly residing in imbalance. In my continuous flow, right at that time, in the absence of Alessio, I was falling in love. I was producing my strongest emotion, the flow, the force inside myself, everything inside the boundaries of this body, without my even knowing that I was leading myself towards the destruction of my peace in the absence of everyone else, alone.

I had to speak to Alessio. What we had started just couldn't have a future. I already had my plans with Elias, my life, my future. This would evolve to my marriage, my children and my house. But what was right and what was wrong? I felt alone. I could not speak to Alessio, I had no clear decision, I did not even know what to say. I could not speak to Elias, he did not know and best it remain so. I thought about my friends. The thoughts would break my head. I should have stayed away from Alessio. But suddenly I heard a knock on my door. Maybe it was him?

- Good morning, Elias said with a bright smile.

Oh my God! What was he doing there? Maybe he understood? Maybe somebody saw me coming out of Alessio's house in the middle of the night? My speech was gone.

- Did you just wake up? I don't see you in the best mood. Are you ready for church?

Oh yes! How stupid I was! It was Sunday morning, it was time to go to church. We were attending with Elias every Sunday the morning mass. It was the place where all people of Malvasia would meet, pretending their devotion to God's Word. In reality, they would go there to gossip, the "important" people would criticize the others, but never themselves, for what happened in town, and the "wannabes" - just regular people - were listening with great interest, nodding their approval from time to time. It seemed that the older and "mature" people had found there an audience in their effort to "put things in order". But it seemed as if the regular people were just agreeing in order to have their approval, in order to be one of them, in order to belong to this small group of society, because they felt unimportant, they felt like helpless ants that needed to go with the flow inside their colony in order to survive.

But I was not. Even as a young child I was never going with the flow. Sometimes I think I was going against it, even if I knew I was wrong. People like me were the most popular topic at these Sunday meetings, that their participants were calling a religious mass. If only they knew that last night I had slept with Alessio, I am sure that there would be no other topic. Of course they would speak about us only in our absence. They would be glancing from time to time towards our side, always making sure that their look would not be apparent, thus making it even more apparent. And if we approached their side we would always notice that a new topic had just begun, usually about the weather. What a group of fakers. These fearful beings who were deemed to be important and powerful would not even have the power to express their always "right" opinions in front of their victims. I just wondered how unimportant the rest of the people should be in order to follow them. But I had also participated in this game last night. I left in the middle of the night from Alessio's house so that nobody would notice. For the time being I needed some peace from their silly mouths. Weird. What kind of thoughts were crossing my mind? Why was I even part of it? Why was I attending church?

-Come on, Mikhaela, we will be late.

Today it seemed that many people skipped the church or would attend the mass later than we. Seats were readily available so Elias and I chose two separate seats and sat far away from each other. In orthodox tradition the men needed to sit in a separate section, away from the women. It seemed that God and sex would not fit together. If I were to think about the night before with Alessio, this was definitely the case. It was obvious that every traditional norm had a well thought-out reason for existence, even if this reason was not always apparent or applicable. But most people would follow tradition religiously, without a second thought, especially in a religious place. And this gave me the opportunity to have some time on my own.

Yes, this is what I needed. Some time to be alone, to digest what had happened. I did not need time with Alessio nor with Elias. And no, it was not yet time for my friends. I wondered: How come that the result of a fierce encounter is always to end up alone? Life is a constant paradox. Yes, a constant duality, a balance between the hot and the cold, or rather an imbalance that would result to the flow, the creation of energy. Falling in love. What an intense illusion. The more the imbalance, the stronger the love. The wider the difference between hot and cold places, the stronger the wind between them. Yes, that would match. Nature is a great teacher.

Strong wind. That was the result of my encounter with Alessio. How could I sleep in such a strong wind? White nights and the craving for tranquility. The craving to be alone. And when I was alone? The craving for excitement. The craving not to be alone. I was imbalanced. When there was silence, I would crave for the wind, and now that it was blowing, I was looking for shelter. There is no such an experience as satisfaction in life.

When the mass was over I realized its importance: An excuse to stay alone. Alone with God? How can I be alone and at the same time with somebody, even if that somebody is God? Unless God was not somebody else. Until today the church was for me a boring place, a waste of time, a place that I would sit in disquiet, watching people pretending to pay attention to some supposedly wise words, which nobody fully understands, which were written some thousands of years ago and which are repeated every week, as if the preacher knows that the attendants are not paying attention and thus he needs to repeat what he already chanted last time. But today church was different for me: Alone with God. Another paradox indeed.

I was looking forward to the afternoon, where I had an appointment with Alessio outside the city walls, near the lighthouse. Alessio was not religious. Although there was a catholic church in the upper town, Madonna del Carmine, he would not find it important to attend the mass. He was saying that God can be found in any place, if you pay attention to yourself and your surroundings and if you know the direction towards which you should look. Most people would look up towards the sky. Even in the church the frescoes of Jesus Christ and the apostles are placed in the dome. But Alessio never looked up. For him God was inside. He was weird. But interesting.

When I approached the lighthouse, I saw him sitting on a rock, staring towards the sea. He seemed peaceful. How could he be? We shared the same experience yesterday. I was shaking and puzzled.

- Did you find God in church?

He noticed my presence, despite my slow and careful steps. I thought he was less alert.

- I am not sure. I don't think so. But I wasn't looking for God today in the church to be truthful.

- That explains part of the reason. While you were in the church I was sitting on this rock staring at the sea. Today the waters are calm.

Indeed it was one of the few days of the summer when the wind was calm and the sea was quiet.

- In this sea I was able to find God.

He was definitely weird! Anyway, in ancient Greek religion many of the twelve Gods were connected with elements of the nature. Poseidon, the God of the seas and Aeolus, the God of the winds. Maybe he was right.

- Look at this sea, Mikhaela. It looks tranquil. But it is not. Its water is full of currents. They are flowing between the hot and the cold, eternally, in an ever-present effort to terminate duality. Huge masses of water move every second from the hot to the cold and from the cold to the hot, as if the water is craving to balance its omnipresent imbalance of temperature. And even though this is happening for millions of years, duality still exists in the water and we know that it will never cease to exist, no matter how furious the flow is. The water will need to accept the hot, the cold and the flow.

» The flow is energy, it is the result of imbalance, the consistent product of duality, the vessel God created in order to bring to us life. Energy is the will of God, His desire for us to become Him. Energy is the single ingredient of mass, but because it is ever flowing, people have not yet observed or measured it.

» Imagine a river. The river is neither the water nor its banks. It is not even their combination. The river is the flow. The flow of the water between the banks. And so are your feelings. Your feelings are the flow, the flow that results from your imbalance. Without imbalance you would be lifeless, in other terms dead. Your feelings are pure energy. And as such, they are your vessel towards your rescue, your encounter with God. Your imbalance is to be blessed.

This man was special. This is what he was seeing inside this sea? For one thing I was sure: If God was to be found through my feelings then God should be residing in hell.

- Through the hell comes the paradise, Mikhaela.

Did I think out loud? But what did he mean? The priest was not talking about this. That was weird. I decided not to continue his thoughts. At least for now.

- I have a question for you, Alessio, I finally said.

He must not have been surprised. I was only questions. He was telling me that this is what he admired in me. He was saying that all people have questions, but most of them just accept their presence or even deny it. Only a handful of people decide to take the dangerous path of finding the answers and even fewer overcome their fear and take this path all the way to the end. For him, small children were admirable, because they would always fire their questions like catapults.

What happened with ageing was not that people were finding answers but that people would stop asking questions. People would gradually lose on energy. Instead of growing up they were just growing old. And losing on energy, people would gradually become asleep. Until one day everything would come upside down. An external event, some important news, a sudden death, a depression, anything unexpected and strong could lead them to this moment. Then they would wake up and see the light, get blinded from its intensity, recognize it from the time they originally had it. They would become full of fear and they would grasp tightly their fists on their bed in a pointless effort to stay asleep. Alessio was calling this the "awakening". The questions would rise, all at the same time, a revolution that would be impossible to ignore.

But my question now was only one.

- Alessio, do I love you?

III.4 The vision of reality

My question was followed by silence. A calming silence, like the harmony that follows a storm. In front of us the seawater was calm, around us a light breeze of air, even the seagulls were sitting still on the rocks gazing towards the horizon. It seemed as if everything along with me in this scenery had finally understood that their knowledge is incomplete, that what they possess is only the unimportant, and what remains hidden is the essence of life.

I contemplated this silence. I observed the clouds, constantly changing formations, the sea, constantly in motion, the birds, constantly flying without a real target. Everything moving, constantly moving, but at the same time still. And in harmony. Except my own mind.

- Mikhaela, he finally said. If you look around you, nature is constantly talking to you. It has all the answers.

- Nature is lovely, lovelier than ever, but in my eyes it is silent, Alessio.

- Let's take a walk, Mikhaela. I will lead you to your answer.

We walked hand in hand. The surroundings were so lovely, the time had stopped. Everything was still, we were the only beings moving. I remembered the day we had been swimming in the sea. He had grabbed me around my waist and had been turning me around in the water. It seemed that time had stopped, that nothing else had been moving. For an instant I thought that now even the seconds had stopped, that I would meet people on the street, but I would watch them standing still, frozen in the same posture. Everything was magnificent; it seemed as if nature was built for us, as if everything around us was meant to be perfect, except for our own selves. Islands of hell inside the paradise, disturbing an eternal harmony that has been maintained for billions of years, intact.

He picked up a flower. Its color was violet and its leaves were small and wide. It was simple, but focusing on the little details of its leaves, it seemed that a whole miniature world was hiding inside them. It was so beautiful!

- This one is for you, Mikhaela.

He was in love with me, this was obvious. Why was my own love not obvious? Did I not love him? For sure my mind did not think of picking up a flower for him at random. But my mind was never away from him. Every instant of my day he was there, right in front of me, whispering in my ears with his sweet calming voice. I had never felt such an intense feeling before, not even with Elias. If that was not love, what was it?

- Love is all around. It is found in this little flower, which you are holding in your hands. It is found in these clouds that make you feel small and unimportant in a world full of grace and harmony. It is found on this tall rock of Malvasia, which is rising proudly from the sea, it is found in the trees with their millions of leaves that fill your eyesight with color, your presence with protection from the sun, your ears with a calming sound of tranquility.

» Everything around you is made in perfection, full of love and harmony. Except one thing, Mikhaela.

» Your thoughts

» In such a beautiful day with harmony extending everywhere from our two little bodies to the endless horizon there is only one thing that is not tranquil.

» Your mind.

That was absolutely true. Everything around me was perfect, the nature, the weather, even he himself; he was the perfect companion. All girls in the town envied me because Alessio was paying too much attention to me. It seemed that everybody wanted him. What was wrong with me?

- And here is the answer to your question:

» Having incarnated your other self, you neither know nor love yourself. You do not think that you deserve perfection. You are detached from this harmony.

I did not know why or exactly what he meant, but I agreed.

- Look in the eyes of your small dog. What do you feel when you are looking at her? You get immense joy, a whole sea of love penetrates you! Look at that little bird. It is jumping around, from branch to branch, it is staring left and right, it is doing absolutely nothing and it fills you with love! Look at the face of a little baby. Even if it can't stop crying, even if it gets the ugliest expression, the smile just cannot disappear from your face! You just look around you and you are in love! You feel love.

» But then go and look at the mirror. Do you feel the same?

Amazing. If I felt the same? Of course not! Usually whenever I looked at the mirror I would notice all my traits. Even if the smallest mark appeared on my face I would notice it and I would feel angry or frustrated if I could not remove it. Then I would look away and I would quickly forget it. But a look at myself would never bring me complete satisfaction, joy. It would never emit love. Not like a baby. Never like a bird. It seemed as if everything was perfect, but me? Not in my eyes. Maybe in his.

- I don't feel the same, I finally said. I try my best to make myself better and better but I am never satisfied. I cannot get the love that I am getting from a baby out of my own self. Maybe I don't love myself enough yet, just as I love a baby.

- And this is exactly the reason that you cannot love me yet either. You cannot accept that you are worth it.

In a sentence I received my answer, its reason, and the reason behind the reason. I could now understand why the wise were telling me that I first need to love myself. Just as a baby, I thought. Why was I finding perfection in a small common bird, practically identical to all the birds of its kind, and I could not find it in my own distinct and unique self? Why did I want to be distinct? Why did I want to behave and to look unique, when common was so lovely? Who was this

"I", this distinct thing that was hiding in my body trying to behave differently, competitive to the others? Maybe the reason lies in separation. Maybe the separate, separates itself from a harmonious and lovable whole.

- And how about you? Do you feel love when you look in the mirror?

- Not every time, he said. But at the present yes. I am very proud that I found you.

- You found me?

I felt very attracted to Alessio. When he was around, I felt complete, like a puzzle that has found its missing match piece. When he was away I missed him. I feared that the day he would go I would suffer from my own incompleteness.

- Alessio, are we incomplete? Is there such a thing as our other half? Walking somewhere around on this planet? And we are trying to find it?

- No, Mikhaela, we are complete. But we do also obey the law of duality. In that sense there is a missing part of us. Better said: a hidden one.

» And this is what you feel now, Mikhaela: An explosion. Two particles that attract each other so intensely that they collide, and when they collide they explode, unleashing such a dynamic, that they are forced apart even harder than they were forced together, gazing back during their whole outward journey, vainly attempting to return, trying to explain what happened, how such a powerful force of attraction suddenly transformed to a force of separation.

» Everybody in their life is meant to meet their other half. The whole universe will conspire, the fire will turn to water and the earth to dust, until the encounter happens. The Reencounter of the whole. And when you meet your other half you will experience the moment of utmost tranquility. The time will come to a halt; you will understand the unimportance of the material, without somebody reasoning it; you will transcend to paradise without making a single step from your doorway; you will unite with God without even going to the church, without prayer or meditation; you will look at the mirror and you will just feel happy. This is your bonus, a glimpse of the reality, your vision of paradise, the truth behind your journey, your reason to live and to grow.

» And this is exactly why it happens. To give you a reason. To show you the goal, the sea that you will merge when you, the river, will reach your destination, your unavoidable return to God, your destiny of completeness.

» But you are not bound to stay in this moment. It comes only as a glimpse in the material world, it may last for minutes or hours or weeks or months, but it cannot last forever. As if it would, there would be no reason behind the journey of life, no reason behind action. This will be your gift, your compensation when you mature; when you become again a baby; when you will merge with the dog and the bird; when there will be no more boundaries between you and the sky, the trees, the sun and the sea. All this wonderful surrounding that is composed out of one element: Harmony.

This was what I was feeling now. Time was absent, everything and everybody stood still, my surroundings were beautiful. I felt happy, without knowing why, I felt complete in my incompleteness, I felt that there was nothing else to strive for, that this is the goal, paradise itself, the highest feeling that can be felt. I felt that there was no need to work, because there was no value in anything material that can be gained with the money. I was experiencing the highest feeling and in that moment I wanted nothing more.

- Mikhaela, this vision of Love will show you the end. There is nothing higher than it and you shall instantly realize it. It is the feeling of completeness and you shall know that there cannot exist anything more complete. The vanish of your ego, the final fall of the Other, the return to your Godly presence.

» In this moment you will realize the utmost Truth: That there is no self, you are a Union. That there is no time, time is an illusion. That there is no distinction between you and nature, between you and the other living beings. You will be able to feel them as one, you will be able to love them and you will not be able to do anything else. In this vision of Truth you will realize that you can only love. There simply is no other feeling. In this moment, even if somebody hits you with a rock on the head, you will feel no pain or anger. Because these feelings do not exist either. You will be protected and you will feel this protection. Standing on this moment you will realize that the material is just an illusion, that it does not exist. Just like the time, anger, pain and fear, you will realize that the material's birth and seizure happen concurrently, governed by an illusionary time that permits them to illusionary exist. But in truth they don't. Just as you know that pain has a beginning and an end, you will realize that you cannot define either the beginning or the end of love, because it simply neither begins nor ends, it only exists. God is Love is Truth, it has no beginning and no end. And in this moment of Love, standing on the timeless dimension, you will realize that only beauty exists. To your eyes everything will be beautiful!

» In this moment you will see reality. And since my presence has brought you to this moment you will deem yourself incomplete without me. This is an illusion, since you have brought yourself into this moment looking through me inside your own whole. At the moment you deem yourself incomplete you shall fall, reality shall terminate for you, and you shall return to the illusionary material world. Fear of loss will penetrate your body along with all other illusionary feelings. Time will return. You will believe that completeness is found in me, not in you. And ever since you fall you are bound to lose me and to always seek for me.

Tears came to my eyes. This was all true.

- However, Mikhaela, this is only part of the truth. This is the truth as your mind understands it. The truth is that your being is complete, you are complete. You are both a male and a female. I am the male inside you. In me you see your missing part. In fact this part is not absent, it is only hidden.

I am only reflecting in front of your eyes what already lies behind them. And as long as you are not in love with what lies behind them, you cannot be in love with what lies in front of them. As much as you want me, with your actions you will push me away. And with my reaction, I am bound to do the same. That way our collision will explode. From thence forwards we shall crave for each other pretending that we don't care. But craving will be in vain, because our destiny is apart, not together. Our destiny is formed on earth, our goal is to mature, our end will be the paradise. And what we will really crave for is not each other but ourselves. Our true selves. Our egoless selves. Union. God.

I could not help stopping my tears coming from my eyes. I remained still and it was true: Inside his eyes I could see myself. He was my other half, right here, right in front of me.

- Now you have realized that I am the unseen you and you are the unseen me. Just now you have seen the unseen. From now on you shall behave to me like you behave to yourself. But now you are not you, you are your social Other. The Other is dominating your body. And as such, you shall seek advice from the others. You shall not listen to your own emotions. You shall conform to what you were always conforming. You shall push your own true self away from you. And as part of your true self, as your exact opposite, you shall push me away as well. Searching God you shall take distance from Him. But know this:

» To take distance is the only way to observe.
» Through the dark tunnel comes the light.
» Through duality you realize the One.
» Through the hell comes the paradise.

Tears were dropping from my eyes by now. They were tears of truth. After all, a tear itself is truth.

- So you answered my question.
- I did.
- I want to love you.

- I know you do. This is the purpose of life. We all want to love. But there is a path to reach there. One day you shall love me. It is just not the time yet.

- Alessio, do you love me?

- I do.

- Can you keep me with you forever? Can you just fold me in your luggage and take me wherever you go?

- I can't.

- Why?

- To be with God is a choice. Even if finally it is not possible not to be with Him, the illusion of time permits you the illusion of your being away from Him. And so you have the choice. And even if He knows that you can only be with Him, he shall respect your time-governed choice not to be with Him. He will challenge both your choice not to be with Him and your choice to be with Him. And since God is Love, your love shall be challenged. And if you choose to be the Other, you shall push Love away. You shall attract fear. But you also shall be given the vision of Love. And in its memory you shall suffer. Suffering is your depressed love. And as such it is energy. This energy will be fueling your journey, which will lead you to your savior. Isn't everything made in perfection?

- I hate you.

- This is a good sign. It means you have feelings. And it means you can hate yourself.

- God is mean.

- He is. If God is everything, He is both good and mean. At the same time He is high and low, black and white, hot and cold, He is all there is, He is one and you see Him as dual because you are dual. He is the harmony that results out of the furious energy, He is the reason for the flow as well as for its end, the sea with which the river is bound to merge, the destination of your journey, the glimpse that you are receiving now, your true and utmost goal, your own self.

- Alessio, I love you.

- I know you do. You can only love me, there is no other way.

III.5 Love and marriage

I had my answer and it would make sense. I could only love him. But how could I love two men at the same time? I was supposed to have one boyfriend and later one husband, one father for my children; I was supposed to be half and seeking my other half. Or was I two quarters seeking for my other two? Isn't that supposed to be the same?

By now it was clear to me: This whole game of love was wrong. The goal was marriage and everything in this game was moving around it. To create a family, to serve the spouse, to make my parents happy, to have children. Everything was fixed, predetermined. But where was I in this game?

It was the norm in our town that men would decide about the future of the daughters. The groom goes to the father asking for the bride. The father examines the economics, the social status, the degree of trustworthiness. Without asking the bride, the father decides and marriage follows. Marriage was clearly a business deal, a contract. Luckily, our father was different. Having four daughters and a wife, he showed some understanding to emotion. He allowed us to select a man on our own and even maintain a relationship before marriage. For many people in Malvasia this was unacceptable, especially for those following the Islamic traditions.

But marriage was still there. It was still the hidden goal of our relationships and everything was silently turning around it. Where was love in this game? Nowhere, not even behind this weird invention of marriage.

It was clear. The decision was not about whom to love. The decision was about seizing love. The decision in fact was between love and marriage, with them being mutually exclusive. When I was ready to give up love, I could get married.

After my encounter with Alessio, I felt as if love woke up inside me. Having four years of relationship with Elias, I saw our love having its ups and downs, but the feeling was generally declining. Our relationship was extinguishing this sparkling love that we had in the beginning. I felt my heart going stiff like an ageing man towards his end, freezing its motion to a rock. Sometimes I would justify Elias saying that I loved him mechanically.

All this until Alessio came to my life. My encounter with him was like a breeze of fresh air. My heart softened suddenly and I began feeling again. What I didn't expect was that I began having feelings for both Alessio and Elias. Elias seemed pleased and surprised, but he couldn't attribute the reason for this sudden change to anything. I was once again happy.

In this world that I created, I felt comfortable. I had my work, my family, my friends, I loved and I was being loved at the same time. Elias was there, stable like a mountain, solid like a rock. With him by my side I had a reference, something that was always there, a home I could always go, a future and a family. Security. That is what he was. My medicine against an ever present fear, the man ensuring that I would never be left alone. And beside me Alessio, a sparkle, a breeze, a river of fresh water that would relieve any thirst in the blink of an eye. With him I had found a reason to love, a reason to live. Why couldn't I feel both for one man only?

The reason was me. I had well understood from Alessio that inside me I had two personalities coexisting, fighting to prevail, the Me and the Other. The Me was an ambitious girl, full of interests, dynamic and loving; it was attracting growth, risk and challenge. The Other was a creature of society, an always craving entity, a pursuer of stability, wealth and company. An entity that pursued marriage as the single insurance that I would never be left alone, unsecured. The Other was fear. The Other was craving for security because it didn't have it. The Other was craving for stability because it didn't feel it. The Other was craving for marriage because it believed that beauty was declining with age, leading to an unavoidable loneliness in life.

The Other was craving for children, because it was craving for somebody to continue its erroneous existence after my body would die. It was craving in fact for reincarnation, its settlement inside a younger body, my child, that would live after my death, constantly being inherited from mother to daughter, an ever-existing crave for the daughter to look like the mother, behave like the mother, talk like the mother, finally be the mother, after the mother's death. The Other was craving for continuance because it knew that one day it had to die. The Other was mortal and for this reason the Other was fear.

It was clear. The Me and the Other had different needs. And for this reason the Me and the Other were sleeping with two different men.

In this contrast I had found a balance. A balance between two entities inside myself, a balance between Alessio and Elias. I would spend some time with Alessio and some time with Elias, keeping both parts on par. But I needed to keep those two lives separate. I was trembling with the idea that one day they might meet on the street.

Alessio knew about Elias, I wanted to be honest with him right from the start. Even if I could sense that he wanted to be my boyfriend, he seemed to be adjusting to the role of the lover, at least for now. Sometimes I would feel jealous about him meeting other girls, but then he would remind me that I did not allow him to be my boyfriend. One day I did want to be his girlfriend, in fact I was even dreaming of it in my sleep. But I feared of losing Elias. Even if I craved to fly, I still didn't want to let earth go. Having both of them, I did have both wings to fly and feet to walk. Interchangeably, in a sequence, like the day follows the night, and the night follows the day, I would be with Alessio and Elias in two separate worlds, sequencing each other.

From night to day and day to night one month passed in a flash, in a dream, in a world where I could walk and fly whenever I wanted.

III.6 The moment of choice

Until it came to an end. I always feared that this moment would one day come. Even if I always judged it to lie in the future, there comes a time when the future becomes present. The future cannot always stay in the future.

Everything looked as if that day would be a normal working day of the summer. I went to work and afterwards I passed by the house of Alessio. I was feeling more and more secure with Alessio and I always preferred to spend the evening with him. Of course, I had to spend time with Elias as well, but this usually happened after some kind of complaint from his side. He was complaining more and more about me not spending enough time with him. What seemed weird to me was that Elias started behaving like a sponge: No matter how much water I would pour, the sponge would absorb it. Enough was never the case. Many times I felt guilty about it and I knew that one day I would have to make the choice.

That day was today.

- Welcome Mikhaela, Alessio said as he opened the door to me. He was smiling, as always when he was greeting me to his house, but I immediately got the feeling that something was wrong. He kept on smiling while I kept on standing at the door. It must be me, I thought, and I entered. Sometimes I do get feelings without a reason.

- Please sit down Mikhaela, I need to talk to you.

My feelings were never wrong.

His house was relaxing and warm. At least this is how I was feeling in it. His furniture was placed in such a way that enough space would be left inside each room. I was feeling that my emotions could expand in this house. I selected one of the soft cushions on the floor and I sat down. He sat opposite to me, extending his hands to touch mine.

- Mikhaela, a letter came today from the government in Venice. My department will be staffed with new people who will be coming from Venice soon. In one week my assignment in Malvasia will come to an end.

I remained silent looking at him. I didn't get any expression, neither did I feel the need to cry. The tears were already dropping on the inside.

- Mikhaela, I don't need to return to Venice immediately and after all I am a free man and I don't need to return at all. I would do anything to be with you and to organize my life in Malvasia would only be a small part of it.

» But, Mikhaela, I need you to make a step towards that direction too. You need to make a choice. The choice between Elias and me. If I stay here, I will stay for you, and commitment cannot come from one side only.

A change is never partial, that much I had understood from life. Either everything changes or nothing and changes do have implications. He was leaving and I needed to choose. I could keep him by my side, but I needed to hold my hands firmly on his, just like he was holding mine now. And if I would let them go, he would flee.

- Mikhaela, I think the best way to make a choice is to be on your own. Being with me, like right now, will bias your choice towards me and being with Elias will bias your choice towards him. Only alone will you be able to make a firm decision.

Alone? I was never alone. That word was blacklisted in my vocabulary. I was four years together with Elias. And before that with Marcus. And before that with Nicholas. And before that? I didn't need to count. I only needed to count how much time I was alone. It was only adding up to some months, not even a year.

- Alone, Mikhaela, means to really have time on your own. Everybody else except you comprises the Other. You already know what the Other is, you already know that it is not you, do you want the Other to decide for you?

Even when I was not in a relationship, even for these few months, I had numerous friends. And somehow I would remember them more frequently then. And when I was not with my friends I was with my sisters. My family was big enough so that always somebody would be available to talk to. Alone. For me, this situation was to be avoided.

- How can I be on my own, when I am splitting my time between you and him?

- For my part I decided to help you. I will make a journey to Egypt. I always wanted to see the pyramids and learn about their ancient culture and I think now it is a good opportunity for me to do it. For the part of Elias, this will be up to you. You need to explain him, and he should understand. This time needs to be time on your own. If you stay with him, your decision will be biased towards him.

That night we made love passionately. I don't know if it was because I feared that I would lose him or because I wanted to prevent him from going away. Most of all, I was afraid of myself. I was afraid that if he would let his two hands go from holding me, I would just let him go, watching him getting lost in the distance. With his two hands around me I fell sound asleep.

III.7 The drama

Alessio was going away and what I needed was time to think. I remembered my grandmother. Letting her go, I was watching her getting lost in the distance. Is it all about a replay? The same, again and again, from different people, in different situations, but always the same? I always feared that this moment would one day come. But I know what made this fear grow inside me: I had lived this in the past and I couldn't stop it, I was living it in the present and I couldn't stop it. I feared that I would live it in the future and that I would not be able to stop it. I once was unable to stop separation and this situation was coming again and again when I was least expecting it, challenging my ability to stop it.

- This moment, this repeating situation is your drama, Mikhaela.

Was I thinking out loud again? It was already morning when I woke up next to him.

- What is my drama, Alessio?
- Your drama. It is a situation that happened to you in the past. That time you were unable to handle it. Your reaction to it was inadequate and you were led to a painful experience. You know you could have done better but you didn't, perhaps because you considered yourself weak or because you were lacking experience. You resent the situation itself but most of all you blame yourself for your action or inactivity. It was painful and you don't want the situation to appear again in your life.

» But this situation is coming again and again. From different people and in a different context, but it always requires from you the same reaction. It is the reaction that you could not and still cannot perform. In that manner, your drama is stronger than you. You are still not able to cope with it. And therefore you fear it.

Abandonment. My parents who abandoned me in Sparta when they left for Malvasia. My grandmother whom I abandoned when I left for Malvasia. My little dog, my only company during my early childhood years, when our father took her to his workplace and she got sick and died. My little puppet. My first boyfriend. What did I do to prevent it? Nothing. What could I have done? Much. I was thinking over and over what I could have done in all these situations and I was coming up with so many alternatives. But all these alternatives stayed in my mind, in reality I had never reacted. And the situation was happening again and again in my life, in a replay, in a drama that I would participate as an actor, a drama directed by a higher force and me, only reading the script out loud.

- Do you think I could have acted in a different way, Alessio, I said irritated. I felt I was trapped, I felt I was powerless. There was nothing I could do. Or maybe I could, but…

- The past belongs to the past, Mikhaela. What is important is that your drama was then bigger than you and that you did not act otherwise. The situation happened just as everything external only happens in order to create an opportunity for you to act and through your action to realize your thoughts, realize yourself, define who you really are. If you failed to act according to your thoughts and feelings, then you resent. Resentment means that this action was not you. You could have done otherwise and even if you couldn't back then, you need to make sure that in the future you will be able to. It is an inner contract with yourself, a contract of change, a contract to stop resenting and finally fight what seems to be invincible: Your drama.

» As much time as you feel unable to fight your drama, thoughts and feelings are circulating in your mind. Why did you do this? Why didn't you do that? You fear that the situation will be repeated, that you will fail again and you will get the same results. You feel less powerful than the situation and therefore you fear it and you don't want it to repeat.

- True.

- But it will, be sure for that. Your biggest fear shall realize, Mikhaela.

- The law of attraction.

- Exactly. Subconsciously you fear the situation thus attract it in your life. Your drama is replayed. You start getting used to it, accepting it. You think it is your destiny, your karma. You develop a set of responses, which seem reasonable in your eyes. Responding like that you already know what will happen. You know that this will be painful, but the more you get used to that pain, the less you feel it. The sudden pain is always worse than the expected one. You get familiar to that pain, in a way numb. And you start blaming the director, God, that He keeps on sending you the same drama. You think you deserve better.

Correct.

- This is all wrong, Mikhaela. You don't deserve better. Not until you outgrow your drama.

» Life is a wonderful dance of joy and you do get what you deserve in order to grow. Every situation comes to you in order to make you think and react, in order to first create in your mind and then in the world and afterwards receive the joy or the sorrow as an inner indicator of whether your action was right or wrong. Every sorrow, every wrong action is an opportunity, an opportunity to grow. Or more precisely: An opportunity to outgrow it.

» Once you outgrow your drama you are stronger than it. You know your response was right, you could do no better. And even if the outcome was not pleasant, it is pleasant that whatever was in your hands was done properly. You decide that if the situation comes again, you will behave exactly in the same way, because this behavior is the best you can do, there simply is no better.

» Once this happens then you have outgrown the situation. You don't fear it anymore and most important you don't fear your response to it, simply because you know there is no better. When you stop fearing it, you stop having it circulating in your mind. When the thought ceases, the action ceases as well. In a world where everything is created as a thought in first place, there is no more space for your drama again in your life. You are ready for a higher challenge, another more difficult and more interesting situation. And this will come in order for you to grow higher. This process is called evolution.

- Alessio, do you believe that everyone can overcome their drama?

- Everyone can but not everyone does. It is a process and many people either quit during the process or, more commonly, they get used to it. And with it they get used to blaming others or God for it. But your drama needs to be passed, either in this life or in another one.

- Reincarnation?

- If you believe in it. It comes along with your karma and your karma is in fact your drama and the destiny of your river is the sea and the river can never reach the sea going round and round. You need to go through.

- To go through is painful.

- It is, and that is why it is easier to keep going around. But life needs you to be a warrior. What you try to avoid keeps coming to you because you fear it. Isn't this game designed perfectly? The only way not to fear it is to outgrow it, to go through it. Evolution is the only alternative in this game. Only when you incarnate your thought and your true self, you can see the light on the other side of the dark tunnel.

With these words he left me and I let him go. Abandonment. Once again my drama was there, the boomerang came back and I was challenged. I managed to see the boomerang more clearly this time. The boomerang was in fact my drama. And its design is such that it keeps coming back, no matter where and how strong you throw it. The boomerang is the essence of this life.

When I left his house, I felt that I had just entered the dark tunnel.

Deep inside Mikhaela knew what was right for her. But if only there were no other factors. If only there was one decision simply right, and one simply wrong. But there was not. She knew that the one defining right and wrong was only herself. Or better put: The feelings she would get after her decision was made final. The feelings of an assassinator lying in front of a dead body, knowing that there is no way of undoing her act.

She cried. No, she didn't want to be the killer. Once again, she didn't want to take the decision. With the boomerang in her hand, she felt once again weak.

III.8 The school of sorrow

On the next day, I woke up with a nightmare. I was standing at a crossroads. Alessio was on the road in front. He was walking forward. Elias was standing beside me at that crossroads. On my left side I could see a signpost. It had many signs, all confusing. Some signs were pointing to a direction where there was no road. Alessio was moving on forward looking at me frequently, nodding me to come. Elias was standing beside me looking at Alessio. He was sad. I felt like hugging him, but my hand was going through his body, I was not able to touch him. Alessio was walking away, getting lost in the distance. Perhaps he was heading to Egypt or somewhere else. He was nodding at me to come with him. On the road in front of me I saw a dusty sign. I could hardly read it. With well-worn letters it said: "One way". I then looked at the road on my right. It was curvy and heading uphill. It looked tiring. I looked at the road on my left. It seemed like a dead-end. The paved road ended in the distance and some narrow dirt paths seemed to start from there. Probably some people created them by walking their own way after the end of the beaten path. I looked front again. Alessio was already lost. I trembled. The old signpost on the road was still reading: "One way". I looked towards my right. Elias had vanished into thin air. I collapsed. I was standing alone at a crossroads in the middle of the desert. I woke up. It was a dream. My heart was beating fast. I felt relieved.

Taking an early breakfast I realized my need to talk to somebody. But to whom to talk? Elias did not even know about my affair with Alessio. And Alessio had already left. My friends were good at keeping company but too strict on advice. They would tell me exactly what to do, but if they were in my situation, I am sure they wouldn't do it.

I thought about my mother. She once told me about a monk who lived on the other side of the thin passage that separated Malvasia from the mainland. He was known for his ability to look into the future. He had a small house next to an orthodox chapel and although there was no regular mass in that chapel, he was there every day for his morning prayer. Very seldom would people cross the thin passage to the mainland to visit him and usually they would be asking for some kind of help or guidance. The monk was always kind and asked nothing in return. His name was Jeremias.

As it was early on this Saturday morning, I decided to pay him a visit. The road was long, but I enjoyed the morning dawn. I was walking slowly, following Alessio's advice. Thoughts were crossing my mind and in between I was able to contemplate the sunrise. In between. This very small timeframe, where Alessio would say that the Being was hiding. In between my thoughts a magnificent sunrise was taking place.

When I opened the door of the chapel, I saw Jeremias bending in front of the image of Mother Mary, whispering prayers. I sat on a bench inside the chapel. I was his only visitor.

When he finished his prayer, he blessed the rest of the images with incense smoke coming out of a metallic censer.

- Good morning, young lady, he said turning towards my side with a bright smile on his face.

- Good morning, Father, I said.

- It's always a pleasure for me to see visitors in this small chapel.

He was looking straight into my eyes. His eyes were shining. I remembered the eyes of Alessio when he was getting obsessed in his word.

- You seem worried young lady. A lot of thoughts are crossing your mind. You came here for advice?

- I have heard many things about you, Father, I said. I need your advice. I feel confused. I woke up early in the morning.

- Oh, worries, worries and worries. People worry because they don't know. And they don't know because they don't have a clear mind. Too many thoughts, too many worries.

Leaving aside his censer, he sat down opposite me, touching both my palms. Closing his eyes, he murmured some prayers. Then he said:

- Let me guide you inside your dream.

His face had a smile that was not coming through his mouth. It was like the smile of a happy baby. As if he had seen my dream himself he started talking:

- You seem to be facing a choice; at a crossroads. Crossroads always come unexpectedly in the walk of life. You think that your path is straight, but in fact it is full of dead-ends and crossroads. You are standing too long on them young lady. You are indecisive and while looking at the various roads, they change, they become different.

» I see a young man in your dream. He is standing firmly next to you. But he is not looking at you my dear. He is looking towards another man in the distance. I can see the other man, he is a foreigner. He is leaving. He is going back to his country. But he loves you. He loves you a lot. The man next to you is not looking to you anymore. He is looking towards the foreigner too. You are taking too long to decide young lady. The signs show your way. You are looking at many ways, but there is only one way, I can read it clearly. But while you are taking your time to decide, the foreigner is going away. And even if you see your friend next to you, it is only his image. He is not there, he is looking towards the foreigner. You can't touch him, in reality he is already gone. At the end you stay alone. Both vanish but the crossroads are still there. Don't worry young lady, your path is full of light.

He opened his eyes again. Tears were welling up in my eyes, ready to flow. At the end would I lose both of them?

- What is your name?
- Mikhaela, I managed to say.

- You have a beautiful name, Mikhaela, he said with a bright smile. You are named after the Archangel Michael, the warrior of light. He protects and guides us, when he sees us in need. His image stands in every Orthodox church. There!

He pointed towards an old image beside the inner door of the chapel. It was a handsome male with big wings dressed in full armor. In his right hand he was holding a sword. In his left hand he was holding the soul of a man, He was firmly stepping on a dead body.

- The body is the body of the Greedy. The myth says that the Greedy in his life was not willing to share anything with anyone. He was lost inside his belongings. The Archangel is there to separate the pure from the fallen. In his hand he is holding the pure soul of the fallen man. Purity lies always inside the sinner.

He stayed in silence for a moment. With a serious expression he looked at me and said:

- Mikhaela. The Archangel is your guide.

I felt confused; I was too unimportant to have such an important guide.

- You are so confused, Mikhaela, you are like a baby. This is normal. But you need to grow out of it. We all come to life for a purpose, we are here to evolve, and this counts for you too. Everything happens for a purpose, this purpose, evolution.

» In your path you need to have faith. Every time you doubt, it is because you don't know and you have lost your faith. Then you need to go through the school of sorrow. The purpose of this school is to provide you with a lesson, a lesson that you learn through experience, a lesson that will help you guide yourself. Knowledge lies in faith. Faith that nothing can go wrong, faith that God is with you, faith that you are protected. Faith makes you feel strong, it makes you trust your feelings and without fear choose the right path at the crossroads of life.

» But sometimes, even if you sense your path, even if you see the signs, you fear. It is when you lose in faith that you fear. And when you fear, you lose love. And when you lose love, you lose everything, even if you can't understand it.

» I will tell you a parable from the Bible. The apostles were on a boat, while Jesus was praying alone on the mountain. Suddenly, during the night, a strong wind blew on the sea, causing big waves to rise. The apostles were in danger. They got desperate, fearing that they would drown. Then they saw Jesus approaching them, walking on the water. They couldn't believe in their eyes, they thought they were already seeing ghosts, how could somebody walk on the water? And Peter said: "If it is you my Lord, order me to come to you". And Jesus said: "Come". Then Peter stepped off the boat and started walking on the water. But the waves were high and fear penetrated him. Suddenly he started to sink in the water, asking for His help. Jesus came closer and giving him His hand He asked: "Where is your faith Peter? What made you hesitate?"

» It is when we lose faith that we fear, Mikhaela. And when we fear we need to sink and understand that our body can only float on the sea if we don't move it.

» The whole universe conspires, the black turns to white and the sun becomes a moon until you enter the school of sorrow. You need to realize it, accept it and with it, accept sorrow.

» Like the word also says, this school teaches through sorrow. You go through a period of sadness when things couldn't go worse, when everything happening seems to be negative. What is weird but explainable is that you can't go out of it, even if you want to. It is like the moving sand. The more you move to go out, the deeper you sink, the more you lose in force. Anyway you are in this school because you are not feeling strong enough, so don't think that you are able to fight against it. But if you do, pushing your limit, then you continue to go deeper in this moving sand until you drown.

» Mikhaela, in the school of sorrow you have nothing to fear, except your own self wanting to go out of it without taking the lesson. Crossing your limits you can literally die.

But this is up to you. You can fight as much as you want, anyway you will get zero results, but obey your own limitations. When you feel tired, stop. Climbers know very well that if they cross their limits, death is waiting at their footstep. You should know that too.

» The lesson really starts after you stop denying it. After you stop moving, the very fact that you were moving against it comes to find you; sorrow. You go through it, you feel it and without stamina you can only feel it, nothing more. You feel surrendered. In reality you have surrendered to the hands of God. And even if you feel sad, you are watching God giving you a lesson. Watch it carefully and you will see that the lesson is given with so much love and perfection! Of course, the lesson is given to you by Him, it cannot lack perfection, neither love. The whole universe is dancing to your lesson.

» The school of sorrow ends once you are ready to graduate and only then you do realize its value. You realize that without these experiences it would have been impossible to get this lesson, to be who you are now. Everything will look distant and most of all you will have abolished fear. Remember, Mikhaela, God is Love and its opposite is fear. Since in reality only God exists, fear exists not. And the school of sorrow serves God, it is there for you to abolish fear and to bring you closer to your Father, Love. Once you have lived it, you have won it and once you have won it, you can't fear it. You feel and you are stronger. This is the purpose of the school of sorrow.

» The sign says "One way", but you are still reading official signposts. The signs are there only for you but the signposts for everyone. The signs draw your attention, the signposts are screaming. The signs, if carefully looked at, reveal your way. The signposts put your mind into force and your logic can only confuse you. This dream was your sign, but more than that, it told you that you need to go to the school of sorrow.

» Your fear is that you will stay alone and God is not satisfied with your fear. You need to live your fear, you need to live alone, you are about to enter into the school.

» But don't worry young lady, this old man in front of you can see the future. You are gifted, you will not withstand, you are not one of these immature, silly students who say to their teacher "I know". Even if you will withstand a little bit, like everyone else, you will be able to graduate. I am happy for you. Just as your dream says: You will stay alone. Don't be sad, Mikhaela! You do have guidance.

By now tears were flowing from my eyes. Was that a blessing or a curse? I shouldn't have gone to him, I shouldn't have listened to this silly dream. How would I stay alone? I had two men in love with me. I could choose one and be with him. Why would I stay alone? It was in my hands to choose the one, I was the one with the power.

- The whole universe will conspire, Mikhaela, Jeremias said grabbing my thoughts. You have fear, you feel that you are weak and think that you don't know; this is the perfect recipe for the school. You cannot avoid it. But I understand that you want to avoid it young lady.

- Thank you, Father, I said and got up to go.

- Don't forget the sign, Mikhaela. It reads "One way" and it points to the way you won't follow.

I had already run away from the chapel, my mind had already left and skipped those final words. I was running towards Malvasia. This stupid school needed to be avoided. Elias was there, next to me. Alessio had gone. The answer was clear.

III.9 The elephant

One month passed in a flash. I was meeting with Elias and our relationship was stronger than before. I blamed myself for not being faithful to Elias and I tried to be nicer to him. After all Elias had been nice with me too; he was in love and his mind was not complicated like that of Alessio. With Elias I was feeling safe, I was feeling wanted, I was feeling a beautiful lady next to a handsome man. Isn't that what everyone wants? Wasn't that a blessing?

Elias was a simple person. For him everything was either black or white, there was nothing in between. He believed in God, he was following the Orthodox religion and traditions and he hated all these new philosophical ideas of the Renaissance that had come from Venice. His friends were mainly Greek and he scarcely socialized with Venetian or Turkish men apart, of course, from work matters at the port.

With Alessio being far away I had returned to my old peaceful life. I had even forgotten about my dream and the prophecy of Jeremias. Of course many times my mind would travel to Egypt. How was Alessio doing? But my thoughts would quickly disappear, he was too distant for me now. I knew that Alessio would come back soon, but this date seemed distant too.

Until this date got a number.

- Mikhaela, are you inside?

I heard the door knocking. It was Anna. Why would my colleague need me on a Sunday? I opened the door. She had news.

- I was at the harbor today to get fish for the week. I swear, I am telling you the truth, I saw Alessio.

Anna was one of the few friends I had in whom I confined about Alessio. She too knew that he would come from Egypt one day, but none of us knew exactly when.

- He was there, carrying two big pieces of luggage. He didn't see me, but I am sure it was him.

I didn't know if I was happy or sad. I wanted to see him, but my life now was peaceful, even if not full. For sure I needed some time on my own to digest the news and think. I locked the house and went to the lighthouse. It was my usual meeting spot with Alessio. I sat down watching the sea extending as far as the horizon. I didn't have an answer for him. How did one entire month pass? It felt like a day.

I am not sure how much time I was sitting there. I was lost inside my thoughts, until a voice broke my silence:

- Good morning Mikhaela. I was almost sure that I'd find you here.

It was Alessio in the flesh.

He told me of his experiences in Egypt. He stayed some time in Alexandria. He also went to Giza to see the pyramids and he also visited the cities and villages across the river Nile. His stories were so interesting! As always he was passionate about his new experiences, he was so descriptive that I nearly felt I was there. I was listening with interest. He finally said:

- Mikhaela, the purpose of this trip was for me to challenge myself. Even if I am talking so much to you about walking slowly, following the signs, following love and not fear, this is easier said than done. During this trip I decided to challenge myself only to find that I too had fears, I too subconsciously increased the pace of my walk, I too feared that I would not fulfill the purpose of this journey: To cross through the desert and meet people who have merged into nature, who can communicate with humans as well as with birds. I too thought that my destiny was lying ahead in the distance when it was lying right in front of my feet. In this trip I challenged myself to face my own weaknesses.

I had almost forgotten my thoughts. I was lost inside his experiences. Until he came to the question I was expecting for such a long time:

- And how about yourself? Did this time help you think, make some decisions? Did you manage to get some time on your own?

It was like waking up from a dream. My breath stopped for an instant. What should I tell him? That I stayed all this time with Elias as if nothing had happened? That I avoided at all costs staying alone? That once again I had thrown the boomerang in the air with all my force, hoping that the inevitable would not happen, that it would not return again?

- I have not made any decision, Alessio, I still don't know.

- I had guessed so, Mikhaela. And therefore I already have the answer.

I could guess the answer from the expression of his face. The executioner had already lifted his sword in the air.

- You have twenty four hours to make your final decision. You need to decide whether it is to be me or Elias. If you choose me, I will stay in Malvasia. Then we will decide together whether we stay here or in Venice or anywhere else. You will inform Elias about your decision and that will be the last time you will communicate with him, at least for the short term. If you decide it is to be him, tomorrow will be the last time you will hear from me. This will also be the case if you cannot make a decision until tomorrow night.

With these words he left. I don't know if it was better to be given more time or to be executed right away. The boomerang was again in my hands but this time it was too heavy to be thrown. I was standing at the crossroads. And he was leaving in front of me, nodding me to come. The dream was coming true.

I didn't want to think about my choice. I didn't even like the situation in which Alessio had put me. Who told him I liked deadlines? And who told him he was able to constrain me?

The next morning I met with Elias. He was part of my life and my life was my best distraction. In my life I would forget the big and important decisions, my life was a constant occupation of things that would distract me from what Alessio was describing as the single reason to live: Evolution. And so I met with Elias. We took a walk, we cooked and we ate together until the evening. The time was passing by and the thought of the choice was constantly returning to my mind, but I was trying to push it away, even if this only could barely last for some minutes. Alessio was describing this effort as the effort to avoid the elephant. He was saying:

- Sometimes, Mikhaela, in our lives we have an elephant in front of us. He is so big that he blocks our entire view. We know that we can't remove him from our way, he is huge. We are trying to see life from the left and right of the elephant and somehow we do manage to oversee him. But the elephant is there, still blocking our clarity, still occupying our brain, capturing our life force. We live constantly occupied with everything that lies on the left and right of the elephant, believing that life is it.

» But, Mikhaela, the elephant is life. More accurately what lies beyond the elephant is life. Since the elephant is there, you need to focus on the animal and try to find out how you can convince it to leave. The elephant is your burden, the single most important reason that prevents you from seeing life with a clear eyesight. I can assure you, Mikhaela, that whatever is able to come is able to go as well. And since the elephant can use its feet and come in front of you, it can use its feet to go away.

The elephant was there and life was behind it. I felt that my choice was too heavy for me, how could I lift an elephant? My mind was constantly occupied with the past, how could I bear the weight of a future? I understood why the executioners of all times and religions were men. We are not made to kill, we are made to create. How could he ask me to kill, how could he ask me to choose, how could he ask me to execute the non-chosen? I felt depressed. That role was clearly not for me. He could execute whatever he wanted, but not I. I felt angry.

On the other hand he was right. If I were not to decide about my own life, who could do it? I felt angry with myself. How could I drag the lives of two handsome men behind my indecisiveness? I felt more insecure than ever about myself. At this moment I needed security.

"Security", said the voice inside me.

"Security will take away your fear", somebody whispered into my ear.

"Security is what you need now, later comes the rest".

Beware of this moment, as it is well planned, in order to bring you in front of your fake savior: The Lucifer. Right at your utmost point of desperation, right in the middle of the emptiness, the Lucifer appears.

It was already late Sunday. I was exhausted. I took a small piece of paper. I wrote on it: "Security is my choice. I am sorry, Alessio". I ran up to his house. I didn't want to change my mind again. I slipped the note under his door and ran away. The decision had been taken. That night I did not sleep. It was the worst night I can remember.

III.10 The path of pleasure

And suddenly the turmoil ends, the storm calms and nothing can tell that right here, just a while ago the wind was blowing relentlessly taking away everything blocking its furious way. Nothing but remnants of wood and branches lying around the alleys on a sunny calm day. After the fierce waterfall there comes the calm lake.

And so the days were passing and there was no response from Alessio, no communication, no sign of life. He really kept his promise. I was feeling weird. Why did I do that? I had to choose something and so I did. Why should I feel like this? I missed him. I started to see Elias as an enemy. If it was not for him I would never have let Alessio go, not in a lifetime. But I had. All this because of Elias. I could feel that my anger was now turning towards him, though he was not directly aware of it. Only through my weird reactions.

I remembered Alessio saying:

- We are just drops in a vast ocean, Mikhaela. Do you think you can change the flow of your river? You can only delay the river, you can choose whatever you want and the river will correct its journey to head again towards the sea. It is only important to let the river flow, not to impede it. At the crossroads, whatever path you take will end up ultimately at the same point. Of course, your journey might be less pleasant or more pleasant depending on your choices. But even so the river will keep on flowing towards the sea, it can only flow down.

» When you are at a crossroads you need to observe the options. Look at all the streets, but only once, since taking too long to make a decision can only make it more difficult, the scenery is constantly changing. Some streets look interesting, beautiful, green. Your path is there. Some streets look tiring, difficult. Your path is not there, but you can take them too. You can also create your own path. In life everything is permitted and that's the joy about it. But whatever road you take, Mikhaela, remember that you are the only one responsible for your choices. Never blame others for them and most important: Never blame God. Remember that God is the final destination and, no matter which road you take, you are bound to flow downwards. All roads meet at some point. The only question is: Will you enjoy the journey?

- But sometimes Alessio we need to sacrifice, we need to strive favoring a higher goal.

- Of course! Why do you think you are at a crossroads? The goal makes you move, the goal keeps the journey alive. And what you describe as a sacrifice in reality is a pleasure. Look at a man in the dockyard building a boat. He sacrifices his time, his money to buy the materials, he feels frustration when he finds leaks. You deem it as a sacrifice, but in his world he is happy. In his mind the boat is already there, crossing the seven seas and he is a captain. For him this road is a road of pleasure, a path full of trees and flowers.

» But imagine if this man was a slave, forced to build a boat. He would be sad, doing exactly the same tasks, but not serving his own goal, his dream. It's the dream that powers the journey, the one defining the path. Without the dream, the path is useless.

» When you are walking your journey you will encounter many crossroads. Always you will feel that one of them is more pleasant. Even if you don't, there is no need to worry. It means that you are yet immature and you can't listen to your feelings in advance. That's natural for the beginning. Just take one path, if all look the same, and go. After proceeding to this path it is always certain that you will get a feeling as a response. This feeling will be so intense, that you won't be able to miss it. In your path remember this mantra:

» If you follow the signs you are on your path. Your path is a path of pleasure.

» My master once told me to repeat this word whenever I am in doubt. Following this I go through my own life.

I was puzzled with his logic.

- Does this mean that we should never strive?

- Quite the opposite, Mikhaela. When we don't strive for something, when we don't have a dream, then we feel bored, not pleasant. It is the goal that defines the pleasure. Just remember the man with the boat or a mother feeding her newborn baby. In this striving, in this sacrifice, love is born. Love for the goal. In the mother's mind the baby is already a professor. Love is being created. The mother loves the dream, she loves the professor. The gardener loves the plant, even when it's just a seed. God loves you as God in the flesh of a woman. Without a dream, life is useless.

» Your path is a path of pleasure. Striving is pleasure when striving with love.

Indeed. What is the value of a life without a dream? A pointless journey. Yes, I was taking too long to decide. I didn't know what to do. But did I have a dream? Yes, I did. But did I take my decisions according to it? I would not bet my life on this answer.

- Many times striving can be unpleasant, Mikhaela. And usually this happens when you lose your contact with the goal. That is, when you go for the means to a goal. Have you seen a compass losing the north? It keeps turning like crazy.

- Most people have a goal; they are fighting, Alessio, I objected.

- Most people are fighting for the means to their goal. And many of them are losing the true goal in the process. Go to the harbor and look at the boatmen. Some of them are smiling, but most of them are sad.

- Of course they are sad. They stay such a long time away from their families in order to earn some money.

- Exactly! Money is the instrument. It is used to buy something, it is used as a means to a higher goal. So what is the goal? Why do they need the money?

His words made me think. Everybody has a dream and for most of their dreams people could also use money. But only money? Probably not.

- I once went to a sailor and asked him: "Why are you traveling on this boat?". He said, "I want to build a new house". And I asked back: "By now you should have enough money to sell your old house and build a new one, I have seen you working very hard all year round, I scarcely see you in the city". And then he said: "I want a bigger house so that my family can be happy, but I don't want to sell my old house. I want to rent it so that I can stop working".

- Most people are like that, I said. That's normal, he is striving for a goal!

- He was confused, Mikhaela, and so are you. His goal was to live together with his family without working. And he was doing exactly the opposite.

True. I decided to stay silent.

- This man drowned last month on a shipwreck while sailing to Venice.

That was shocking. I remained silent.

- His wife is now seeing a man from the upper town. He has a mansion.

I don't know why, but I expected this ending.

- You see, his wife was on her path, she wanted a bigger house for her family. But he was confused. He loved his wife, he wanted to be with her. But he was doing exactly the opposite. He was going for the means, Mikhaela.

I was doing the same. Right now. I wanted to go out of this small town and experience the world. I wanted to live in Venice. Instead I was staying in Malvasia and I was working hard all my life in order to earn money. In order to see the world and live in Venice. Later. But now I was moving to the opposite direction of my goal, hunting the means to it.

- Remember, Mikhaela, you can pray to God for your dream but you cannot tell Him how to realize it. Just watch for the signs. They will be there to show you the way.

» If you follow the signs, you are on your path. Your path is a path of pleasure.

One way. The sign was clear. It was dusted but clear. Alessio was always telling me that we could live in Venice, travel to Rome and Florence, visit the harbors of the Mediterranean. He was even telling me to join him on his trip to Egypt.

I was sad. I had just abolished both the man I loved and my childhood dream, coming from a shortcut. To choose what? Security. Since when was security my goal? Only recently. I was not dreaming of security when I was young. But of love? Of travel? Of living in Venice? What did I really want?

Alessio was saying:

- Remember, Mikhaela, of the purpose of life. God is defining Himself through you, through me. Who you really are is defined by what you really want. And you cannot know what you really want unless you do what you might want and receive the resulting feeling as an input. Pleasure means go on, this is what you want and who you are. Sorrow means stop, this is not what you want, this is not who you are. Stop for now and also, don't do it again.

» And this is the value of crossroads. Crossroads make you select between the good and the better. Of course if a good was given without a price, you would always take it. But that wouldn't define the answer to the question: "Do you really want it"? Remember what the ancient Greeks were saying: "The goods come through striving". Everything good comes with a price. And the price lies at the crossroads. What will you choose? The non-chosen is the price you need to pay. Your love is being challenged. Who would believe your love if it wouldn't be challenged? Not even you.

Yes, I was at a crossroads and I had made my choice. And I was receiving my result: Sorrow. That was not what I wanted. I had made a mistake. In the evening I went to the house of Alessio. Three days had already passed. Three sleepless nights, three days of sorrow. I didn't think that it would be so difficult. When he opened the door he seemed astonished. Behind him I could see a large leather trunk. He was about to leave Malvasia. I had already guessed that.

- Come in, he said. Sorry, there is nowhere to sit down.

- Are you preparing to leave?

- I was actually planning to leave in the morning. I just changed my plans for tomorrow, because I needed to meet my friend in the upper town today.

- Okay. I came to give you some clothes that you forgot at my place and your guitar.

- Thank you. You found me by chance. I was not supposed to be here now.

Silence followed. I was not good in these moments. It was now or never.

- You know I was thinking a lot about you since I left you that note. I was crying a lot. I feel sad.

- It was your choice.

- It was, but I am not sure about this choice. I chose security, not a person.

The expression on his face suddenly changed. I could still recognize it; he was a man in love.

- Mikhaela, just as I told you, you need to choose. Either him, or me you cannot fit both of us in your heart.

I was not sure about this statement. But I needed to choose for sure.

- Will I be able to meet Elias once in a while even if I choose you?

- No, at least not for the beginning.

But would he spy on me? How would he know? Maybe I would be able to talk to him only once or twice. I could not imagine not talking to him after four years of relationship.

- I have already arranged a trip to Sparta with him for the next week.

- I would prefer you to cancel it, but if there is no other way, we can make an exception.

Silence followed.

- So do I take this as a yes?

I hugged him.

- I love you, I finally said.

He hugged me as well.

- I will cancel my trip to Venice. We can stay together at my house.

I had not said yes. Neither would I have said, had he insisted on asking me. But I managed to prevent him from going back. I felt relieved. That night we made love and I felt happy again inside. "If you follow the signs you are on your path. Your path is a path of pleasure", I thought to myself. I could feel that my path was the path in front of me. But I didn't walk there. Standing still at the crossroads I had managed to pull Alessio towards me.

III.11 The choice comes back

I was always swinging back and forth, this was me, especially in front of a future. But it was true that now, after I managed to keep Alessio in Malvasia, I was feeling better. However I had one more task to do. I needed to inform Elias.

I was always reluctant to end. I was lacking the knowledge of emptying, I could put aside, but never completely dismiss. Even in my room I still had some childhood toys and puppets that were hidden inside an old wooden chest. They were not used, but neither distracting me, nevertheless, they were there. And such was the case with my relationships. Never in my life had I asked from a boyfriend to split. Whenever a relationship ended it was due to them, not me.

But this was not the case right now. After four years of relationship with Elias, I needed to draw the final point. As I knocked on the door of Elias he greeted me with a smile. But I was not smiling, my mind was full of thoughts.

- Elias, I need to talk to you, I said instead of a greeting.

Elias was used to this kind of conversation. I used to have a lot of complaints, even before meeting Alessio.

- Come inside first, he said. Let's discuss behind closed doors, you never know who is passing by on the street around this time.

I stepped inside, but I didn't feel like sitting down.

- You must remember my colleague, Alessio.

- Of course I remember. That superficial guy who used to work with you in the government office. Didn't he leave Malvasia already?

- Well, he is back. He came back for me.

Elias stared at me with an obviously puzzled expression on his face. He was always jealous of Alessio when I was telling him about our discussions. He never agreed with Alessio's words, he thought that all these new ideas, which came from Venice, were applicable only for a nation that was living in abundance out of the wealth of its colonies. He disliked Venetians and he disliked even more my lunchtime encounters with Alessio.

- Elias, I am in love with him.

The news fell like a rock on his head. It was clear that I was not good at introductions.

- What do you mean? Are you in love with him or with what he says? Do you really know this person? Do you really know who he is? Do you really know if he has a family back in Venice? I think he is just spending his time with you dressing you with romantic compliments, like all Venetians do.

I stayed silent. I knew that he would explode. He walked around the room before sitting on a chair.

- Have you made love with him, he finally asked.

That was such a silly question. A woman makes love with a man in her mind a lot before this happens on her bed. A man can only understand actions. What is the value of feelings for a man?

I have never told lies, nor did I wish to start now. What would happen, should happen based on truth.

- Yes, I have, I said with my eyes looking down.

I could see the earth disappearing from beneath his feet. I could see his world getting destroyed and him vanishing in unconsciousness. Just like after a strong injury of the body the feeling goes numb, the same happened after this strong hit on his heart. I could see that he went blank.

- Tell me the truth, Mikhaela, I need to know everything, he managed to say.

And, just like he told me, I poured out everything to him. As I was talking I was feeling relieved. I remembered the word of Alessio: "You will always get a feeling in response to your action. This is your true self speaking". My true self was prompting me to continue.

I saw that he was about to cry, but he didn't want to let himself go. I was staring at him, feeling sorry.

- You have already made your decision, Mikhaela. Thank you for informing me. So I guess that we need to stay apart now. He is back again for you and you are in love with him. I think that I am redundant for you now.

- I am sorry, Elias, I finally said.

I turned around and left his house right after these words. After all these years together I had to draw the final point. I had to choose and now I had to tolerate the emptiness, the big gap that replaced what once used to be my present and my future. A gap that I could not fill in myself. A gap that Alessio could not fill in either. "You will always get a feeling in response to your action. This is your true self speaking". Emptiness.

That night I wanted to stay alone. I was feeling unstable. My anger was still there, but this time it was pointing back to Alessio. I could foresee that it would be a tough task to forget Elias. I would need to strive. I remembered the man building the boat: He was striving with love. I was not.

III.12 The glass world

And so the days passed and the weeks with me feeling everyday happier with Alessio by my side and thinking from time to time of Elias. I did not want to stop communicating with him, and neither did I. Malvasia was small and from time to time I was learning about Elias. Sometimes I could even find an opportunity to meet him. My door to him was not closed. I was happy about him, he managed to stay proud in front of me and he even managed to find a new girlfriend. That news came to me as a surprise, but I knew that girl. She was always speaking with very charming words about Elias, even when I was present. But Elias didn't seem to care much and so I had never become jealous about her. Neither did I become jealous now. Strangely enough, I had never felt she was a big threat to me, not even now.

The days were flowing but in this flow I felt that I was not participating. It was a feeling of peace, of inner tranquility in which I could find security. I could not explain this feeling, but during all the days that comprised this period I felt like I was somebody else. Somebody who did not care about security, because she was already feeling secure. Somebody who did not pay attention to the matters at work, in the town and in the world, because she felt that none of these things could affect her happiness. Somebody who didn't know how to get angry, jealous or sad, because these feelings simply could not be felt. Somebody who was being, just being and the time passing, just passing without affecting her at all.

The feeling of tranquility was like a big glass all around me and the world was constantly moving outside it, people would get angry, stressed, noisy, but inside it only me, observing, with my eyes and mouth open, just breathing and watching, but hearing and feeling nothing, just tranquil. It was a feeling I had never experienced before, I didn't fear of anything, not even of its end. Where was my old self? Was it still outside that glass, in this weird ever-moving world or had it simply disappeared? One thing was sure about me: There was nothing I wanted. There was nothing I didn't want either. There was no goal, no dream, no journey, I felt like I was already there. I was feeling like an unborn baby inside the womb of its mother. I wondered if the falling from paradise was taking place at birth.

Alessio seemed pleased too. He had renounced work, anyway the government office had replaced him with other people from Venice even before his trip to Egypt. But he didn't seem stressed about finding something else. In Egypt he had met wise sages and they had taught him a new technique called meditation. He said that using meditation he could go into a state of tranquility and observation. I wondered if this was similar to what I was feeling now.

We had developed a new routine, but what was new to me was that we did everything together. We were walking together to my office early in the morning and he would come in the afternoon to pick me up and walk me home. We would eat dinner at his house, he would tell me some of his stories from Egypt and then we would go to the lighthouse to contemplate the sunset. This routine was like a room of pleasure with all its doors unlocked. I could open a door anytime, get away alone, go meet my friends, even Elias and return in this peaceful world, close again the door and feel warm, secure and tranquil. The time was flowing, but I was not. I was feeling free.

Alessio described this feeling to me when I asked him:

- Mikhaela, God is Love and God is the sea, the dream, the final destination of the river that is flowing, the purpose of the journey. What your feeling shows you is that the river is already there, it has already reached its destination. You are the river and you are already there.

» You might think of time as something linear, but it is not. Everything is happening right now, right now the river is on the mountain, right now the river is in the sea. Whatever you think will happen in the future is only an observation from your current state. In fact what will happen in the future has already happened. The river is already in the sea and since you are the flow itself, you are both on the mountain and in the sea; you are already there.

» And since you are already there you are able to feel it. And your destination is love. Once you feel love, you feel the dream, you feel that you are there, you feel that the flow has stopped. You can see the others flowing, striving for a goal making a journey, but you cannot understand why they are moving. You are the observer. The time has stopped. You have no goal to strive for, you have no journey to take, you feel that everything is pointless, your work, your money, your belongings, everything but the state you are, the state of Being.

» And it is true, Mikhaela. In reality, when you are forming the sea, everything is pointless.

In fact the state of Being had come to me. But everything that comes, goes.

And so one day Alessio told me:

- Mikhaela, I will need to make a short trip to Venice. My father's health condition is worsening and I want to visit him. I am not sure how long he is going to live and since I decided to stay here in Malvasia with you, I want to visit him before the winter comes. My trip will last only for a few weeks, that shouldn't be a problem.

I worried for an instant, but then I realized that a few weeks wouldn't be long.

- If you want we can use this as an opportunity. If you want you can come with me and I can show you Venice. You can also meet my family and my friends! If you are able to do it, then you will have a chance to feel how life is in Venice. I can provide you with the cost of the trip.

I always wanted to go to Venice! That would be a great opportunity. I could almost imagine the canals and the gondolas, people singing Italian songs on the street; that must be truly romantic! In my mind, I was already there. And with him for company, that would be ideal! But how about my work? I could manage. I decided not to miss this opportunity.

And so the days passed until the day he had to leave. I could not go with him though, as leaving work for such a long time was not permitted. So he decided that I would travel alone one week later and meet him in Venice.

I had never travelled alone, not even to Sparta. And even if I didn't feel comfortable with his decision, there was no other way and finally I accepted it. I wanted so much to go to Venice that I decided to take this risk. Alessio made all the arrangements for my trip, he also managed to find a boatman, who was a friend of his, and who would even pick me up from my home. In this glass world in which I was living there was no such thing as a barrier. Everything was possible, it was only a matter of will. There was no threat inside, no fear, nothing could go wrong, everything was being taken care of.

Alessio had already prepared everything and we were ready to go. He was not taking many things with him, the trip would not last long and he would be back soon. I was so happy. I was happy that I would meet him in Venice, that we could walk together in this beautiful part of the world. We walked to the port side by side early in the morning. The vessel was already there and people were embarking. I gave him a last kiss and he too embarked.

As I was watching the boat sailing away, I felt my glass world breaking apart. Fear returned in an instant. There I was again, waving away. My drama returned. The summer ended in an instant.

Part IV: The autumn

Look around and contemplate. It is rainy and humid, but the earth is thirsty for this water. The leaves are falling from the trees, it is their time to go, but look at their fascinating colors! The earth is emptying, the birds are abandoning the sky, the butterflies are leaving, the cicadas are fleeing underground. Even the sun is preparing to hide behind the clouds.

May you find tranquility in this silence. May you look back to the summer and contemplate it, free your boldest feelings. In the silence comes the sorrow and deep inside it, the love. And love is really contradictive. As are your feelings, as is nature, as are the leaves on the trees, prepared for their last trip, but wearing their most cheerful costume. In this beautiful, silent time of the year, the summer is drifting away and the winter is preparing to come.

May the Force be with you in this contradictive silence. May you accept that the summer is over, that the winter is coming and that the only way to the summer is again through the winter and the spring; the earth can't go backwards, neither can you. May you let these feelings penetrate you, contradict you, may you remain still and understand that the winter has to come too and that one day, along with the autumn, your bold feelings will also be gone.

IV.1 The moment of the Lucifer

After Alessio left Malvasia for Venice, I started having doubts about what I was planning to do. Was I ready for this? Was I really ready to follow somebody I had met only a few months ago to a remote city, where I knew nobody but him? How would it feel to be there with Alessio and still thinking about Elias? My memory was playing with my feelings, bringing sometimes moments with Elias and sometimes moments with Alessio, but all of them happy. An invader of my tranquility that was stealing on my behalf the most valuable from the chest of the past, leaving in it only what was not worth bringing out.

However, even without being confident in what I was doing, my travel to Venice was already planned. Alessio had prepared everything and he was waiting for me in Venice. I had also arranged with my supervisor in the government office to be absent from my duties for this trip, which, to my surprise, had been accepted. Having that in mind I started making my preparations to go. The boat was leaving the next morning.

Was I fearing to love or was I loving to fear? Both, two sides of the same coin. After packing my travel bag, I decided to go to the upper town and sit on the verge of the cliff next to the church of Madonna del Carmine. From there I could extend my sight to the horizon, feel the breeze in my hair, imagine Alessio being somewhere there in the distance, waiting for me to arrive. A whole ocean was separating us, my love was feeling distant, the sea between Malvasia and Venice was drowning me in its vastness. I needed time to think.

Alessio had been sitting with me at this same spot, only a few weeks ago. Looking far into the horizon he had said:
- When you contemplate the horizon, you are already there.

- How can I be in a place that does not exist? The horizon is an abstract line. The more you travel towards it, the further away it moves. You cannot reach the horizon! You cannot be there!

- The horizon is the gateway to love and in love there is nothing to reach. You just need to contemplate it and then you are already there. You are Love. But to be there you need to oversee this vast mass of water, which separates you from it. You need to oversee what seems to fill the entire picture and focus only on the thin line of the horizon. The horizon separates the earth from the sky. In fact it is the gateway to the sky.

» However, as soon as you manage to focus on the horizon you remember again the presence of the sea. Remember the parable of the Bible about Peter walking on the water. Walking on the sea, he realized what he was doing. How was it possible to walk on the sea? Doubt penetrated him. Focusing on the sea and the absurdness of his action he began sinking. In your effort to focus on the horizon, you too get distracted by the sea. And then you lose your focus, you start feeling separated from the horizon, once again you start looking at the sea. The sea is your fear. When you lose on faith you grow on fear. Then you lose the horizon. Then you lose the vision of love.

» The way to reach the horizon is to focus on it, forget about the sea. The horizon becomes then your driver, your dream, the compass that shows always the direction of your life. You feel it in the distance, the need to cross the sea grows inside you. This is indeed your journey. The whole universe is there to assist you in your efforts! The stars reveal your direction, the seagulls indicate the land, the islands invite you to rest, the full moon lights your path. The astrolabe is guiding you, the compass always shows the north!

» And following your direction towards the horizon, one day you reach the land, one day you cross the ocean, one day you step your foot on America! And from there you look back towards Europe and you contemplate again the horizon over the sea. And in this instant you discover the real value of your journey. Looking at the horizon you say: I won the sea! The horizon is the same, in that same distance, but the difference is that now you know you are able to defeat the sea. This is the purpose of your journey. To win over your fear, to overcome the doubt and to be able to focus on the only reality of life: Love.

In my heart I was already there, in Italy, I could see the narrow canals of Venice, cross over a thousand bridges, float inside long gondolas, I could already breathe Italian air! My heart was telling me to go. But the sea in front of me looked immense. I felt I was already drowning in it, even without stepping a single toe on its waters. Sitting on the edge of the cliff, I remembered sitting there with Elias, talking about remote worlds. It was our favorite spot. We were talking about going to Venice, just to leave everybody behind and sneak one day into a boat and go. Just the two of us, young and in love, traveling around the world. Talking about travel we were hugging each other, smiling and waiting for a colorful sunset. The sun was setting now too. The memories of Elias were alive in my mind. I felt the sea expanding, the horizon getting lost. How could I go to Venice? How could I go to Alessio? I was not ready for it. I was feeling terrible. I was about to open a new door, but my hand was trembling on the handle. The memories were drowning me.

It was already dark. My boat was leaving in the morning. I got up to go home, I needed to get some rest before the long trip.

Arriving at my house I saw my family gathered around the dinner table. They seemed worried. As soon as I closed the door my mother started talking:

- I just met Marcus, the boatman, on the street. He told me that his boat is leaving tomorrow and that he will be picking you up in the morning. Alone!

- You know, Mikhaela, my father said, your mother is concerned. It is dangerous for a young lady like you to travel alone.

My mother interrupted him in higher voice:
- You could be raped! Do you know how many drunken sailors are cruising on these boats? How many lonely old men? Girls are not traveling alone.
- Our mother is right, my younger sister continued. You never know what can happen during the trip. I know how much you want to go, but you might even get robbed. A friend of my schoolmate got robbed last year whilst on his way to Venice. He lost all the golden coins that he carried with him and didn't even have money to return.

I had not even put my bag on the floor before they started firing at me. I immediately went up to my room.

Indeed I was in front of a change. Should I proceed? I didn't know. And I didn't know because I had never been in Venice, I had never had any plans to get married to a Venetian, I had no idea of how it would feel to be far away from my family and my friends, together with a person whom I had only just met. How could I decide between the familiar and the promising?

Alessio was describing the moment of the Lucifer:
- In front of every beginning, in front of every new path, in front of every open gate there is one single obstacle between where you are standing and where you need to go. And even if you have walked hundreds of kilometers, even if you have spent thousands of hours to reach to this point, there is still this single gate you need to cross. And in front of it:

» The Lucifer.

» The fallen Angel, the object of fear of every living animal and human of this planet, the ruler of the abyss, the devil, he, himself is waiting in front of the open door. Behind him: The Unknown. Your journey. Where you need to be. Where you were always fighting in order to be. In front of him: You.

» Right at this moment time stops, doubt penetrates your mind and you need to make a decision. Should you cross the gate or not? Should you continue? Should you follow your heart?

» "I am here to protect you", the Lucifer says. "I am here to warn you that what you are about to do is not reasonable. I am not here to prevent you, the gate is open and you can go; I am here just to give you my advice."

» But he is not. He is there to distract you. He is there to stand in front of the gate that separates you from your feelings, you from Love, Truth and God. He is there to hide the beautiful valley that lies beyond the open gate, the valley of which you were always dreaming; he is there to hide it behind a cloud of doubt, which blurs your vision.

» Your feelings will tell you to proceed. He will tell you that your feelings are irrational, there is no sense, what you are doing comes with a high risk, a high cost. And it is true. Crossing that door means that you need to leave everything you have behind. And the cost is exactly this: Everything you have. Nothing more and nothing less. You can only cross this gate naked. You can only proceed if you leave everything behind.

» "Don't you see? What you are about to do has no sense". He is right. It doesn't. What you are about to do is your single reason of existence, what you are about to do makes your heart beat, in front of it you feel powerless, in its imagination you feel numb.

» Every person on this earth needs to go at least once through this moment, which lies between every significant ending and a new beginning, during a small period of transition. Even earth has to go through the moment of the Lucifer, twice every day: At the end of the night, just before the beginning of the new day, the morning star, Lucifer, appears in the sky. He is so bright that you can't miss him. All other stars fade away and he remains the only one to be seen. And at the end of every day, just before the beginning of the night, the Lucifer appears again. Again he is there alone, the evening star in the sky, the sun has set, the moon has yet not risen, again he is the only visible star. Every dawn and every dusk is a silent moment of transition, a moment of ending, a moment before a new beginning. And in every dawn and every dusk the Lucifer appears.

» But earth knows what to do, earth is the female Goddess, earth is wise. Earth knows when the day has to come to an end. Earth knows that the night needs to come so that thousands of beautiful stars can appear in the sky, so that the moon can reflect its romantic light of silence on the sea, so that the tranquility of the night can penetrate the living beings. And earth knows when the night has to come to an end too. Earth knows that the day needs to come in order to bring its warmth to the people, fill the landscape with color, reveal the energy of the sun. And once the day or the night comes, just after earth crosses the gate of the dusk and the dawn, the Lucifer disappears.

» Mikhaela, the moment of the Lucifer is a holy moment. It won't last long, but it is able to destroy everything. If you listen to the Lucifer and don't cross that gate you will return to what you always had. You will fall down from the mountain you were climbing, back to its feet and staring at it you will feel the sorrow. The Lucifer will disappear and you will be back at the beginning. You will have to climb again. Again you will have to exercise the same effort, but maybe not on the same mountain.

» The moment of the Lucifer is there to prove your readiness. The proof that you possess wisdom. The proof that you are ready to leave everything behind in order to follow your heart. The proof that you have no fear of losing. The proof that you know what you want and you are ready to sacrifice everything else for it. This is why the moment of the Lucifer stands before every ending of the old, guarding the gates of the new: To test you. But even if you fail Mikhaela, know that the Lucifer can only delay you. A worm will always become a butterfly, it is in its genes, the river always finds the sea.

» For these moments you need to remember: The Lucifer talks only with the words of reason. And if you want to cross his gates, close your ears and ignore his reasonable advice, even if his voice comes from your dearest beloved ones.

I was in front of the gate. The gate was open. Alessio had arranged everything. In a few hours I would be going to Venice. In a few hours I would hear the knocking and I would open the door to it. In front of the open door I would be required to cross it, to leave Malvasia and go to Venice.

In front of the door my family, saying that I was crazy to leave a man in love, Elias, following a Venetian traveler, a person who was just living the opportunity, talking some cheap words of philosophy, which were nice to hear, but not applicable in the real world. Where was the Lucifer? Was he in the words of my family? Or in the indulging eyes of Alessio?

Alessio fought his way back into my thoughts:

» For the moments of doubt I will give you a precious gift and you need to keep it well guarded in your heart, ready for access when you are standing in front of the open gate. I will tell you how to distinguish the Lucifer from God.

» God always speaks silently, you need to pay attention and listen. The Lucifer talks loudly, he tries to draw your attention. God only comes to you if you call him, if you pray and pay attention. Lucifer always comes uninvited. For God, you need to wait, learn to be patient. Lucifer provides you an easy and affordable solution. God only gives you an indication, a potential path leading towards a better but unknown world. Lucifer always gives you the entire path with crystal clear indications on where to go, how not to get off track, he will even remain by your side to ensure you will take his blessed route. For God you need to work, to be challenged, to strive. For Lucifer everything is easy, the knowledge comes preprocessed right into your mouth, you need to strive for nothing. Lucifer always claims he has advice especially for you. God's gifts are for all. God will always wait for you at the end of the path, Lucifer stands at the beginning.

» And most important of all, Mikhaela: God talks with feelings. While listening to His Word, you can feel its correctness. You always get the feeling of understanding the Truth, even if you are not sure why. You know what to do next but you don't know what to do last. After He is finished you always get the feeling of tranquility and familiarity, His words sound as if you are remembering something that you already know. His voice seems to come from within, not through your ears but through your heart.

» On the contrary the Lucifer only talks using pure logic. After finishing the only feelings you might get are doubt and fear, but he is smart enough to hide the fact that it is he who lies behind this fear. You will perceive that the fear comes from his distancation after you cross that gate and this can pull you even closer to him. You will never, ever, feel fear in front of the Word of God, Mikhaela, because God rules through love not through fear. God lies inside you, you need to reach nowhere to find Him, God's clothes are those of a beggar, He begins only when you are silent, His speech leaves you breathless.

» Do you still confuse God, Mikhaela?

After his speech I got the feeling he described: Understanding.

» For the moments of doubt, I will give you one single advice: Close your ears, listen to your heart, leave everything behind, undress and continue.

I was not ready. I was not ready to close my ears to my family. I was not ready to accept that the Lucifer always wears a mask, even if this could be the mask of my mother. I was not ready to go to Venice. I was not ready to avoid the Lucifer in this single, smallest moment of transition, the dusk and the dawn, a moment where everything can change, where the summer can turn to winter in an instant.

I could not go on. My mother was right. My planned act was not backed up by reason. My heart started to fear.

Alessio used to say:

- God is always just. Through our experiences we receive the knowledge, we apologize for our actions, we get our lesson, we resent. We then pledge ready. If it comes again, we know how to react. But the path of God is full of challenges and He does not accept our pledge unchallenged. And out of the blue the boomerang returns, the same situation appears under different clothes, waiting for our immediate reaction.

» The moment of the Lucifer: When we get hit by the boomerang, right in the forehead, falling unconscious; and upon waking up God is absent. The challenge. The absence of signs. Lack of future and past. The uncertainty of the present. God in the opposition, unseen, but observing, waiting for our reaction. An open door that calls us to proceed.

» The moment of the Lucifer: Because we asked for it. We once pledged we were ready. We once thought that we had learned our lesson and that we are one step closer to the Truth; we can do it alone. And there we receive it. A contract of the past. But we are not alone. Lucifer is there with us.

» And so history continues, with our being challenged, our understanding of Truth being tested and certified, the same events happening again and again, in a chain of inevitable incidents, in the cycle of samsara, until one day we wake up and decide to behave like What We Really Are, until one day we can prove that we are the Truth, that fear is not part of us. And this is when we receive the control of our lives, overcome our karma. The inevitable will not happen again, for we no longer need this challenge. Our actions are truly us. We don't resent. We are one step closer to Him. Contemplating the horizon we are already there. Incarnating Love we incarnate God.

But I was not ready. I was not ready to leave what I had, I was not ready to go to Venice, I was not ready to follow a future of uncertainty and leave my life, my family and my friends to follow a stranger, alone, in an undiscovered country.

I was determined: I would cancel my trip to Italy. I was not ready to move on.

IV.2 The loss of the opportunity

I had just woken up when I heard a knocking on the door. It was Marcus, the boatman. Alessio had prepared everything for my trip to Venice. He had arranged with Marcus to pick me up from my home, help me go to the harbor, and had even paid him in advance for my trip. With my hand trembling on the handle I opened the door.

- Good morning, Mikhaela, he said with a bright smile! Are you ready to go? The boat is leaving in an hour. I can help you with your luggage.

I hesitated. I was not good in these moments.

- Marcus, I am not coming with you. I decided to stay here. I am not ready for this, I am not sailing to Venice.

Marcus froze still. He was a short man with a belly and a long mustache. He was constantly smiling using his whole face, even when he was just talking. But now his smile had disappeared. He was surprised. He didn't expect this. Neither did I. His eyes remained fixed at me. With a different tone in his voice he responded:

- Has anything happened to you my dear? You look scared.

I was not sure if it was he or I who was scared.

- No, thanks Marcus. I am fine. I just decided not to go. I don't feel ready for this yet.

I opened my hand and gave him a folded note that I had just written.

- Please give this note to Alessio. Please don't open it. I want it to be kept private.

The note said:

"I am sorry. I am still in Malvasia. I didn't make it to the boat. I am really not ready for this. I am sorry. Please don't contact me. I have no words to describe my feelings now."

He put the note in his pocket. His eyes were wide open. He still did not seem to understand what was happening. Neither did I. What was happening, was happening on its own. I felt as if my body was moving alone, as if I was an outside observer. I could see the action but I could hear no sound.

With a quick gesture he lifted his hat and turned around, closing the door behind him. I was left alone. Returning to my body I understood: Everything was final. There was no return. The dice had been thrown.

*****

I spent the weekend thinking about Elias, about Alessio, about my life. What had I done? I had abandoned my relationship, I had been going around with a stranger, a person whom I had met only a few months before, and I was about to travel alone to find him in a foreign country, so far away, somewhere I had never been, somewhere I did not even understand the language. I must have been crazy. How did I decide all this? Was this me deciding, or was that somebody else, having penetrated my body? Who was I?

I was clearly contradictive. Sometimes I wanted this, sometimes I wanted that, but I always wanted it in deadly earnest. Anyone would assume that I was really decided, that I was going for my dream. But my dream was constantly changing. Before I would be able to reach it, the dream was already different. And again I was going with all my force towards it, hunting a moving goal, being determined to live the undetermined. I was tired of myself. By now it was clear. I was not one person. I was two persons in one body. Totally contradictive, interchangeably decisive. Sometimes the one had control, sometimes the other. I wanted neither of them. I wanted neither Elias nor Alessio.

What was I thinking? I needed to see Elias. I needed to tell him that I loved him. I had just cancelled my trip to Venice, I had just forced Alessio out of my life, I had done all this for Elias. I loved him. He needed to know. Maybe we could even spend the weekend together and maybe I could make up for all the frustration I had caused him.

I ran up to his house. I knocked at his door. I knocked again. The door remained shut. Nobody was in. I felt as if I was in front of a wall. I felt that I had put myself in front of a thick wall, in a dead end from whence the only way was back. The door was still closed. Elias was not there. I sat down on his doorstep. I cried.

I don't remember how much time I was there. Nor do I remember why I was crying. Was I crying because I lost Elias or because I had just closed the door to Alessio? I was for sure crying because with my weird behavior I had stopped everything that was going on in my life, I had put a final dot and most important, it was me, I could not blame anybody for this. "But which dot, Mikhaela", I thought to myself. The dot that I drew after four years of relationship with Elias to follow a stranger to nowhere? Or the dot I had put only a few hours ago, a dot to my dreams, a dot to a fortune where everything was exciting and new? I did not know. But for one thing I was sure. That I had put a full stop. And after this dot there was only a dead end, a wall, a closed door in front of the house of Elias, a future that existed only in my mind but in reality was behind a door, which remained closed because I closed it. I was crying loudly. I didn't care if somebody heard me. In front of a closed door nothing matters.

I remember somebody passing by and offering to help. I did not want any help. I wanted to stay and feel helpless, because this is what I was. He told me that Elias was not there for the weekend. He was out of Malvasia with his new girlfriend. I only wanted that person to go. I wanted to stay alone. Elias had found a new girlfriend because I had left him. What had I done? I left at his door the necklace, which he had given me as a gift for our anniversary. I stepped up to go. I needed to realize that he was not there for me anymore.

I spent the whole weekend with my close friends. At least that was what my body was doing. My mind was on that boat. My soul was traveling on the Adriatic Sea to Venice. Where would I be now? Where would I be if the full stop was a comma, if I would not be putting ends in my life but beginnings? My friends were concerned.

The weekend ended and my feelings were still raw. I could not go to work. My supervisor had approved my absence for my trip to Venice, how could I go there again? What would I tell them? To go to work was not an option. I thought that maybe I could correct my mistake, maybe there was another boat, maybe I could still go to Venice. I tried to sleep.

The next morning I ran to the harbor. If I could find a boat to Venice, I would immediately board, by now I was decided. Reaching there I saw a lot of people standing on the docks, all sailors. The harbor was full. What was happening?

- Can't you see, a sailor said. The waves are huge. Please step aside.

The sea was angry, the waves were splashing at the docks of the harbor smashing the boats against each other. The sailors were trying to rearrange their boats and protect them.

- It started this morning, another sailor said. At least we are lucky to be inside the port. And this can last for days, even weeks…

No boat was sailing out of this harbor. I thought that by now I would have been sailing in the safe waters of the Italian coast. My mind was still at the boat of Marcus. No, there was no other boat. There was no way to repent, there was no second chance for me. I thought that when an opportunity decides to go, it destroys the path behind it, so that nobody who has not taken it can follow.

I returned home. I must have stayed the entire day inside my room. What had happened? I had just destroyed my most precious gift, the opportunity for which I had always been waiting to travel and experience the unknown. I always wanted to live in Venice. I had just denied the man I loved. To select what? A day in front of a closed door crying, a terrible weekend, supposedly a weekend with Elias, a weekend of repentance, but only a weekend planned in my mind. The opportunity had been there, everything had been planned, but I had said no.

The opportunity had been calling me, telling me: "Come!" I hadn't gone. The opportunity had been insisting: "Come, I am here!" I had pretended not to hear. As if the opportunity understood, it had been nodding me with hands and feet to go to the other side of the bridge that separated us, the bridge over the Adriatic Sea. The opportunity had been standing there, nodding me to go along. I wondered why opportunities want you to walk to them, why don't they come closer to take you hand in hand. The opportunity had been nodding at me. But I had looked away. And when I'd looked back again, it had gone. I remembered my dream. The sign was still reading "One Way" but Alessio was not there anymore.

Alessio was talking about the vessel of opportunity:

- Mikhaela, opportunity is a boat, and as such, she is a female. Like every lady, the opportunity lives in periods, just like the earth. When she comes, she brings the summer. But even before that, when you see nothing, she is getting prepared. And yes, like every lady who respects herself and her partner, she is taking a long time to prepare, and thus you need to wait until she appears, because she knows that the secret lies in the preparation. In the preparation she is formed. While she is dressing herself up, she is thinking of you. The spore is transforming, the caterpillar is growing, it is the time of the spring.

» And when she comes, she comes for you. Of course! She was even thinking of you while coming, how can she come for somebody else? She ties herself to your dock and welcomes you with a beautiful smile. She comes unexpectedly and surprises you, for what is the charm of an opportunity if she is expected? A beautiful lady always comes unexpectedly, as does a beautiful opportunity. She is beautiful, you have to admit. She says "come" and you are looking around to find out to whom she is speaking to. You think: "Did she say this to somebody else? Do I really deserve it?" Looking around you see that nobody else is there. It is only you and her. She came there for you only.

» She insists. You just stand and stare, you even deny her. Of course, you didn't expect her. She came 'out of the blue'. You have other plans. But even though you keep on delaying your decision, trying to think, she still stays around. She will put on her best clothes, do everything that she can to attract you. But respecting herself, she will not hunt you. She will stay there long enough, showing you her beauty. And indeed she looks magnificent, you will have to admit. And even if other people want to embark her boat, she will deny them. You will ask: "Why me? All these people want you and I don't, why me?"

» Mikhaela, this is because she is your opportunity, she came as a gift from God only for you. You can recognize her, because she is shining. No matter how blind you are, you will for sure admit that she is pretty and even if you are totally blind, you are not deaf, so you will hear the others praising her. You might feel that she is not exactly what you want. Of course, you don't know her well, she just docked at your port only a while ago, how can you know if she is exactly what you want or not? You will feel that you are not ready to receive your dream, that she can't be it, because your dream only exists in your mind.

» Looking away, you will try to hide from her. You need time. You need time to think, to observe, to digest, but she is a boat, her place is in the sea not in the harbor. She came to the harbor for you, she came there to take you, she came there to take you to the sea, to the sea where every river ends, to the sea that connects every land on this earth. She is there to take you everywhere and everywhere is the only place you can be with her.

» While you are hiding from her, she will put on her autumn clothes and leave. She will not leave because she decided to quit. She will leave because, even if she wants you, she respects herself, she knows that she is beautiful and she knows that only beautiful people deserve her. And nobody beautiful is hiding, nor is she. Watching her sailing away you will immediately notice that you should have been on that boat. You will try to follow her but it will be in vain. Your opportunity is the fastest vessel and once gone you cannot grab her, no matter how hard you try. If something in this world is impossible, then this is to grab a lost opportunity.

» Going home you will immediately notice that everything is happening as if you had entered that boat. Suddenly war might start where you live and you will need to go, or you might learn that your friends are on their way in another boat going to that same destination. Everything in nature will confirm that you should have been on that boat.

» But even if you try, there is no way to follow that boat, the boat is gone. Returning to your initial plans, soon you will realize that the wind is against you. Your plans cannot be realized with ease. It seems as if the opportunity has taken the summer with her when sailing away and that you have been left with the emptiness of the autumn.

» And exactly this is what you feel. Emptiness. All the fruits have fallen, all the leaves have gone, the cicadas are no longer singing, the birds are abandoning the sky. You try to do something else, but there is nothing to do. Emptiness is what the autumn is.

» The autumn is the time to remember the summer, to contemplate, to feel, to experience. To be true and confess that the opportunity was there for you, but you were not yet mature enough to take it. And to accept that the opportunity is now gone. Even if you can't accept that the summer is over, you will for sure notice the cold. You need to realize that the earth is female and she lives in cycles and as such it is certain that the summer will come again. But the summer will never come by going back. By refusing to proceed forward, you can only stay in the autumn. The only way to the summer is through the winter and the spring, and then again a vessel of opportunity will come to you, unexpected, uninvited and pretty.

» For the cold winter I will give you my advice, Mikhaela. Forget this opportunity. She is gone. Remember that once lost she can only hurt you. Never look for substitutes, because the substitutes can only make you remember what is forever gone. Enjoy the winter, even if it is cold, it is also fresh. And have your eyes open for another opportunity, for the summer will come again, this is as certain as the rotation of the earth.

» And when an opportunity comes again, do challenge her, see if she is there for you. Listen to your feelings, not to the others. Only you can feel if this opportunity is really for you. And if she insists, don't let her go again. Don't hide again, be true to her and to yourself. She is another opportunity, she is different from the previous one, but she too looks magnificent. Take her on time. Mature as you are now, you will know that she came there for you and that if you don't take her, she will go.

My opportunity had now gone and standing over the dead body I realized that it would never revive. I had just killed my love with Alessio. A glass, once broken, can never be repaired. Yes the sages are wise.

I wondered why opportunities have to come and go so fast in life without leaving me time to comprehend and digest them. And instantly I heard the voice of Alessio in my head: "It is not the opportunity that passes by fast. It is you who have not yet learned to walk slowly".

IV.3 The path of confusion

I needed to talk to Alessio. I could not stand the ghosts in my head anymore. I closed my eyes hoping that by reopening them I would see him standing again by my side. I decided to write him a short letter. But what could I write about? My thoughts went to the note I had written to him, the note I gave to Marcus. I did not even want to imagine his expression when opening it. I wish I were by now in Venice, I wish that note didn't exist. But I was not and that note was the last news he had heard from me. I put pen to paper. I was not good at introductions:

Monday September 16th, 1709

Dear Alessio,

I hope you are fine. My thousand apologies for not coming to Venice. I know that action has crossed your limit of tolerance. I could not forgive myself for taking such a decision either. I guess I have painfully paid for that by losing my loved one. However, I appreciate if you could listen to me for the last time.

My parents were shocked to know that I was taking the boat alone. It was my mistake. Things would also be different had they met you in advance. I understood their concerns. Anyway, after explaining to my parents over the weekend, they finally realized how much I have grown up and am now ready to walk my path alone. It was not easy to convince them, but I did.

I know it's my journey and on this journey I have to walk alone. I am now totally prepared to begin this journey. But I sincerely hope that you can be my guide along the way. I would appreciate it very much.

I also tried to take another chance to come to Venice, but I realized this was not possible. I am wondering, why do I have to understand my opportunities in life only after they are gone? Why do I keep on pushing them away? What happens actually to all people when they deny what is there for them, taking only what requires effort? I love you, why did I let you go?

I might not be good in writing or expressing myself but I would really appreciate if you could understand me and give me another chance.

I love you

Mikhaela

I decided not to write anything else on that letter. I also decided to send it with the government correspondence. This was the fastest way for a letter to reach Venice and I had access to it from my workplace. I needed to return to the office anyway, I could not stay at home all day crying over a dead opportunity. What had happened belonged irreversibly to the past.

The next day I suddenly appeared in the office. My colleagues were surprised to see me. They wanted to know what had happened. Why when something goes wrong, does everybody want to know the details, making the feeling of it even worse? I invented an explanation about my health and served it to them. They didn't seem satisfied with it, but they accepted my excuse. I told the truth only to Anna. She showed understanding.

It only took a couple of weeks for Alessio's answer to arrive, but it did seem a long time to me. I feared that he would never want to talk to me again, after what I had done. While reading his answer, I felt as if he was next to me. In his letter he wrote:

"Mikhaela, understanding your own behavior, your feelings, your dream is probably one of the biggest achievements of your journey of life. As every journey, life as well is solely powered by a dream. Take the dream out of your life and you will see that your life will instantly become meaningless, boring, a life not worth living. It is the dream that defines your behavior, everything that seems weird and absurd to people, even to yourself, is perfectly explainable once your dream reveals itself. Because in your dream you already are. Everything you do is intended to bring you closer to it, to bring you closer to your own dreamed reality, to what you already really are in your imagination, away from a world in which you don't want to participate."

"It is when you understand that you can't go for your dream that you start behaving irrationally, when you convince yourself that what you have in your mind can't be reached, at least not for the time being. It is then when you invent a plan and it is then when the intermediary is born. The intermediary is a battle that comprises the war, a war carefully planned by your mind, strategically including many battles, which, once won, will ultimately lead you to your dream. Your mind convinces you that you are not able to receive your dream without winning a series of intermediary battles. But, Mikhaela, every day that comes brings to you an unnoticed opportunity to realize your dream right now."

"Starting to fight you realize that you are not good enough and that the battle is not as easy as it seemed. This battle has opponents and losing is part of it. Your mind then focuses on winning the battle. Your mind is prepared to do anything in order to win the battle, setting aside everything else, including its very reason, the war. It is exactly at this point that the war is traded for the battle; the dream is traded for the intermediary. Your mind doesn't know that sometimes a battle needs to be lost for the war to be won. Your mind has already planned a series of battles for this war, an entire path to your dream. I call this, the path of confusion."

"And this is where the opportunity is lost. Every opportunity comes as a bug in your life. It comes uninvited, unexpected and it is trying to deviate you from your mind's plan, sometimes to an extent that it becomes molesting. The opportunity is something new and does not fit to this magnificent, perfect plan of your mind. And since an opportunity is always a choice and never an obligation, you don't choose it."

"The reason that you keep on missing your opportunities is that you keep on living in a plan. The reason that you created your plan in first place is because your mind believes that your dream can't be reached directly. But would you trust a commander for your war, who does not believe in your ability to win?"

"Mikhaela, you see here the very source of the flaw of your mind. Your mind invents the plan because it does not believe in the dream. How can your mind win if it does not believe in it? How can you reach the horizon by looking at the sea? Your mind is faithless, your mind is a machine, a servant; your mind is simply not able to have faith. Your mind is a warrior, but you are the dreamer and a warrior knows how to fight, but you need to direct him, encourage him, show him the way. The commander is you."

"But even if you get convinced that the war cannot be won, then look around, and right at your utmost point of desperation, you will see her, sitting on the other edge of the battlefield, your opportunity, your bridge over the battle, not through it. This battle must be sacrificed, the opportunity must be caught, the target has to change. The ability to succeed follows the ability to accept failure."

"The path of confusion is a construction of your mind, a path constantly adjusting towards a goal constantly shrinking to something more tangible, a battle to win the war and later a battle to win the battle, an intermediary, a stubborn warrior refusing to accept loss. Observe your plan and you will see that it only resides in your mind. You never communicated it to anyone, even if other people are participating in it. You are playing chess alone, Mikhaela, and even if your smart mind has planned ten moves in advance, an unexpected move of your opponent can make your entire strategy vanish into thin air. And life is full of surprises once you place God in the opposition."

"You need to understand that there is no opportunity that will make you look through it. Opportunities have to be experienced or lost to reveal their virtues. There is no preview. And your stubborn mind, following the path of confusion, going for the intermediary, knowing what it wants, an egoist solely wanting to win, does not like misty paths. It prefers a difficult, but clear path, over a pretty but uncertain one. And opportunities are both pretty and uncertain."

In fact this was true. I had never travelled alone. I had never been to any country where my language was not spoken. And what if something happened on that boat? What if there was a storm? What if I would go to Venice and I would not be able to return? What if I went there and I ended up thinking only about Elias? What if Alessio didn't love me and he was telling these sweet words to all girls? What if we got married and he would dump me or travel away from me to another country with me staying alone? My mind was already confused in its planning. My mind was never satisfied with uncertainty.

My mind was full of questions about Alessio. But not about Elias. In four years of relationship everything was certain. And right when I was in front of the opportunity all these questions came to my mind. And I drowned in them. That is what happened.

I continued reading.

"An opportunity is a shortcut, Mikhaela. It is the answer of God to your dream. It is the means to reach where you need to be, directly and more pleasant than following your mind's path of confusion. Because your mind focuses on constraints and this is why it leads you to such a long and strenuous path. But for God there are no limitations. His opportunities are always supported by actions of the entire universe. Your mind's path of confusion is lonely, in it you are the only actor."

"And this is why you are losing your opportunities, Mikhaela. It is because you are not yet humble. It is because you are convinced that you know what you want, you are convinced that the battle needs to be won, it is because you have not yet mastered the art of losing. Not having mastered loss, you fear it and fearing it, you are constantly thinking about it, thus attracting it. And by fearing, you don't let your heart express. The voice of your heart stops at your throat."

Indeed I had a lot of problems with my throat. I had gone to many doctors, but none of them was able to give me a cure. My throat was frequently aching.

"Letting your mind define your life is a certain path to confusion. For your mind there are too many constraints. For God there is nothing that can stop the dream, there are no threats, even threats are opportunities. God listens to your heart. He does not listen to what your mind wants, because He gave you the mind as a tool, a servant to help you follow your dream, go for the path of pleasure, understand the signs. But let the servant guide you and soon you will understand that your own wish is over, soon the mind will be controlling your mouth and your hands and the voice of your heart will accumulate at your throat."

This was all correct. So many thoughts were coming to my mind when I was standing in front of him. Staring at him, I was admitting that he looked wonderful, but what was inside? For my mind risks. For my heart dreams. In reality? The Unknown.

"Mikhaela, the opportunity for you to come to Venice was lost. I am sure you tried your best to follow her after she was gone. I am sure, standing on the harbor you dreamt of that boat, I am sure, standing in front of the dead body you tried to resurrect it, only to find yourself in front of a vast nothing, what I call the lake of emptiness."

He always liked to use new terms when he was talking.

"The lake of emptiness is the place you end up after your opportunity is gone. It's a full stop to your river's flow. It's a lake after a waterfall. In this lake you realize you can't go back, climbing up a waterfall is not a choice. In this lake you can only imagine the path you have not chosen, the path of the opportunity. In this lake everything and everyone is absent and you are the only one moving in a slow and unnoticeable flow."

"The lake is there for you to learn. And you can only learn if you don't rush and if you meditate. The lake is there to force you to walk slowly and understand that indeed you have made a mistake, you were confused, your mind led you to lose the opportunity and follow the path of confusion."

"I know you would have done otherwise had you but known. And everybody would have done so. Everybody can value an opportunity after the opportunity is gone. That requires no special skills. But the mastery of life lies in your ability to listen to your heart and value the opportunity when she is right in front of you. Maturity lies in discarding your original plan in front of every opportunity that comes for you and go for her while she is there. Walk slowly in order to decide on time."

"And always remember that every opportunity looks pretty from the outside, she comes at the beginning and her only opponent is the plan of your mind, the path of confusion. She always comes alone, it is not a choice of alternatives, it is a choice between proceeding towards the dream of your heart or following the planned path of confusion. An opportunity never lets you look inside before committing to her, as does every woman who respects herself. An opportunity comes uninvited and unexpectedly and she waits long enough for you to take her, because she wants you as much as you want her. God wants you to be with Him, not away from Him. You never go to find an opportunity, in contrast she comes to find you. And know that an opportunity is a shortcut. Losing her does not mean that you will not reach your dream. But it does mean that you will reach it in a more painful way. A river always leads to the sea and even a still lake has a downward current."

I had lost my opportunity. For that I was sure. But of course, as he said, I realized it only after I lost her. I needed to learn a lot. In fact I thought of all the opportunities I had lost in my life, Why did I lose them? It was lack of knowledge. If only I knew. I could understand what Alessio was saying, that knowledge is for the stupid. I was stupid too to lose so many opportunities in my life. But it was true, every single of these opportunities insisted before disappearing. In one way or the other every one of them was trying to open the closed gates of my mind. And all of them without real cost. I only needed to sacrifice my original plan, what Alessio was calling the path of confusion. I only needed to accept the risks, I only needed not to fear it. But Alessio was saying that this was also part of the mastery of life. To be able to recognize risks but not fear them. And that virtue was given after gaining the mastery of failure. I decided that in the future I would never leave an opportunity to get lost. And as if I could sense it, right at the time of my decision, God was preparing to challenge me again.

I decided to devote myself to Alessio. Elias was anyway seeing somebody else, he was not there for me anymore. I decided that if I was given an opportunity to go to Venice again, I would take it. I decided to change. I decided to devote my life to Love, not to fear. And just at that time I felt unease in my heart. My heart was telling me that God was preparing for me His next challenge. He was not satisfied with the pledge of my mind.

IV.4 The return

As if nothing had happened, I began communicating again with Alessio. He was in Venice with his parents, taking care of his father, meeting his school friends and sending me letters. He also started helping his family business, which was left headless after his father got sick.

I was always eagerly waiting for his letters. I wanted to show him my love, to show that I wanted him in my life, to tell him that I missed him. He was also responding with love to my letters, he never delayed his answer, he was saying that he loved me, that I was the single thought present in his mind, that he felt close to me even from so far and that he wanted to return to Malvasia and see me.

I also wanted to be with him, I was in love with him and I was not hiding it. By now I had decided that my future was in Venice, that my future included him. After I had let him down, staying back in Malvasia on the trip he arranged for us to Venice, he decided to change his plans. He would still return to Malvasia, but not in order to stay. He said that I was too volatile and that he could not base his future on me. Instead, he would return to Malvasia in order to discharge his obligations, give up his house and take his belongings to Venice. He offered me the opportunity to go and stay with him in Venice for some time and then decide together what to do next.

I did appreciate that he was giving me a second chance to prove my love to him. I did appreciate that after all I had done to him, he was still talking to me. Even if he had decided not to stay with me in Malvasia, I could understand him, I could see that this was not what he really wanted, but only his reaction to my indecisiveness. He was telling me that if our relationship went well, we could return one day to Malvasia and I did believe in his promise. He also told me that he could place me in his family business and that he could even give me a salary for my contribution. I could see that he was making his best effort to make things easier for me to decide to follow him to Venice and I did appreciate it.

I showed understanding of his decisions and this time I decided to prove that I was not volatile, that I was devoted to him, that I was thinking about him, and that I loved him. And that was true. After I stayed back in Malvasia I blamed Elias for my weird behavior and I decided to stay away from him and devote myself to Alessio. But that was not always possible. Alessio was far away and my only communication was through letters. Elias was living in the same city and we had many common friends. So, I continued to see Elias, sometimes with other friends in public, and sometimes in private.

Even if I feared to make such a big change in my life, I knew that my feelings for Alessio were strong and that Venice was a wonderful place to live. Thus I decided that this was the way to go. To implement my decision I informed my manager at the government office that they would have to find a replacement for me. I decided to resign. Venice was waiting for me.

My parents did not approve my plan. My father said that I was crazy and that he had taken so much care of me all these years, striving to provide me with the necessary education in order for me to succeed in life and not in order to renounce everything and go for love. He was saying that my job at the government office was too good to be lost and that I had strived a lot in order to get this position. And he was right. Everybody envied me for my job, my compensation and the security that this job provided.

But as Alessio was saying, everything good comes at a price and I was prepared to pay it in order to be with him, in order to show him that I was there for him and to show to myself as well that I was devoted to my dream and that I was now ready to accept any social cost that this decision could bring.

However I could not immediately go to Venice, even if I wanted to. I needed to wait for two months until the government office would find a replacement for me and until I could train this person for my job. And so the time passed by with my exchanging letters with Alessio, dreaming of the day I could advance to my next step, hating this time away from Alessio and close to the temptations of Elias, but at the same time getting courage from Alessio's letters and the approaching date of his planned return to Malvasia.

*****

Even if it was only one month since I missed my opportunity to go to Venice, to me it seemed a lot longer. It was a transition period, a period that I would have to remember, resent not going to Venice and wait for Alessio to come to Malvasia. Wait for his letters, wait for him to come, wait for the government office to find a replacement, wait always for something external, something I could neither provoke nor speed up.

I remembered the lake of emptiness that comes after the missed opportunity. I felt exactly this: Empty. Even if I wanted to hide this from Alessio, from my parents and from my sisters, I was feeling empty. There was nothing that I could do to go out of this vast lake, only be patient, wait for an unnoticcable, slow flow to take me out of it. I was not good at waiting.

Until one day I received a letter from Alessio saying that finally he was about to come for one week only, in order to collect his belongings, give up his house and settle down his taxation issues. It was only one month more until my own trip to Venice, the government office had already found a replacement, and I did need him by my side for this important change of my life, I did need him to stay here in Malvasia and accompany me on my trip to Venice. However he claimed business issues at his family business, saying that he could not be absent for an entire month. I was wondering if he would give me any attention once I would land in Venice or if he would be too busy with his family business.

For one thing I was sure. With him I could never be certain about something; with him I could not feel secure.

My parents wanted to meet Alessio. After I told them that he was about to come, they insisted on meeting him. Although I did not want to show a negative image to Alessio, I found their claim fair. My father promised me that he would be gentle with him and keep to himself all the negative comments that I was hearing about him every day. I wanted Alessio to feel welcomed in my family, so all this time I decided to stand in between, hiding an unwelcome reality.

IV.5 The parents

The next morning Alessio would be arriving at the port of Malvasia. I was excited. After such a long time he would be more than just letters to me. Even though I missed him a lot during this time, I was still happy, because my path was finally clear. In only one month I would join him in Venice, in only one month I would advance, change, go with him and finally be with him. And tomorrow he was finally coming. I was happy. Just as every night I fell asleep hugging my pillow, but tonight I squeezed it tightly, snuggling it to my face.

Immediately after the boat of Marcus docked at the harbor, the passengers began fleeing outside, running towards the land, looking for relatives, touching the ground and cheering. Some were returning again to their homeland, while others were migrating to this small but busy and flourishing city. My eyes were fixed at the moving crowd, searching for Alessio. Immediately when he saw me, he smiled and began walking calmly towards me. He was still handsome and as always, not very expressive. He usually refrained from appearing overwhelmed, but in his core he was still a child. As he was walking towards me, I could see that everything on his face was smiling. My heart began beating faster. He was finally here.

The next day I had arranged a dinner with my family. They were increasingly eager to meet him and I had already informed him about that, asking if I could introduce them to him. By now my parents had stopped criticizing my choice and I could see that they were really looking forward to this dinner.

Alessio belonged to the upscale society of Venice, had received thorough education, and had even attended the University of Padua, which was only for the privileged few. My parents had completely changed their opinion about him and about my choices once they learned about his profession and social status. They had even begun indirectly encouraging me, which I found quite annoying. I used to be always in conflict with them about my private life and this exception did not make me feel comfortable. However for the time being it was convenient and so I had accepted it with pleasure.

The dinner was arranged in one of the well known restaurants where people from the upper town would arrange to dine, usually talking over financial affairs. My parents wanted to present to Alessio a good image of our family, especially when they learned about his proper background.

Arriving with Alessio at the restaurant we found everybody sitting at a big round table. They had already ordered wine. Once we entered the room they immediately turned towards us, as if the groom and the bride had just entered the wedding hall. I still can remember the elegant appearance of Alessio that day. His clothes, carefully selected, were both modern and classic, all made in Italy, giving him a distinct appearance as compared to the rest of the guests. I was proud to have him by my side.

As soon as we sat at the table my sisters began chatting and smiling with each other, giving quick looks towards his side. Alessio could not understand Greek, but he kept smiling back at them, regardless of whatever they were saying. The dinner went better than I had expected. Alessio was talking with my father, who could speak a little bit of Latin, mainly about business issues. My mother was also pleased with Alessio and she even invited him to her birthday celebration to be held in two days' time. I was happy to see Alessio integrating in my family. In this way I felt him coming closer to me.

We spent the rest of the days together, I was helping him to pack his belongings and empty his house to give it back. I felt sad to see this house getting emptied; for some time it was our house and it had formed part of our life and memories together. However I had already accepted that we would need to move to Venice, that the preparation was done in Malvasia and that our relationship would really be formed in Venice.

And by now everything was on track. I had quit my work, I had introduced Alessio to my family, I had the blessing of most of my good friends. I felt that I was flowing safely and steadily on a river towards what was already prepared: My life in Venice.

The week passed by quickly and Alessio was set to go. Accompanying him to the harbor, I was holding him tight. I am not sure if I was holding him because I didn't want to let him go or because I didn't want to stay back. For one thing I was sure: I did not want to be apart from him, not at this volatile point. Even if less than three weeks remained until my trip to Venice, there was one weak link in the chain:

Me.

As the boat was leaving Malvasia, I remembered my daily duties and my arrangements for the rest of week. On the weekend I had already arranged to meet Elias.

IV.6 The labyrinth of life

I still remember my last weekend in Malvasia before my trip to Venice. I was sitting on the outer wall of the east entrance of the city, waiting for the red colors of the sunset. What a magnificent place in my city. Sitting on the brink of the wall I had the view of the entire town on the one end and of the vast Mediterranean Sea on the other. What an inspiring place! That day I had to make the most important decision of my life. And nobody could be there with me, because nobody knew the entire truth; this was buried deep inside me. I was guarding it like a precious treasure.

I never lied to anybody. But I was fooling myself and others, saying and believing that I was honest, when I was only sharing part of the truth. The part, which would avoid my being criticized. Even if Alessio was now far away, I would often remember his words:

- The only way to be honest is to share the entire truth, nothing more and nothing less. The exact moment when you fail to be True you are creating the Other. The Other is created because of your need for the love of the others. But even if you finally receive love by sharing part of the truth, know that the others don't love you. They love their creature inside you, the Other. And your real personality is being replaced thus making you lose your real self.

» If one attitude is important in life, then this is to deny the love of the ones who do not accept you as you are, the ones who want to change you. Change only when you yourself understand the need to change. The ones criticizing you are like closed shells pointing always towards the others, hiding behind their extended finger, when they should really be only pointing to themselves. While they are pointing at you they keep on looking at their pointer, failing to recognize that their three other fingers are pointing back at them. Show them the path by ignoring them, making them have nobody to point at, apart from their own self. God is Truth and He wants all people on earth to become Him. Always be true and always help others to only be true. Don't accept your dishonesty and don't accept the dishonesty of the others.

Even at a thousand miles away, his voice was still in my head. I felt as if he was next to me, on this same wall of Malvasia, guiding me through a world made untrue. A world I was criticizing, but also forming, hiding from Alessio the very fact that I was still meeting Elias. Because I was afraid of being criticized, because I was afraid that he would lose his interest in me, if he found that the single thought when I was with him was Elias. I was afraid, this is what I was, constantly fueling the presence of the Other with my fear. Why couldn't Alessio understand and accept the very fact that my heart was still attached to Elias? Why couldn't I accept the risk of losing Alessio and be true to him? If this was me, then why didn't I accept my own behavior?

But I was not only hiding from Alessio, I was even hiding from Elias. I was hiding the fact that I had introduced Alessio to my parents, thus making my relationship official. I was talking to him about everything else than Alessio and he had accepted this behavior. I was also hiding from my friends, because some of them communicated with Elias and some with Alessio. I was hiding from my parents, because I had just introduced them Alessio, I had just convinced them that I was in love with him in order to receive their approval for my trip to Venice. In a world surrounded by people, I was alone, trying to hide my thoughts, my feelings, and even my body, sitting at this very moment on the loneliest spot of Malvasia. I was seeking these moments away from the others, because I was seeking to stay away from myself.

The sun was setting. The day of my departure to Venice was approaching and I had to make this decision alone. Elias was a nice person. After all I had done to him, he still loved me. I also cared about him, I had him in my mind, I knew that he could make me happy; he was a man in love. Alessio felt now distant in my mind. But his voice, his wise voice, his omnipresent advice were always with me, even right now as I was watching the sunset alone, he was beside me. Regardless of his physical presence, I would think that if I extended my hand, I could touch him. He felt distant, but in a strange manner he was there. Who was there? He was saying:

- The Truth is always there, it is your shadow. More correctly put, you are the shadow of the Truth. Even if it feels distant, it only feels distant in your poor mind, the Truth is always there, always right next to you. Is it the first time you hear that God is omnipresent?

The Truth was here. Yes, the Truth inside his words. But he was not here. He was in Venice. And I had to decide. Should I stay or should I go? Should I be what I was or become what I was not? Should I proceed and accept the risk or remain in the safety of knowledge?

I remembered what he once claimed to be his most precious advice:

- Mikhaela, today I will give you my most important word. You can use it anytime when you find yourself in difficult situations, in front of tough decisions. Even if you fail in everything else, you cannot fail in life if you only observe this advice.

» Life is like a huge labyrinth of rooms. At any certain point of time you reside within a room. If you like this room, enjoy it! Don't think about anything else, don't let your mind travel outside its furnished walls, don't look at its closed wooden doors. There is no need to open them, this can only make it lose its romantic ambience and its rich smell. Sit on every couch, contemplate the view of the paintings, roll your body on its Persian carpets, enjoy! Don't hold yourself back, surrender to its beauty and fall in love!

» But if you can't fall in love with it, if something does not feel right, if this room feels depressive or the air is too heavy, if the carpets look worn out and the couches are not soft anymore, then it is time to place this room in your past.

» To master the life and enjoy its divinity you have to learn both to start and to finish. If you are afraid to change what needs to be changed, you will become like the stagnant waters of a lake, you will have a dirty smell, you will become muddy and blur, and mosquitoes will gather around you. You will not be the crystal clear water of the flowing river.

» Every room has many doors that lead to the adjacent rooms. These are the doors to the Unknown. I call them the dark tunnel, because if you open any of them, you will only see the dark. Yet this is natural, as there is no candle lit up inside.

» Stand in the middle of your current room. Admit it; yes it is time to leave it. The more muddy and smelly you become, the more difficult is it to leave. Observe the doors around you. All doors look the same. Behind them: Always darkness. The Unknown. But meditate and observe yourself and you will see that what is not the same is the feeling you get when you are looking at them. Place your fantasy behind them, imagine that you are already there. For some you will feel indifferent, for some you will feel interested, for some tired. Try to observe your different feelings, not by trying to invoke them, but by letting them to slowly express; they are only sleeping. Imagine yourself turning the handles and opening the doors, losing yourself behind them. Make your imagination real by bringing in all the details, get lost in it. Abandon your logic and forget your rush, take your time not to think, but to feel.

» And by doing this always remember: It is not important to open the right door. What is important is to overcome your fear preventing you from opening any door, forcing you to become stagnant only because you don't know which door is the right one. Of course you don't know. You can only feel. Even if you are not sure about it, proceed.

» Open the door and look inside the dark room. The only color you can see is black. Observe your fear. Observe your mind begging you to stay where you are. Tell your mind that you have already made your decision. Your current life situation is not thrilling, not stunning, not exciting. You know already that life itself is thrilling, stunning and exciting; it is a dream put into action. When you really live your life, you live the dream. God created the world like this for the brave.

» Combat your fear and enter the darkness. Most important of all: Close the door behind you. What is known to your mind is known to be imperfect. Life is perfect. What is known to your mind is not life. Put a lock on the door behind you. The candle is still not lit, it is still dark, you are inside the Unknown, you want to go back. You stare at the closed door. Don't ever go back. Always go forth. What lies back is not life and your ultimate goal is to discover life, accept it as a gift. Try to find the candle. I want to ensure one thing for you, Mikhaela: Every room has a candle. It takes some time to find it, but if you keep that door shut and you give it your best try, you will find it.

» Life is a sequence and no one can guarantee you that the next room will be more elegant than the previous one. In fact I can guarantee you that many of these times, it will be less. However you have proven that you are brave, that you don't like the smell of the stagnant, that you have the will to discover and thus, you shall discover. It is very probable that this next room is just a passage. A passage that will lead you to the room you will really enjoy the most.

» This process is never ending. It can only end by you, when you realize that you really live the life, when you realize that you are in a mansion, an exciting mansion. What can end this process is not fear; it is Love. It is God. It is You. Looking back you will see that all the rooms you have entered and all the passages you have crossed were necessary to reach where you are. As was necessary your honesty and braveness when you left them. Blessed are the brave.

After the sunset, I carefully walked down the steep staircase of the wall, hiding in the narrow streets of the lower town of Malvasia. As I was walking slowly down the street, tears were falling from my eyes. Maybe someone would see me? I tried to hide. I stopped. Deep inside I knew that my relationship with Elias was loving, caring and sweet, but thrilling, exciting and passionate? No, it was not it. I was convinced that exciting would not last for long, thrilling existed only in tales. Even the exciting sunset on the top of the fortress of Malvasia did only last for minutes. Why should I risk what I had for a temporary excitement? It was already getting dark.

Alessio insisted that life is indeed exciting all the time. I could see it in his eyes: He was emotional, passionate, loving; for him life was a discovery. But not for me. Maybe life was not the same for me as it was for him.

I feared in front of my choice to go to Venice. I was tempted to open the door and go back. I could not stand the darkness of the unknown. Elias was waiting for me. He was the only one familiar in an unfamiliar world.

I decided to pass by his house and knock at his door. He opened it; he was still there. He was always there and I was sure: He would remain there, even if I decided to leave. Standing in the darkness of the dusk, I saw the light of the candles coming from inside his room. As I stepped inside, he closed the door behind me.

- I missed you, I said looking him in the eyes. My eyes were still wet.

- I almost thought you had missed your Italian friend. I learned that he is already in Venice. What happened? Did he go back to his wife?

- He has no wife, I said irritated. He is a nice person, please don't talk like that about him. Maybe I should leave. I just passed by to see you before traveling to Venice.

- No stay, I am sorry. I didn't intend to be mean. I am just concerned by all the things you have told me and I have heard about him. I am concerned that he is brainwashing your mind with all these humanistic ideas about serenity and tranquility and now you are even talking about this nonsense yourself. The humanists and their ideas were even abandoned in his home country, in Italy. Maybe that is why he came to Malvasia to preach. But it seems that he has found in you a follower of his great ideas.

- Please don't talk like that about him, I said. If only you could try to be more open. Not everything is exactly as it appears. If only you were not stubborn. If only you were not stuck in your small little world, I might not even have to go to Venice.

In my anger I was revealing myself. But I decided to continue.

- Please try to accept something different from what you have learned in school. Not everything is the same in this world and for the different to exist, there must be something true in it. Even in this little peninsula, in Malvasia, there are people of three religions, Orthodox, Catholic and Islamic. There must be something true in each of them. I can't just accept that only one is right and the rest are wrong. I can't just accept that only we are smart and the rest of the world is fooled. Behind every opinion you can find a truth.

He sat back to think. He was irritated and I could understand him. After all it was I who had brought him to this turbulence with my own behavior.

- I am just concerned about you that's all, he finally said. I just want you to know that I am here for you. Your friend has already left. I am concerned when I imagine you living so far away from Malvasia and even traveling there all by yourself. Who knows what could happen to you in Venice? Who knows what could happen if he falls in love with another girl, leaving you there alone? You won't even have money to return back to Malvasia. You might even have to work as a prostitute or something. I don't know. I am just concerned.

Approaching me, he hugged me, placing his head next to mine.

- I love you, Mikhaela, he said.

While he was hugging me I kept my eyes open looking towards the back. Even if confusing thoughts were coming to my mind, I could find security in him. He was right. Anything could happen to me in Venice. I could not depend on Alessio. Not yet. With my mind I convinced myself that my swing between Alessio and Elias had to terminate. I decided to stay in Malvasia. I hugged him too, but I didn't find the force to hug him tightly.

Years after this I would realize that there are two types of people: Those who decide based on fear and those who decide based on love. For the first category life is dangerous, suffering, unfair, a constant race. They have to strive hard for a living. For the second category life is exciting, full of surprises, a real journey of experiences, a challenge that can only be won. Both live the same life, but their life is different.

Still now I can remember that day, myself crawling on the small alleys of Malvasia. It was the last time I decided based on fear.

Part V: The winter

May the citizens of this fortress endure the cold winter, be patient, have faith. May they have prepared the wood to be burned, may they use wisely their supplies. Because wisdom lies in the knowledge that the winter too will cease and the supplies need to be used for they are useless in the spring.

May you understand that the winter too is necessary, for those who have never seen it are unable to contemplate the warmth of the sun. May you understand that this is not the time to plant your seeds, as the soil is not yet ready to receive them. The earth will not appreciate them, she is a female and she is not always fertile. May you endure and keep your seeds safe for the spring. May you be patient.

V.1 The Challenge

In the morning Alessio woke up with thoughts in his mind. Mikhaela was his daily visitor. Either as the memory of a distant dream or as a thought, she was always there. He wondered, who was producing these thoughts? He was neither their author nor their director; he was a mere listener. He was only receiving messages, messages sent from somewhere distant in this inappropriate early hour. It was half past five in the morning. As if this was the time that the universe was waking up every day, sending its messages to the unfortunate recipients, who had to wake up in order to listen. Alessio didn't want these thoughts to appear. Not at this time of the morning. It was Sunday.

Stepping out of his house for his morning walk, he heard the bells ringing. Alessio lived in the parish of St. Giovanni Nuovo and the bells of the St. Marcus basilica could be heard even from within his house. It was the day of the Epiphany, the day that the light comes from the skies to earth, the day to celebrate enlightenment. As if the bells were calling him, he decided to go to the church. His morning thoughts were still there. They were saying "Listen to me, I am here, I am important". He was answering "Go away. You are just an illusion. You come from a world of dreams and fantasies". And thus were they repeating, until they would be heard.

On his way to the church he was followed by questions about Mikhaela. She had just vanished. He had no news from her, no letters, she had disappeared, as if she had never even been there, nowhere but in his fantasy, coming from the same distant world of thoughts. He was not sure if she was doing well, he had no news from her or from Malvasia. Was she doing fine? He was tempted to write to her, but no, he knew this would not help. He had already sent her one letter, which received no answer. A second one would not bring anything new. If she was not fine, his friends would have informed him. Even Marcus, the boatman, would learn and inform him if something wrong was happening. But no, there was no news, she was neither well nor unwell, there was just silence. Absolutely nothing, but questions following his morning walk to the church.

The ceremony of the Epiphany had just finished and people were queuing up to receive the holy bread and wine. Each one of them was waiting patiently to receive the sacred flesh and blood of God. Alessio also queued up.

While he was patiently waiting in the line, Alessio felt suddenly ready for it. Although he was not a frequent visitor of the church, he had eaten and drunk the Holy Gift many times in his life. But for the first time he had the feeling that he was ready to receive the flesh and the blood of God. To receive God in flesh and blood.

Standing in the line he was able to feel the present. The thoughts had disappeared. The questions had been left outside the door of the church. Alessio was just watching the crowd, the church and the priest. He was thinking of nothing and he was feeling nothing else than ready to receive God in the present. Realizations appeared in his mind. He could feel the difference between a realization and a thought. A thought comes from the outside world, it screams and insists. A realization comes from inside, it is silent and trustworthy. Alessio remembered the moment of the Lucifer. The Lucifer is screaming. God talks silently and with feelings. He was sure. The Lucifer had stayed outside this basilica.

Waiting patiently in the queue he realized: God is Love and receiving His flesh and blood was indeed an act of receiving love, or as most people describe it, the act of making love. He remembered his past intimate experiences with his love mates. No he was not always receiving the flesh and blood of God. Sometimes he was just eating bread with wine, although the ceremony held was roughly the same. He looked in front of him. All those people in the queue were waiting to receive God. He had been in this same queue many times. But he didn't feel the same today. Indeed, this same ceremony, in this same cathedral, with this same bread and wine was a wholly different experience for each one receiving it. But for the majority of people, this was the time after the mass or the time before going back home. For Alessio this was the only thing that existed now, the present, the time of receiving God. By now he was sure: It is not the bread and wine that is holy. It is the person receiving it.

After the ceremony he sat on one of the benches of Piazza St. Marco. People were passing by in front of him on their way home. He closed his eyes to make his morning prayer.

"God, my Lord, my Almighty, now I know why I live, my ultimate purpose in life. The source of all my thoughts, all my feelings, the driver of my actions, is my desire for mutual love. Today I know that I am ready to receive and honor love. Please guide me towards her encounter."

In that morning prayer he was true to himself, he had realized and named the purpose of his being, his true motive of all actions. It was not an intermediary goal. It was the single true purpose of his life. He didn't hide behind a life for money or fame, a life for pleasure, a life to help the poor, or a life for children and a house. For the first time he discovered and told to himself and God the truth: A life for mutual love.

A thought struck his mind:

"Your will shall be challenged. Your devotion shall be shown. And you shall receive Love."

It was the voice of his master. Even though he had talked to Mikhaela about the voices in his mind, he had never told her about the voice of his master. It was his teacher, his guide to life and spirituality. He had discovered this voice during his journeys across Egypt; the voice of his master was his guide through the desert. He was speaking with words or feelings, but he was not always there. His master was there only when Alessio was able to release himself from all past and future thoughts. His master did not appear when Alessio was stressed. The only voice appearing under stress was the voice of his thoughts combating his mind, forcing him to raise walls against the outside world and hide, not from the world, but from them. By now Alessio was not confusing these voices with the voice of his master.

His will would be challenged. What did his master mean? He remembered Mikhaela. He also challenged her love. Though never expressed, his true reason behind leaving Malvasia was to challenge her love. If not challenged, thus is not proven.

"Alessio, God is always by the side of those practicing the Truth. When you are true towards a being, you can see God inside it. You can find God in your partner, in your father and your mother, in your teacher, by staring at your own baby; God resides in any human being. You can find God in a cat feeding her small kittens, a dog always being vigilant of the street. God resides in any living animal. You can even find God in materials and landscapes, in mountains and lakes, on the earth or in the skies, as He is the Love expressed in everything that exists. You can find God inside yourself. The only reason that you might not be able to see God is that you have lost your very own ability to be true. You can contemplate God everywhere, but only when you are true. Because God is Truth itself. God and Truth come together, it is the same Being expressed with a different word. God is not true, God is Truth."

"You can never receive the Truth unchallenged. This is not possible, as the only way to distinguish Truth from the untrue is to challenge it. Truth will always withstand any challenge, it is impossible for the Truth to fail. However, even the slightest deviation, even the tiniest piece of untruth will eventually lead to failure. It will only be a matter of time. Challenge will cause eventually and with time everything untrue to terminate. Thus challenge is the weapon of the Truth to distinguish itself from the untrue and remain. The untrue can only be temporary. In a timeless present, the untrue does not exist. Thus, the untrue is only an illusion."

"Alessio, what is not True is indeed just an illusion. It cannot exist. Truth is God and God is everything that exists. Only God can exist. Anything else cannot. Only God can withstand any challenge. And Love. Because this is the holy trinity: God, Truth and Love. The same meaning expressed in different words, the trinity of the One. Only Love can exist. Fear is deemed to be temporary. Only God can exist. The Lucifer is deemed to go. Only Truth can exist. The untrue is deemed to cease. The whole world, everything material is deemed to be temporary. The material world is just a playground of continuous challenge, a game revealing the Truth, using the illusion of time to give to the untrue through birth and termination an illusionary existence."

"Alessio, the untrue is born and ceased. And challenge is the cause of its seizure. Time only brings challenges, nothing else, challenges are the ones that cause your body to die, the Other to vanish, the lies to reveal, the sex to finish, the material love to terminate. Challenge will kill anything but God, Love and Truth. Because this is the only thing that can ever exist."

"What exists is not born, thus cannot die. What exists can only be discovered. Remember when you feel love. You can never trace the moment of its beginning. When did your love begin? Was it love at first sight? Is a sight enough for this breathtaking state to be born? You thus come to the only possible conclusion: You felt this love even before seeing the person. You come to believe that seeing her only brought up what already existed. Did you meet in a previous life? Was there even a previous life? The only thing you know is that there was no start, not in this life, it is just impossible to find a beginning anywhere. And this is true. You cannot begin loving anybody. Neither can you finish."

"Love, God and Truth are to be discovered. They can neither be created nor ceased."

Alessio sat back to think.

What is not True is an illusion. What is not God is an illusion. What is not Love is an illusion. Living in an illusionary world, governed by illusionary time with everything getting challenged and failing with time. Everything dying, everything staying only in memory, in the morning thoughts of Alessio, in the love of Mikhaela. What were all these thoughts? Illusions, appearing and disappearing in an instant, sometimes even remaining unnoticed.

Alessio was realizing more and more. What was this memory of Mikhaela? An illusion. She was not there, not to be seen, not to be heard, not to be touched, she was only in his mind, thus an illusion. Yes, this was it, an illusion existing in his mind, an illusion brought up by circumstances that in reality had nothing to do with her. In the timeless present everything is deemed to pass, to remain only in memory and thus reveal its single property: That it is nothing else but an illusion.

"Alessio, the end of the world is foretold. As is its way of termination. Challenge. This is what will be used for separation, separation of the Truth from the illusionary, the self-realization of God."

And so Alessio realized: God challenges. So does the one who loves.

"Alessio, life with God is not easy. He shall challenge your love, though He shall never face you with a challenge that you are not able to withstand. In a challenge, what is proven is your readiness. Once not ready, you are given a second chance. And a third chance. Until you are ready to pass the challenge and love too. Or avoid the challenge and suffer until you break and return to it. But the one who loves, never leaves, he is always there, seen or unseen, ready when you call him. So is God."

"Because God is Love and he wants you to be Love too. To incarnate Love, to be Truth, to become God. He challenges only your readiness, and in the moments of your limit, He is there with His full Love. A conscious parent raises parents. And a conscious teacher prepares teachers. So does the Lord. He raises the God, human, the incarnation of Himself."

It was Sunday noon already and Alessio rose from the bench upon which he was sitting. Once again he was one step further in his long path. He realized his true purpose of life and realized why he challenged Mikhaela. He realized that Love could withstand any challenge. And he realized that she did not withstand it.

It was the end of this weekend day of the Epiphany. He wished to receive news from Mikhaela soon. He wished to be able to see her, feel her, communicate with her.

V.2 To be or to become

The next week was beginning. Waking up Alessio opened the curtain of the window behind his bed. It was still dark. Again he woke up too early. Again, his first morning thought was Mikhaela, the good-morning thought. By now he had realized that there was no point in trying to sleep again. With the good-morning thought in his mind he could only twist and turn in his bed trying to abolish it. But what is deeper than the memory of love? Sitting straight on his bed he closed his eyes, not to sleep, but to meditate. Concentrating his mind on his breathing, relaxing his tense body, he began observing his thoughts. Observing the pain, feeling it, understanding that the pain expects to be tolerated, not buried. And by observing it, see it growing, threatening, rising, culminating, becoming unbearable and suddenly: vanish. There is a limit in pain and crossing it, the miracle happens, the body and the mind numb, the pain suddenly disappears.

His first thought came fast. How was Mikhaela doing? She is fine with Elias, he replied to himself. No, she is not fine, his mind told him. He started to hate this voice in his mind. Why couldn't this voice agree that she was fine, why should this voice only pose questionable answers, without any logic, just questions faking the form of an answer, questions that in reality could never be answered? She is not fine then. Why is she not fine? He knew that his mind could not sleep with a question.

Opening his eyes, he went to the kitchen to prepare his morning coffee. This day, like the others, he would go earlier to his office. His family business was depending on his questionable presence. The answers he was trying to find were not for his business. Why wasn't she fine? If she wasn't fine she would have told him, not hide for such a long time. "She must be fine, she is having back her old life, she is not thinking about me anymore", Alessio said to himself. "She is not fine, she is thinking about you every day, she feels helpless and abandoned", the voice said in his mind. He indeed hated this voice. It was once again time to ignore it and drink his morning coffee.

Again his day in the office was unproductive. His innovation was lost inside a labyrinth of thoughts, full of questions, guesses and supernatural answers. He was smart enough, he could solve the daily problems, respond to the requests of the customers, find answers to their queries, but he was not able to innovate anymore, invent new ways, seek for new clients. His innovative thinking was shed by the question of the day: Why wasn't she fine? That could not be true.

On his way home he realized that in the evening he had nothing to do. It was a cold winter evening and his friends were not in the mood for meeting people. Alessio disliked the winter, not because of the cold temperature, but because of the cold feelings of people during that time. After all, there was nothing wrong with the cold, there was nothing more refreshing than the rain, more appealing than the snow. Yet, people in the winter would hide their smile behind a long face, suppress their feelings, ignore the present and focus on a long wait for the next summer. He decided to walk around the city, just walk without a destination, think about life, maybe try to make some decisions or try to find some answers. He was walking slowly, cruising for over half an hour, when he found himself again in front of the theatre of San Giovanni Grisostomo. It was the last day of "Hamlet". He hesitated. He noticed that the show would begin in short time. A well dressed old man was selling a single excess ticket in front of him. Should he go? It started to drizzle. He should go. Even with his mind blurred, Alessio was still able to read the signs of the Universe.

He remembered when he was passing in front of the same theatre one month ago, on his way to meet a customer in Cannaregio. An advertiser started talking to him:

- Come to see "Hamlet" from William Shakespeare. A world famous tragedy, now in Venice for one week only. Reserve your ticket in advance sir!

Alessio was fed up with these people. The performance seemed interesting but he was not interested in the happenings of Venice. His mind was still in Malvasia. What if he would need to return by the time of the performance? If he received a letter from Mikhaela he would go to Malvasia and meet her, so he would not be able to see the performance. But a letter never arrived. And today he was again in front of that same theatre, completely by chance, at the right time, with the performance and the rain starting concurrently. The Universe talks with signs, he needed to obey. Buying the ticket, he entered the theatre.

It was a tragedy. He was obsessed with the plot. To be or not to be? Yes, that is the question. He was able to understand what prince Hamlet meant. Yes, the meaning of death is far beyond the material ending of one's days. To be or to become? That is the real question. To accept the reality, live with it, yield to a painful life or to dive into what is not yet there, merge with the unknown, cross the border and travel to an as yet undiscovered country wherefrom nobody ever returned? What was behind that swinging door?

He didn't want to know. He loved life, he wanted to be, why not be, why cross the door of no return? His mind went to Mikhaela. Yes, it made sense. Why should she cross the door towards him, why should she leave her settled life, the known, Elias, her family, her friends, her work, to follow a promising stranger into an unpredicted future in the distant Venice? Yes, for her that was death, it was a suicide, the permanent killing of what is, towards what is not yet, the undiscovered country, the great Unknown. Wherefrom nobody ever returned. Out of inability or out of own will?

To be or to become? If nobody ever returned, there must be a reason. But even so, his choice was to be. His choice was the security of life, even a life of disappointment, a life of injustice, a life where the goal was never to be reached but merely to create a wobbling journey. The known. Including the knowledge of its certain termination. Is it really a choice to be? Or is it perhaps a façade, a dream where we insist on staying until a certain and foretold awakening? But his own choice was to be, to be even now in a life of pain, where he was not fine. He didn't want to discover yet what is behind the door of not being.

And yes, this is what Mikhaela did as well. In front of the Uncertain, the Unseen, she chose security, she chose what she already had, she chose Elias. Just like Alessio, just like everybody else considered sane, she chose to be. And yes, just like Alessio, in this "to be", she was not fine. The morning question was answered and matched. She was not fine.

At the end of the tragedy, Hamlet dies. Is that what life is supposed to be? "If it be now, 'tis not to come; if it be not to come, it will be now; if it be not now, yet it will come. The readiness is all."

Is choice then just an illusion? In a timeless present isn't there only one choice, not to be, to become? Of course, in the long run we will all die, that is more than sure, there is no question. He wondered if this applied as well to Mikhaela. Did this mean the promised end of the suffering, the unavoidable path of becoming, the obligation not to be? Did this mean that one day, sooner or later, she would leave her life and her work in Malvasia, she would let Elias go, her family, everyone, in chase of the Unknown, a life maybe in Venice, a pure becoming, written on some large books of faith? Was it worth the waiting?

In the darkness of the theatre, Alessio found the space to cry, release, express his sorrow, maybe because of Hamlet's readiness to die, maybe because of Ophelia, maybe because of Mikhaela, maybe because of his own choice to be, but no, he started crying when he remembered how he was forced to become, to become a visitor of this performance, to leave behind his gray days of winter, to not be in his winter depression, even for some hours only, to become.

His mind went back to the promoter; his memory was more vivid than the play. That day he had been walking on the one side of the canal on his way to a prospective client. In front of him there had been a lot of people gathered, so he had decided to cross the bridge to avoid them. The promoter had been standing on the other side of the bridge. He had offered him to buy a ticket. He had stopped, even though he had been in a rush, he'd thought for an instant and then gone on. On the rest of his way he had been thinking about that performance and the ticket. Why?

His memory went back again to the time he had been standing in front of the bridge, wondering whether to continue through the crowd or cross it. His mind focused on three figures who, it was now clear to him, appeared to be there as well. One of them had been next to him, looking at him. Alessio had been looking at him too, though unable to see him. With his stare the man had nodded to him to cross the bridge. Alessio had crossed the bridge as if on command. When he'd crossed the bridge, two more figures had been waiting on the other side; one of them standing next to the promoter and the other further away, observing the scene. With his mind he tried to focus on these figures. They had been there, most certainly, but why was it only now that he could see them? These figures were neither moving nor smiling and, although he could see them, he was unable to either look at them directly or tell what they were wearing. These figures were bright, not white, staring, not looking, directing him but not using their hands, only their stare. These figures were spirits.

For an instant, Alessio's breath stopped. His memory was clearer than his vision. He was led by spirits, he was led to see Hamlet, he was led in front of the question to be or to become in his divine mission to confront it and to understand it. The performance had ended, people had already gone, but Alessio was still sitting there on his seat, crying loudly now, releasing energy, getting rid of a painful being. He was subconsciously led to becoming, to not being, not meaning death but life, not an illusion but the Truth. The fire was lit inside him to show him that the darkness is not there, that the reality lies in becoming.

Alessio did not know what to do. All he knew was that he was happy to be crying again, that he did not want to stop, he only wanted to let it be, let it evolve, let it become, transform. Crying and laughing were not far apart, not at all, both releasing energy, a volcanic eruption, lava bursting out and burning what is, what needs to be burned for the new to develop, to become. He wondered why crying is a privilege of the babies, why grown-up people are discouraged to cry, thus keeping everything inside, accumulating rubbish, getting older and weaker, every day of their lives less able to become, to see in clarity, to see that there is not even a glimpse of that question, to be or not to be, to realize that the way is one; to continue. The readiness is all. That is the question: Are you ready to become, or not?

Alessio must have been crying for over an hour, but he was happy. Through a mixture of crying and laughter all his energy was released, his stagnant smelly waters streamed out of his wet eyes, the lake was left empty, ready for fresh water to come, to be was not there anymore, washed away by his tears of happiness, yes to be was cleansed, to not be was not death, it was faith. He was happy that all this stagnant energy had been released. He thanked the three spirits. They were angels.

The theatre was empty and dark by now, as was his soul. After the release, the glass is clean and empty, the human is alert, to be is not anymore and to not be anymore is. He realized that darkness was not negative, it is inherent. It just is, like everything else in the world, neither negative nor positive, darkness is there to be realized and to be lit by the only light there is, the inner light, the light of the soul, the light of God. Darkness is a prerequisite for the light, it is the empty ground that lies ready for the crops to be cultivated. Darkness is the winter. The termination of the old for the new to come. And just like on earth, darkness is terminated by readiness to become, by the decision to let the old go, welcome the new, enable fertility, empty and wait for the light, the spring, to come. It is the denial of readiness that keeps darkness in the soul. And the darkness is to be blessed, for it means that the fields are empty.

In his emptiness his master appeared. It was not a vision, only a voice. It was not a thought, it was a voice to be heard, not through the ears but directly inside the brain, a masculine voice, a guide that only appeared in the darkness. Alessio was seeking for this voice, but when he was seeking for it the voice was not coming. In his utmost emptiness, in the absence from any doing, his master was appearing to guide him to a being through not being, to direct him on a journey that would release him from conforming and bring him to the next level, a more challenging journey leading to a higher state of peacefulness. His master today was speaking even more clearly. The darker was his soul, the clearer his master could be heard:

"Alessio, I sent you these angels to guide you to this place, to this moment, exactly now, to this experience, to this darkness, to make you empty, to take out of you all this energy that you accumulated during the summer, along with its memories, all this noise that was preventing me from coming to you, all this certainty that you are something, that you have achieved to build your own castle in the sand, that you are more powerful, more wise, more mature, more grown-up and remind you that you are nothing, exactly nothing and that your nothing is everything, the only state that resists all challenge, the only state you can be, the Truth. And now that you are empty I am here, because I am pure and I do not mix with the dirty and I can only appear when you walk clean."

"I am not a guide, I am not here to tell you anything, nor to direct you, for the only director of your world is you. I am here only to give you the light that will show the vastness of your darkness, the light which will make apparent that what you are is only a short stop during a long journey, that you not yet are, that the only choice is to be, but not to be what you are, to be nothing and everything at the same time, to be all, thus to become. To exit your narrow mind and delve into the vastness of nothing."

"What you are now, Alessio, is not perfect, is not magnificent, it is nothing like the peace of the sunset and the tranquility of the full moon. You only deserve perfection, Alessio, and I am here to light up what you are, your imperfect being and bring you the desire to be God. For God lies in the Being, but the Being comes through the Becoming. I made you see this act to understand that you are only made to become, to return to your Source, God, not to stay on earth but fly and experience the flight. You are not made to be what you are now. You are made to become. Thus, you are made not to be. In order to be. Do you understand?"

Alessio nodded in agreement. He did not understand with his mind but he got the feeling of understanding. Alessio asked his master for advice. He did not know what to do and he had no more energy in order to discover. His master obeyed his holy wish.

"I can guide you only upon your command and what I shall guide you is your own wish, your wish not to remain stagnant, to move and by moving, to be blessed. "

"You need to go to Malvasia and meet Mikhaela, you are not satisfied here, thus you are not on your path. "

"You will meet a traveler in Venice and you need to host him, you will need him in the future and he needs you now. "

"You are the incarnation of an angel and from now on you need to accept it and honor it with your name. "

"You need to face your darkness and go through it and then help other people go through their own dark winter."

"I am your master, I am the Angel of all angels, you need to be able to distinguish me from the Lucifer and help others do it as well. And for this reason you need to face him and understand what the Lucifer really is."

With these words his master disappeared. Alessio remained silent. His feeling was the smell of the earth after the strong rain. Clean as he was, he could see a beautiful rainbow in front of him, a tranquil rainbow to follow. He lifted from his seat, his seat in the theatre, his seat in Venice and his seat in life. He was now set to go, he was receiving clear guidance, he had a goal. He needed to go through the darkness, he had his energy regained and now he could stand up again and walk forward, deeper in the darkness, knowing now that the darkness is followed by the light. He knew he needed to return to Malvasia. He needed to see Mikhaela. He needed to give her a last chance.

The boat for Malvasia was leaving in one week.

V.3 The beggar of love

On the trip to Malvasia, thoughts penetrated his mind. He was determined to offer Mikhaela a last chance. The sun was already setting, tailwinds were cruising the vessel of Marcus. Marcus had understood that Alessio wanted to stay alone and thus kept his distance, greeting him only before the boat sailed from Venice. Alessio was standing on the stern of the boat, gazing at a beautiful sunset. A breeze of fresh air was blowing through his hair. The world is so magnificent, he thought. Why couldn't his own world inside look magnificent too? Why did he have to fall in love with Mikhaela? What was the reason that his heart ignored so many girls who admired him, directing his attention to the one who was constantly disappointing him?

"Love itself is a butterfly, Alessio. When you chase the butterfly it flies from one tree to another, for what is the value of a butterfly inside your closed palms? But if you keep silent and observe, the butterfly will think that you are a tree and it will sit right on your shoulder."

Alessio looked around. He was alone. That was the voice of his master. He blessed his master for appearing when he was in need. Yes, he was chasing Mikhaela. Right now on this vessel, traveling to Malvasia.

"The beggar will only receive the small change, Alessio. He might receive the spare, but never the scarce."

His mind went to the beggars of Venice. They were abundant, always asking for the same, constantly being drunk, living in isolation, inside their own world, talking to themselves, ignored. Alessio was kind enough, always searching his pockets for some coins. Offering them his small change, he was glancing into their eyes before resuming his walk. Though they were always returning a smile, he could sense that they were never fully satisfied. No matter what the amount, he could see that their response was the same.

"You give them what you don't need, Alessio, not what you really value. After you leave your coin with them you move on, you go to the theatre and there you spend what is really valuable for you, your time. But did you know that every human has a virtue and maybe this beggar hides an undiscovered teacher, a silent philosopher, a talented musician or a great painter. Everyone, following their path, unleashes their virtues. And really, no one is worth your spare change. They are worth your attention."

His attention. How many times had he paid attention to them? He was always rushing through, giving only a quick look back at them as he was moving away. But he also knew that everybody, even a beggar, has a sacred journey of becoming, a combat over fear, the experience of love and finally, creation. Everybody was able to create with love, the same kind of love that was emitted from a painting of Michelangelo, a play of Shakespeare, a sonata of Gabrieli. Even the beggars were not born to be beggars. They were only lost behind their belief of inability, in reality begging for attention, not money, having given up their personal combat against their greatest fear.

"And you know, Alessio, even the beggars of love are beggars and they too deserve attention. "

"You don't deserve the change of anyone, Alessio. Not of Mikhaela. What you deserve is her attention, not her spare."

A beggar of love. That is what he was. Always asking for more, because he was getting only her spare. Enough was never the case. Because she was distant. The beggars on the street were not satisfied with his small donation, and he too was not satisfied with her charity, not because there was more to give, but because the given was the spare.

"You can give your spare to everybody, Alessio, but the scarce is given only to the ones you love."

His mind went to the summer. Mikhaela had been visiting him every day after work, but only on her way home, due to the mere fact that her office was nearby his house. He had only been receiving her spare time, what was left after working, dining with her family, meeting with her friends and spending the weekend with Elias. He had been receiving the remnants of her life, not her life itself. He had been accepting the spare. He was not proud enough to deny it. He was a plain beggar, a beggar of love, receiving the small change of an immature girl.

"Don't worry, Alessio. Like the beggars of the street, you too are a little bit drunk. But that cannot last forever."

Indeed. What makes people more drunk, a sip of love or a barrel of wine? What is more addictive to the human? Is wine or love the worst enemy of the reason, leading people to assume a certainty of existence in the absent and deny what lies right in front of their eyes? Is it wine or love that intoxicates more and condemns the affected to create a virtual reality, a self experienced world, which is bound to expire? But what is real and what illusionary? Is this expiring experience the reality or the escape from it? What is the dream and what the truth? Is the world really supposed to be blunt, a reasonable reality, a picture in black and white?

He looked in front of him. The sun had already set and the sky was drowning in red color, decorated with a flock of orange clouds exploding from the most luminous point of the horizon. The world was a dream. The earth itself was drunk.

"Do you want to hear the truth from someone, Alessio? Make him drink. You may think that he talks nonsense, but what does your limited mind understand about sense?"

Indeed people are true while they are drunk. And people in love as well. And indeed the reality is addictive. And what lay in front of him too. He was addicted to the colors of the sunset. And he was addicted to Mikhaela too. In her absence he felt heartless, the sunsets appeared in black and white, the world was blunt. But it was true that he was receiving her spare change. Both in the sunrise and the sunset of love, he was alone.

"Alessio, there is no problem in getting drunk, but getting drunk alone makes you behave like a beggar."

The voice of his master was shaking his dream, even without touching it, he was talking from inside. The deeper he was delving into this love, the lonelier he was feeling. Yes, Mikhaela was left behind; she was not with him in this journey.

"Alessio, if you drink with your friends you will all laugh and cheer. But if you drink alone, your friends will be laughing at you."

His master was giving hard hits to the dream he was chasing. From the ruins of his surrounding castle he could observe the real world outside. It was more beautiful inside. But inside he was alone. He was hiding the truth from his friends, because they would criticize him, he was hiding his disappointment from himself and Mikhaela, because he was still hoping that things would change, he was still hoping that she would let Elias go and choose him, travel with him to Venice and around the world; this illusionary colorful world of his dream, a world of feeling and romance, a world of happy ending or rather a world of happiness and no ending.

Hiding the true reasons of his visit to Malvasia, he was right now sailing away from Venice into the dream of love, alone, a Don Quixote, conquering the world using a kitchen knife and a pot, discovering mystic worlds and stories of previous lives, the voices of the angels, treasures in the castles, signs of God guiding him into his own dream, a world of illusion, loneliness and finally sorrow, the black tunnel itself. He was fighting alone against unseen beasts that were neither defeated nor winning, just not participating, against the odds with nothing going right, or everything going right but him perceiving it as wrong. Just another drunkard, a beggar on the street; that is what he was. Receiving always the spare but never attention. The escape from a challenging world into a lonely reality.

He turned his head to look backwards. A full moon was rising from the horizon. Its reflection on the sea was illuminating the path of the vessel. It was as if the vessel was following the path of light, heading towards the full moon in the distance, as if the moon could be reached by merely sailing on the sea. Yes the world was a dream, but not a lonely one. In this dream everybody was participating and this certified its existence. An ever changing dream lit by the full moon, the sunset, the blossom of the trees, the white crystals of the snow, a dream resulting not out of the expiring sip of wine or an illusion of love, but out of the hand of God himself, out of the one and only universal Truth: Love.

Going back inside the vessel he saw Marcus, wheeling at the bow of the boat, contemplating the moonrise too. He was a simple person, a boatman, lacking formal education, but having the education of life, showing understanding and kindness. He lacked everything that Alessio inherently had, he was neither handsome nor tall, neither wealthy nor educated, but still Alessio admired him for having found love. His wife had departed with him from Malvasia, accompanying him in his commercial route from Venice to Malvasia, cooking for him and for the guests of the vessel, silently managing the boat, his life and him.

Alessio realized there were three categories of people. Those who fear the black tunnel of life and compromise in mediocrity, those who enter it and confronting its inherent darkness seek for the nearest exit, and those who know that the only exit is through the darkness, requiring tolerance and patience to be reached.

The first category is comprised of normal people. Living in an impermanent fake safety they do everything possible to defend it, relying on a selective God to support their wobbling plans, becoming religious, fearing the wrath of their godlike creature. Entering the black tunnel, they are trying to go backwards, seeking the security of the past, a past already changed.

The second category is comprised of the beggars. Facing the difficulties of the dark tunnel they understand their own weakness. Remaining in the darkness, they are begging for attention from God and whoever crosses their life, receiving only the spare. They feel unable or maybe not yet ready to move the elephant that blocks their vision in the front, the single battle that needs to be conquered in order to move forth, their own proper obstacle, the one that they are not only trying to hide from society but also from themselves.

And the third category is comprised of the warriors of light. Having endured their darkness, they learned to exert faith, patience and calmness as the three most important weapons in the dark. Inside the dark tunnel they form light in their imagination, subconsciously also constructing it in reality, patiently continuing their blind walk to the front with faith, guided by an unseen hand of God and at the end seeing the light, not in front of them, but emerging from within. They then begin lighting the whole tunnel, not only for their own journey, but for the others too, they become masters, guiding themselves and their neighbors to the other end, understanding that the path is still long, but also having the certainty that every single drop of water standing on earth will ultimately reach to the sea.

Cruising on the Adriatic towards Malvasia he realized that he still was not yet ready to belong to the third category. He realized his own weakness, he realized that he was begging for attention, just another beggar, a beggar of love. But he felt happy that he was more advanced than normal people, he felt pleased that he found the braveness to get lost into the dark tunnel of his heart, even getting drunk on love, displeased with the mediocrity of normal people's lives, thus creating a dream to live inside it. He realized that this was just a passage in his labyrinth of life, a passage to be endured, a winter that would certainly end on its own timing, with its own pace. Enduring the winter was the only way to reach the spring, going back was not an option for him, he had already seen life in black and white and he had denied it. Having seen today's sunset he was convinced that life is supposed to be colorful, if lit by the inner light springing out of the heart of the warrior. He was not ready yet to be a warrior. But he was receiving guidance with the certainty that the beggar is to be respected because the beggar is more valiant than the normal.

Returning back to his cabin he gave a last look to Marcus, still driving his boat. He must have once entered the dark tunnel too, he must have won it. Building a commercial vessel certainly requires endurance, but now he was driving it with pride. Instinctively Marcus turned towards his direction too. Seeing him he smiled, as if nodding in agreement. As an experienced boatman he was driving Alessio through his darkness. Standing in front of a magnificent moonlight reflection on the sea he was guiding him with his example into the dream. A dream shared, a common dream in which he deserved to participate, reality itself, life.

V.4 Repeat and rewind

Arriving at the harbor, Alessio contemplated the view over Malvasia. Although it was not his hometown, he felt a strange attachment to this city. It was early in the morning and the smoke from the chimneys was moving rhythmically in front of his eyes. What a peaceful city, he thought. Why did he ever leave this place? Why did he force himself to return to Venice, taking with him the memories of Malvasia, thus living in Malvasia, though physically staying in Venice? He was puzzled. But seeing the city in front of him, he instantly felt that he was returning home, even if in reality he was going there only for a short trip. In this trip he would meet Mikhaela. Somewhere in these houses in front of him she was still sleeping in the arms of Elias, looking forward to a peaceful weekend. He had not informed her about his sudden visit.

Alighting the boat, he directed himself towards the inn of Malvasia. With only six rooms it was the only lodging option for the visitors of the city. The innkeeper greeted him. She knew him from when Alessio lived in Malvasia.

Settling himself in the room indicated by her, he looked outside the window. In front of him the vast Aegean Sea with boats entering and leaving the busy port of Malvasia. He used to sit in front of this sea for hours with Mikhaela, talking about the tranquility that is found in the female Goddess. What lay in front of him was waking up memories inside. What existed right now in the present was being translated inside his mind to experiences, which already lay in the past. He realized that the mind is rarely living in the present; it is always obscuring the reality of the present with a memory of the past or a fantasy of the future, both nonexistent in the single moment which exists: Now.

Turning his head back into the room he thought again about his plan to meet Mikhaela. He was constructing it in his mind for endless hours. He had thought about many alternatives, the potential failures to those alternatives, the questions and the answers. Sitting on his bed he realized that again he was not living in the present. Swinging between memories and plans, his mind refused to obey to his life in the present.

It was already evening and he was ready to go. He would meet Penelope, the best friend of Mikhaela, in the usual tavern where he used to have lunch with Mikhaela. Penelope would have arranged the meeting with Mikhaela, without her knowing the presence of Alessio.

Going towards the tavern he decided to take a slow walk. What would he say to Mikhaela? She would be surprised to see him in town. What was he doing in Malvasia? That would be her first question. He had already prepared the answer: He was on his way to Crete where Yannis, his best friend from Malvasia, was getting married. But in reality he had decided to make this long trip only for her and he was prepared to communicate that as well. He had already decided not to hide behind cheap excuses. He was there to give her a last chance as he was directed by his master, he was there to open the door and say: "Come".

But he would not force her to come. He was not giving her a last chance in order for her to take it; rather he was doing it with the knowledge that she would not take it, so that he could justify his decision to move on, even if she was not yet prepared to come along.

Arriving at the tavern, he saw Penelope sitting at the table. She had just arrived.

- Good evening, he said in cheerful tone.

- Well, look who is here, Penelope said. So you finally made it here. When I received your letter I didn't believe that you would come. But it seems that love can do anything!

Penelope was the best friend of Mikhaela and even though she advised him that it was not the right timing for him to come, Alessio had still decided to take the long journey.

- So the plan is as you wished, Penelope said. Mikhaela will be arriving here in half an hour.

- Are you sure that she will be alone?

- Absolutely. Elias is attending a triathlon, he is not even in the town. Should I leave you two alone or should I stay here?

- Does she know that I am here?

- No, I kept that secret. She will be coming to have dinner with me only.

- In that case you can go. I will explain everything else to her. I have no words to thank you.

- No problem, Alessio. I wish you good luck. You know how much I would like to see you two again together.

Penelope was a very romantic person. She believed in love and she was always moved by the love stories of others, which reminded her of her own painful experience.

It did not take long for Mikhaela to arrive. Entering the tavern she immediately noticed Alessio sitting at their usual table. She stood still for a moment staring at him. She should have guessed it. How come Penelope asked her for a private dinner, she had never done that before. Approaching Alessio's table, she sat down. She did not talk at all. She was just looking at him and smiling in silence. Alessio was happy to see her again.

- So you finally came back, she said.

- As you see I am here, he smiled.

- Did you get a new assignment in Malvasia?

- I might stay, yes, but I did not get any assignment. I came to see you, talk to you, you had just vanished.

- I am truly sorry for that. I did not know and I still do not know what to say. I have decided to stay here in Malvasia. Now I live together with Elias in the same house. We were lucky enough to find a house and I was lucky enough to find a new opportunity for work. As I had work experience in the government office, I found a Greek merchant who was willing to hire me and now I handle his accounting issues and calculate the exchange rates during his trade. It all happened very fast. I did not know what to say, I was thinking about you every day, praying that you would be alright, but I was feeling guilty and I hesitated to communicate with you. I am truly sorry.

Mikhaela was pleased to see Alessio now in Malvasia, although she was almost sure that at some point he would return. It felt as though no time had passed since he had left. They ordered dinner.

- Next week, said Alessio, I will leave to attend the wedding of my best friend, Yannis. But during the whole week I will be here and I will be staying at the inn of the town. I hope that you will be able to come and visit me.

Mikhaela nodded in agreement and Alessio paid the bill. It was time to go. Alessio was there and the chance was there for one week. It was her choice to take it or not.

During the entire week Alessio was trying to keep himself busy. He had many friends in Malvasia and he was visiting them whenever that was possible. Of course they all had their daily duties and they were not able to spend much time with him. Alessio was wandering around the city in the mornings, sometimes going to the upper town to contemplate the vast blue sea from the cliff of the rock and to remember the times when he had been sitting there with Mikhaela, talking about Venice that was hidden behind the distant horizon. Every evening he was asking the innkeeper if somebody had come there to find him. But every day he was receiving the same answer.

The days were passing by and there was no sign of Mikhaela. With each passing day he felt more and more that there was no point in what he was doing. He was always going to Mikhaela, but she had never come to him, not even during the summer. It was always he who was forcing his way towards her, a magnet going towards a metallic pin that would commence its way towards him only once he was nearby.

He remembered that every time he had left her alone, she had gone back to Elias. She had gone to Elias when he left for Egypt, she had gone to Elias when she was supposed to travel alone to Venice, she had gone to Elias even after quitting her job in Malvasia, decided to live together with Alessio in Venice. Alessio was convinced more and more that she was getting attracted to whomever was at the moment closer to her, whether that may be Alessio or Elias or anybody else. And now Elias was living with her in the same house and Alessio was lodged in the inn of the town. There was no chance. His actions were pointless.

As the day of the wedding was approaching, he decided to deliver to Mikhaela a small message written on paper:

"On Sunday I am leaving for Crete to attend the wedding of my friend. Please come to see me tomorrow. I will be at our usual spot, I hope you still remember."

V.5 The Reencounter

I was late and stressed. Alessio was here in Malvasia, he had come for me, he was here for an entire week and I had vanished, disappeared, thinking of him but not seeing him, afraid of what? I was afraid of myself, I was afraid that I would dig myself in the same hole in which I had been lost in the past, once again go inside and get buried. I was afraid that once again I would put myself willingly into turmoil.

Arriving at the lighthouse I saw Alessio sitting on the edge of a rock, looking towards the horizon. I wondered if he was using the same rock every time to contemplate the sea. Approaching him from the back, he greeted me without turning his head towards me. Even when he seemed lost in his own world, he was still alert.

But not me. Today I was again in a rush. Elias wanted to know where I was going. He was not convinced that I would meet one of my school friends and he wanted more details. He began asking questions, so we started fighting and again I was late. I always envied Alessio for not participating in a tense world and for maintaining his tranquility by looking at the sea, while I was fighting my way out of my house.

As I approached, Alessio turned his head towards me. He still looked handsome. His face was smiling, even though his mouth was not. He nodded at me to sit next to him.

- Sorry for being late, I said.

I didn't know what else to say, I was still upset.

- Don't worry, Mikhaela, I used this time to concentrate. Sitting here, I was able to connect to my female substance.

That was the least I was expecting to hear, today, in the state that I was, upset because I'd fought with Elias in the morning, upset because Alessio was leaving for Venice, upset because I once again had failed to let myself free and make him stay here with me for the rest of my days.

What did he mean?

- Do you have a female substance too, I asked in investigative mood. I hoped to hear a negative answer, I did not want any more surprises today.

- As much as you have a male substance, yes.

He was still weird. After almost three months in Venice, he remained unchanged.

- Please sit down. I see you are not calm. I will talk to you about that once you relax.

I sat down next to him. It was like exiting a world of troubles and entering a peaceful green valley of flowers and trees. I wanted to close the door behind me.

- So are you leaving again for Venice, I asked.

- Yes, I am planning to leave. Unless you are ready to commit and make me stay here. I came to attend the wedding of my friend Yannis and to see you. But I have been here for almost a week now and we have only met once. I am not sure if it makes any more sense for me to stay.

- Since the day you came here, I have been thinking of you every minute. I think of you before I sleep, after I wake up, even while I work. I don't know what to do. I think of coming to see you and then I change my mind, I get puzzled, I hesitate. I really don't know what to do.

I felt helpless. He hugged me and I went into his arms. I wanted to stay there, I wanted him to keep him forever. In his arms I felt safe. Next to him I was receiving the tranquility I was missing in my own daily life.

We stayed still, speechless and hugged.

- Mikhaela, your true essence is peaceful, just as you are now in my arms. You are a Being hidden behind a foreign personality. Just before, when you came, you were again the Other. Upset, rushing, trying to apologize, trying to calm down. That is not you. You are always and can only be tranquil. How could I speak to you, when you were not truly you? How could I explain to you about the female Goddess? How could I show her to you in the nature, in the sea, inside you, inside myself too?

I stared with love into his shiny eyes.

- I want you to explain to me about your female essence. I know you are not into men! I have tested and tried it.

I gave him an intimate smile. He smiled back at me. I felt happy.

- Mikhaela, when I crossed the boundaries of my own Other exploring my real essence, I then discovered the female Goddess.

Ever since I was born I had associated God with a male. Zeus, the king of Gods, was male. Even our orthodox priest, when he was referring to God, he was talking about our Father not our Mother.

- If God is everything, Mikhaela, how can God be a male? The female Goddess has been purposely hidden in the religions. In a man's world she had no place. However the Deity, as well as you, has both male and female qualities.

He looked away towards the horizon. I could feel the tranquility emitted from this peaceful horizon in front of us into his straight body and from there flowing into my heart. I felt as though the only two beings in the world were us.

- Mikhaela, the female side of the Deity possesses the quality of Being. As a female you are, you just are, feeling, enjoying or suffering, contemplating what is there, remaining, not moving, refraining from doing. Even while the world around you keeps moving, you remain, like the queen that is being carried inside her coach, looking out of her window with everything moving, but she staying still. From a still standpoint she contemplates and feels, she remains and observes, suffers and laughs. Depending on what is in front of her, she becomes. She has no boundaries with her surroundings, in a sense she is one with everything, connected. She is the female Deity, the Goddess, overlooking earth and sensing the marvel in front of her and inside. She is the gateway to heaven, but the gateway to hell as well. What lies in front of her is perfectly reflected inside. She is able to tune herself to earth, send and receive her pulses, because she is one with earth, she has no walls; she needs protection, because she has no boundaries. She is vulnerable, because she is in constant communication with her surroundings.

» If you look at nature, she is all around. The sea in front of us is female. She remains, feeling either tranquil or upset, always being there at her place. For have you ever seen the sea traveling? Do you think you can ever come here to this same place we are sitting and notice that the sea has gone, that the sea has moved somewhere else? She is constantly in motion, like everything in the world, but her movement is in cycle, an ebb and flood, as is the mood of every female. She does not move herself, instead she is moved by a boat that crosses her waters, by the stone that I threw just now, by the wind passing above her, by the position of the moon. But she always has the quality to bring herself back in equilibrium.

» The moon is female too. Did you know that even if she is in constant rotation she remains fixed towards us? We can only see the near side of the moon. Even in a million years, if you look up to the sky, you will still see the same mountains and valleys on her surface, just like the sea, although constantly moving, she remains fixed. She is reflecting the light that she receives from her male counterpart, the sun. She is beautiful, romantic, tranquil, you look at her and see the Goddess, you recognize that she just is, nothing else, and while you are looking, you just are too.

» You can find the female Deity everywhere around you, nature is a great teacher and everything that happens outside is happening inside as well. She resides in the sea in front of you, in the earth that hosts you and feeds you, in the colors of the dusk and the dawn, every day reappearing in harmony and timeless permanence. She is the female Goddess, the beauty of Aphrodite, the fertility of Artemis, the faithfulness of Ira. Observe the expressions of the female Deity around you and you too will feel female, regardless of your gender. Observe your feelings and you will become a female too.

I looked at the sea. Waves were constantly cruising on her surface, but she remained there. Emitting tranquility, I could lose myself inside her and dream, feel, just be. I did not want to wake up from this dream. I was holding firmly the hand of Alessio and I could feel female, held by and devoted to a male, a male inside me but also next to me, holding my hand, guiding me into the tranquility of the sea, the orbit of the moon, showing me the female Deity on earth and sea, guiding my own journey inside her.

- But no, God is not female, God has no gender, Divinity is both. He is the creator of this world. In seven days He created the light, the plants, the mountains and the sea, the humans and the animals. In seven days He created the world, a universe, a home for Her, the Goddess. Because He knew that for the Being to exist, Doing is a precedent.

» The male side of the Deity possesses the quality of Doing. As a male you create and destroy, you empty and fill, you fight and protect, you penetrate and conquer. As a male you are a king building the city walls, constructing the castle, fighting against the enemy, riding the horse, moving, constantly moving to discover, create what needs to be created, destroy what needs to be destroyed. As a male you move back or forth, but always linear. You have continuance and persistence but never a period or a phase. You insist, you are stubborn and you need to be stubborn in order to fight against the hassles and to continue moving forth despite the difficulties on your way. For you there is only one goal and you don't stop looking at it until you reach it. You are Ulysses returning to Ithaca fighting his way through the Sirens and the Cyclopes.

» Possessing these values, you are a male, the creator, the king of the kings, Zeus, ruling the world with his thunder, Poseidon, guiding the sailors through the wild sea, Ares, fighting the enemies on your straight path, Hermes, communicating the messages with clarity and completeness. Regardless of your gender you can be a male and when you begin your inner quest, you will see that you have male qualities too.

» And look around you, Mikhaela. The male is everywhere in nature. Look at the current of the river. Water that only flows forth, unstoppable, fierce, fresh, ever-moving. Who could ever stop the flow of the river? Listen to the wind. He is also moving in one, single direction, never going around, never staying at a single place, he is a constant traveler, never resting until he reaches his destination. He brings fresh air to the warm regions, he delivers, he moves the seeds for the forests to expand, he moves the boats on the sea, he creates energy, he remains in constant action, a true messenger, Hermes himself.

» And look at the sun, Mikhaela. He is a male too, explosive, supplying us constantly with warmth and light, shining his light on the moon for us to be able to see her and get lost in her beauty. In a way, she takes his light and transforms it into something beautiful, it is his light that we are able to see on her. Without him she would be cold, unseen, hidden on a constant state of sorrow. He is the eagle that hunts, the lion that rules, the horse that gallops in the wild, the donkey that carries the crops. He is the one enabling her to be.

» He is inside you, Mikhaela, in a way he is also you. He is the one who drives your progress, makes you move on, destroy what needs to be destroyed. When you are in front of a door in your life, he is the one that tells you to open it and follow the path. He appears in your dream and whispers to you "I am here", when fear comes to your mind. He was there when you were helpless and unemployed, writing down the application for the merchant's office where you now work, he was absent when you were in front of the boat to Venice and you did not embark. He is the one giving you the energy to move forth, Mikhaela, and for that you need to respect him. He is the male, the God inside you, the sun, your source of light, your guide towards awareness.

He was right there, next to me, guiding me to awareness, awakening me, disturbing my silent waters, preventing me from becoming stagnant, providing me a breath of fresh air, bringing to me in Malvasia the dream of Venice, guiding me with his voice into a journey, accompanying me in my travel. Yes, he was my travel mate and I had denied him, turned my back on him, he was my own male voice talking through a handsome Italian body.

- And here comes the journey, Mikhaela. Right here is your trip to salvation, the return home, your way back to the reality you once left, the paradise. It lies in the discovery of your own male and female side, the understanding of your own nature, the understanding of me, the complete understanding of the world.

He looked back at the sea again. Fresh air was traveling through his hair, and my mind, my thoughts, my entire presence was penetrated by him, touching his soft hair and surrounding him.

- Alessio, how do you connect with your female presence just by looking at the sea?

By now I had understood what he meant. He was more than just a man. He was a male and a female combined. Just as I was. Deep inside me both forces coexisted bringing mixed wishes to my mind.

- Looking at the sea, I observe the female presence outside; and through it I observe my proper female presence inside. By looking at the sea I am connecting to the Goddess, the female Deity, my own self and you. I am looking at all of us concurrently, because we are one. And all of it, right now, is in front of me.

He contemplated for one more moment the waving sea. Then he turned his head towards me:

- You need to find the male and the female inside you, encourage them to coexist, fight and help each other. Don't be frustrated if he is stubborn, he needs to be stubborn to keep bringing you forth regardless of the burdens. Don't be frustrated if she is passive, she needs to be passive in order to feel and contemplate. Don't behave like a woman, because you are not only a woman; don't behave like a man, because you are not only a man. When you destroy your Other self, whatever is not you, you will be confronted with a woman and a man, you, a male and female Deity expressed through this beautiful body that I have in front of me right now, through these marvelous eyes in which I am drowning, showing me the path, the path to you, the path of my salvation, the path of my return home, to her, the Goddess, you.

I could not speak any more, neither think, my lips went numb, I only wanted him to kiss me, I wanted to lose myself inside him, vanish into his body, travel with him not to Venice, but to Love.

- We can only return to paradise together, Mikhaela. In all those lives we have lived we are always meeting each other and every time we are giving each other a promise. But to return home, we need to fulfill it.

Silence followed. Yes I knew what he meant. I got the feeling of understanding.

- Mikhaela, the whole truth is in front of you, right in front of your eyes. If you read Genesis carefully, you will see that Adam and Eve did not fall from paradise when they ate an apple from the tree of knowledge. It happened long before that, when Adam discovered his inherent loneliness. At that time Adam felt that he was not able to contemplate the serenity of paradise alone, he felt the need to share his love with somebody, but with whom? Then he requested God to create a partner for him. But Adam was made in the image and likelihood of God, the whole, everything. How could God create something else that is everything but does not participate in itself? It was then that God decided to put Adam into deep sleep and remove a piece from his side to create Eve. And it was that time when Adam was not everything anymore, when he was only something, something incomplete, craving for completeness.

» Mikhaela, it was not the rib taken out of Adam's left side of the body. It was his heart.

I suddenly felt so emotional that I needed to cry. Yes the man is heartless, hands without a heart, and the woman emotional, a heart without hands. How can we reach paradise separately?

- And right at the time of separation, Mikhaela, the path was defined. To return home we need to reunite. I need to be able to feel again and you need to be able to move on. And the whole Universe, God, is showing us the path. The sun shines and the moon becomes magnificent, romantic. Without the moon, upon what would the sun shine? And without the sun, how would the moon look romantic? Even in nature, our material world, harmony results from reunion.

» Our path is together, Mikhaela. Our path is the journey, the holy journey written down on the elements of the nature by the hands of God, the return home, the return to the timeless present, the defeat of all fears, the glory against death and loneliness, the overcoming of time. Just when Adam felt lonely, he fell to the earth and just when he stops feeling it, he will rise.

» And now, Mikhaela, you will need to decide. Are you ready for this path? Readiness is all. The readiness of becoming. Because at the end of this path lies death, or otherwise birth in the form of an ending. There are people who made it, there are men who reached Love and returned to heaven. They went through the holy path, the journey of Eros, they made it. And as a result they died. In the certainty that they would never again incarnate, they received the bliss of Love. Look around you, Mikhaela, and see. Don't you ask yourself why men in love died young from sudden death? They regained their heart. They joined Eve in heaven. Their mission was complete.

Thoughts came to my mind. Yes I knew of a few men really in love. A love that lasted. But in most cases something happened to them and death came unexpectedly. I was always asking why, why does God never leave love to be, why is God mean, leaving on earth only the unworthy. Today I received my answer. Mission completed.

- And this is the holy journey itself, Mikhaela. The path to God, a returning path, a path to zero, to the beginning, the road towards nothing. The ultimate destination is God. And since God is Love, the destination is Love. And this is the path for us both, I need to come to you and you need to accept me. The holy journey, Mikhaela, is the journey of reunion, the journey of the Doing reaching the Being, the male reaching the female. It is the journey of the male river flowing into the female sea.

» This path is a path towards the female Deity, it is the return path of the water that once evaporated from the sea, now traveling through clouds, mountains and rivers to return, to reunite, to be again the whole.

» This is the Reencounter, Mikhaela. It is where the water finally finds the sea, the only state where Adam and Eve are one again, now wiser from their journey. Having experienced each other they will never again separate, because they cannot anymore, being one they will never again feel lonely. And thus they will rise. They will die. Sleep. An ascending, sudden and natural death.

- Love is the journey, Alessio?
- Love is the journey, Mikhaela. There is no other journey. There is nothing more spiritual than love itself.

V.6 The end of the winter

It was already evening and the time had passed, but I didn't want to go home. I was holding his left arm tightly, watching the colors of the twilight, feeling the energy exchanged between our bodies.

Through his extended arm I could connect to him, pass through his body, take my place inside it, the place of his heart, once taken away when Adam realized he was lonely, when he realized that his mind could not communicate with his feeling and with his heart. And when Adam felt loneliness, then God found the solution and took his heart away to create me, Eve. And ever since I stood in front of him he was able to see me and he fell in love with me, the beauty that was once lying inside.

And since that day his mind attached to me, following my random movement. Passing in front of him, his eyes would instantly turn to my direction, in my vision he would go blind, the background would get lost and I would be the only living being moving in the scene. Ever since I left him, he would be cursed to chase me, he would be unable to control his proper brain, he would be able to manage everything else except me. In my vision he would freeze, like a rabbit in front of a torch, being only able to stare at me. He would stand still, his words would disappear, his hands would go numb, he would not know what to do. His chest would open in order for me to go inside again and fill his emptiness, bring color to his colorblind presence. He would travel all around the globe only in order to find me, making up reasons about work, about commitment, about finance, masculine reasonable excuses, trying to hide the one and only fact: That the only reason for his existence is to find me, to attract me and to invite me to take again my original position inside his own lifeless body. A body without a healthy mind is still alive, but without a beating heart it is dead. Thus, he would travel from Venice to Malvasia only in order to extend his hand and invite me to stay with him forever, feel again, even if only for a few minutes, see the world in color, get lost in serenity, receive me inside, be me.

I too admired his thoughts, his word, I could melt into his mouth, I would happily enter through the passage of his lips and take my original place as his heart, be the most important part of his body, give him life and join him back in heaven. I was always striving to make myself beautiful, develop my qualities, be hard working. But I was doing that to satisfy myself. For him, I needed to do nothing, I only needed to hold his hand, not even talk and I would instantly become his world, he would happily renounce everything to receive me.

Sitting next to him, I wondered if he would stay, I wondered if I would blind his vision and drag him into my own turbulent world.

- Mikhaela, I am traveling to Crete tomorrow, he finally said. I am attending the wedding of my best friend, Yannis. But I will not stay for long there, I will return back here to Malvasia. And from here I will be traveling to Venice.

» Unless, Mikhaela, you tell me that you want me to stay here with you. In this case I will not travel, I will stay and be with you, I will find work, but even if I don't, I have enough savings to stay the whole year in Malvasia without earning any money.

He was ready to sacrifice everything for me, to be with me. He was blind, he was a rabbit and I was the torch, he could see only one thing in his picture. Or maybe two. My eyes. The beggar revealed, a heartless man begging God to give him back what once belonged to him, what was now being denied, the unseen driver of all his actions.

I did not want to say anything, neither did I. I would love this to happen, but I was not sure if this could happen now. In my mind it was so distant; even though he was sitting next to me, I still felt him in Venice. He was ready for me, but I was not ready for him. It was obvious, I had his attention, but I was not worth it. I had failed so many times to be with him, to join him to Venice and he would every time forgive me, offering me one more chance. I wondered how many chances there would be in his basket.

I could imagine him walking alone in the streets of Venice. In such a romantic city he would observe everything in black and white, receiving no feelings from these unique surroundings. Being there he would think, not about Venice mirrored in the retina of his eyes, but about Malvasia mirrored in the corridors of his heart.

- Alessio, it's time to go, I said breaking my silence and my thoughts. We have been sitting here for a long time, do you mind taking a walk?

He nodded in agreement. As we rose to go, I noticed a strange black spot on his neck. I looked at it closely. It was a love bite. I pointed to it with my finger.

- What is that, I asked in an angry voice.
- Why do you want to know?

Why did I want to know? Because I loved him. Because I wanted him, because I felt that he had deceived me, because I felt jealous. But I was sleeping with another man. I even was living in the house of Elias by now. Why did I need to know? Why was I jealous over him? Why was I never jealous over Elias? Why did I think about him when I was emotional, why not about Elias? Why Alessio?

If his heart belonged to me, my mind belonged to him. My thoughts were surrounding him, I cared about him whether I was awake or asleep. My mind was wondering how he was keeping. After he had returned to Venice my mind had followed him there, my thoughts had gone there, and even my dreams would still go there. I felt as if my entire brain activity was being consumed there, in a distant somewhere with a man I had no future, ignoring the man next to me, Elias, who was giving me everything without asking anything in return. I needed to re-collect my thoughts and my mind. I needed to force them to return, but I felt forceless. I felt as if my entire stamina was consumed with this irrational thinking, day and night, always traveling,

traveling around, reaching nowhere, with no return, just circumventing the same distant and unseen place.

And brainless as I was, I was acting irrationally. I had quit my job, I had denounced Elias, I had left my future and when I did this, my mind was still swirling around, unable to bring me forward, unable to bring me either to Venice or back to Malvasia. It was just swirling around, a mindless heart just beating, doing nothing, only beating in dizziness, a senseless state of confusion. If he was blind, I was dumb. All my actions were senseless, no reasonable thought was backing them up, I was just acting, my mind was consumed with an idea that was not even properly thought-out. My mind was not working and my heart was governing my head, always expanding and retracting, making my actions expansive and retractive too. Just at the moment I was stepping forward, I was being pulled back. But I couldn't stay back. As soon as I found myself standing back, I was being pushed forward again, in a cyclical action that had no end. Everybody was puzzled by my actions, I had no reasoning anymore, no brain, my mind was not in my head anymore; it was lost inside a flooded city, taken by a heartless traveler.

I thought that even now I should not be sitting next to him. At this very moment I should have been home with Elias, I should not have lied to my life mate, I should have stayed back, but I was being pushed forward by a constantly beating heart.

I looked again at the neck of Alessio. Yes, it was a love bite. Even if my mind was not working anymore, my eyes could see and even my eyes alone could conclude that he had slept with another girl. He was handsome and he had girlfriends. There were enough girls wanting to hug him and keep him in their closed arms forever, but he always managed to escape.

- It is a love bite, Mikhaela, he finally confirmed.

I felt deceived, I wanted to slap him and at the same time I wanted to kiss him. But I had no right to do either. I just kept silent. I took his hand and walked with him to the inn where he was temporarily lodged.

- I have a letter to give to you, Mikhaela, he said. I wrote it this week, here in Malvasia, when I was thinking about you and you were absent.

He gave me the letter. It was written from his heart. His feelings cried out to me from the paper, I could understand that he was a man in love, that he wanted me to leave the room of comfort and enter the space of discovery, the darkness of the Unknown. Holding his hand, he wanted me to shut the door behind and leave my illusionary safety in order to move forward.

After reading his letter I looked at him and saw that he was preparing to begin talking again, but I wanted to hear no more talks. I wanted to feel him; I wanted to feel female again. I shut his mouth with my hand and I gave him a direct look into his eyes.

- I want to make love to you, Alessio.

And so we did. Passionate, hypnotized, entering the same state of ecstasy, when his heart was once detached, the same state where it goes back to the place it belongs. A state of present, where everything else disappears, with me inside, beating, just beating, being, just being, functioning in a continuous cycle, expanding and retracting, giving life to an otherwise lifeless body.

Why couldn't this moment last forever? I remembered him mentioning the vision of love. Yes, we were not ready to receive paradise yet, the river had long way yet to go to reach to the sea, but the water was already there, mixing with the saltwater of the vast ocean and though distant, I could already taste it. And I was sure he could taste it as well. I was drunk and he was drunk too. Without consuming a single sip of alcohol we had both lost the sense of time and memory. Looking at his naked body, my eyes were traveling into an undiscovered world, a world that appeared intimate, even though completely exposed. I wanted to drink him, faster, more passionately; with my hands I was squeezing his chest, searching for his face, running my fingers through his soft hair. The drink was him, his body, his soul, the expression on his face. I am not sure how much time I was lost in eternity. But I wanted to keep this memory with me forever.

Suddenly he made a pause. Looking me straight in the eyes he broke his silence:

- Do you want to have a baby with me?

I felt shaken. I was not that drunk. I looked back to him. He was serious. I knew it was now or never. And the expression in his eyes implied that he knew it as well. I hesitated.

- It is not yet the time, I finally said.

He nodded in agreement. I was now sober. The vision had ended. Like everything in this material world, this feeling also belonged to the past.

Looking at my chest, I saw a huge black mark. It was a love bite. I felt shocked. What would I say to Elias? I returned back to my fearful body. I just wanted to hide.

- Look at what you have done, I told him in an angry voice.

Did he do it on purpose? Did he want to make me feel conquered, defeated, disposable?

- I love you, Mikhaela, I always will. I am truly sorry.

I needed to go. I was already late; Elias would be waiting for me. Alessio was leaving for Crete the next day.

- If you make up your mind and want me to stay here with you, please write a small note and leave it at the keeper of this inn. I will read it when I come.

- I will, Alessio.

- I love you, Mikhaela.

- I know.

With these words I left his room. Walking outside I instinctively looked over my left shoulder. He was still there looking at me.

It was the last time I ever saw Alessio.

Part VI: The later years 1710 – 1720

VI.1 The awakening

The winter had gone and the fresh breeze of the spring had come to the silent hill of Malvasia. But that first day of the spring of 1710 I was not able to work in the office. I was not sure if it was my new job or if I had too many thoughts in my mind.

One thought was prevalent: It seemed to me that I was walking around the same point, again and again, in a vicious circle that was taking me through the same experiences over and over. As if I was bound on a long invisible rope that forced me to turn around an invisible distant center as I intended to walk forward, forcing me in fact to only walk around without me noticing it. But at a certain point and time I was sure that I was seeing the same situations, over and over, with the scenery always reminding me of something I had already seen. For one thing I was sure: I was not walking forward, I was just walking around.

At that moment I realized: I was walking in time like the indicators of a clock, always moving, never standing still, but always turning around. At that moment I was sure: Time was flying but not me. At some point in time life would again look just the same.

I was shocked. In fact it was not time that was moving. It was me. I was an indicator moving around the clock and time was just standing still. Like the dial of the clock, time did not go anywhere. The only moving part in this game was me in an illusion of walking forward, but in a fact of moving around. I felt helpless. I felt as if my life was a big pond and I was a fish trapped in it, never being able to go out regardless of my choice, just moving around it in an illusion that I was free to go wherever I wanted. Like the indicators of a clock, I could only move back and forth but still around.

I put my pencil down. Yes, I had a third choice too: I could deny this game as a whole and stop moving. I could stop time and make that clock not tick any more. I could show the world that time is an illusion: The faster you move, the faster it flies, and the slower you move, the more it slows down. Until you stop. And consider what I thought at that same moment:

What am I doing in life?

Silence followed the question of Mikhaela. It should not have been more than two seconds, but in that silence her entire life passed in front of her eyes in a flash. She realized what had just happened: An entire life of twenty two years was experienced and revived in her mind in just two single seconds. Time is an illusion. As life was passing in front of her, time stopped and Alessio came into her mind. She had once posed him exactly the same question.

- Alessio, what am I doing in life? I sometimes feel that my life is pointless, but I still continue. I am not sure if I continue out of my own will or out of habit. Can I really do something? Is there something I should be doing?

Alessio remained silent. I don't know if he did this to consider his answer or to force me to contemplate my question.

- Nothing, he replied after some time that seemed long to me. There is nothing that you should be doing. In fact, anything you do, the outcome will sooner or later be the same. Thus you can do anything you want.

- But why do I live then? Am I here just to see a theatrical act, where everything is predefined by an unseen director?

- Nothing is predefined, he replied with a straight tone in his voice. You are the creator of your own destiny. What I just told you is that you can do anything you want. The important part of this sentence does not lie in "anything" but in "you want". And what you really want defines who you really are. In fact I will never tell you what you should do. But I will tell you what you should be, in fact what you can only be. You can only be you. Thus you should strive to be you. You cannot be anything else, at least not in the long run, and the only way to be you is to accomplish what you really want.

Somehow I felt inside that he was right, even though by using my logic I could not understand what he meant. But how could I not be me?

- How can I be what I am not? I am me! It's me that you have in front of you, I replied smiling.

- Not always. You are only you if you seek and incarnate the truth. And you do have the option not to be true. You are only truly you, if you think, speak, and act nothing more and nothing less than the Truth. Only then can you be Truth itself. Only then you are you.

In fact I was never me! I had lived my entire life without being me. What was I then? What was I doing in life? This question was bound to change my life.

- I will tell you why you have never been you.

This man was reading my mind. I felt I could not hide from him.

- It is because of two reasons: The price and the consequence. To incarnate who you really are and to accomplish what you really want, you have to be ready to pay the price in advance and to accept the consequences in return.

» What you really want never comes without a price. This means you always have to choose it among alternatives; decide. In addition, you either already possess the full amount of this price or you readily have a way to acquire it. In both cases the amount can be as high as everything you possess or can acquire. And either the full amount or the way to acquire it is right in front of you, there is never the need to wait. This is a fundamental law of the Universe: You will always have the means to acquire what you really want right in front of you at any given time.

» However sometimes you are trying to acquire the means that will lead you to what you really want, which makes you to inevitably change direction: You are not looking any more towards the goal, but towards the means to get it. You replace the goal with the intermediary. But soon you will find that the more you are trying to reach the intermediary, the further it will go away from you maintaining its equal distance, thus making it impossible for you to actually grab it and move beyond it.

» You can only acquire what you really want and God reserves the right to decide by what means you will get it. In this always remember: What is important is what you really want. If what you currently chase is just helping you to reach another wish, go right upfront for that wish. Be open and look around you for the means to it, since now you know: The means for what you really want have already been given to you; they are there even if you don't see them or can't relate them to your ultimate goal. Because having the means is the only way to discover what you really want. And this is the only way to discover what you really are. You have to accomplish what you really want and be what you really are. This is the only reason for your existence on this planet.

His eyes were shining again. I didn't know if I had a human in front of me or some kind of spirit.

- God has always given you the means to reach your wishes. You are able to pay the price right now. But it may be that you have to devote your entire being for it; it may be that you have just enough to pay this price.

» Pay it, Mikhaela.

I was scared. I felt as though I was having an illusion, his eyes were fixed firmly on me and I thought that he could vanish into thin air at any moment.

- Pay it, for this is the only way to incarnate what you really want, thus incarnating yourself, incarnating Truth, incarnating God. And once you pay it and you are there you will be able to think: Was this what I really wanted? And then you will get the answer. And from there you will ask again what you really want, in an ever-evolving process of creation. And you will get the answer along with its price. And remember the law of the Universe: You will always have the means to accomplish what you really want, even if this is everything you have. And from there you move on. Forward and not around.

He then kept silent. The waves were splashing into the high rocks of Malvasia. It was a magnificent evening with him, I was living in a dream. Someday I would wake myself up. Who can stand living in a dream? Who can tolerate the fear of waking up? Maybe waking up is less painful than living in the fear of it.

- And the second barrier apart from the price is the consequence. In fact consequence has no meaning on its own. The meaning of it lies in the fear of it; in the fear that by doing what you really want, you will have to face the consequences.

» There are four principal consequences that you will need to accept in the quest for your dream. All four consequences are expressed in fear: Permanence, instability, resentment and isolation.

It seemed that the number four was some kind of sacred number. The travelers from the east were saying that four in the Chinese language means death. The number that leads to an end. A sacred number, the passage to a new beginning.

- Permanence, he interrupted my thoughts, is the fear of not being able to return to where you were before. Most people are used not to going forward but to always going around, like the indicators of a clock, to always having to face the same problems, because these are familiar to them; people are afraid of new problems, new situations. In order to be what you really want, you have to overcome the fear of permanently losing the known to enter the world of the unknown. Mikhaela, you can only stop moving around once you close that door behind you.

Indeed I was never closing any doors, unless they were closing by themselves. He had once told me that the female power is by nature unable to close and open doors, but I had also understood that every human being, regardless of gender, possesses both powers inside, male and female, since both powers are needed to face the Divine.

- Instability, he continued, results from the impermanence that you will face after closing that door behind you. In fact the fear of impermanence combined with the fear of permanence is the reason that fear is irrational altogether. You fear losing a stable illusion that is bound to finish and enter an unstable reality that is bound to last. But reality lies in the dream and living it has no fear. The irrational state of fear is felt whenever you reside in the material world and believe that it remains permanent, whenever you are away from Love. In fact your fear is that you will lose what you have always wanted, that you will lose your dream. The dream that you don't yet have.

That was true. This was my thought just now. I felt the fear of losing this dream with him even more.

- In fact the only reason for losing what you have is that this is not what you really want. But this "losing it" will be your divine choice in order to take a path that will lead you towards what you really want. Thus instability is not to be feared, it is to be blessed and it makes the first consequence, the fear of permanence, illusionary. In fact, as you will see, all four consequences are illusionary, as is fear altogether.

» And along with this, I will convey to you one thing: You are not capable of losing what you really want, for this would mean that you would be capable of being what you are not. In the framework of time you are allowed to lose it, but only for a certain period. And this period shall be governed by suffering. This is another law of the Universe: Being what you are not, you can only suffer. In your religion, this is called hell.

I thought he was Christian too.

- I am nothing, Mikhaela, how can I be a Christian? But yes, I believe in the words of Jesus Christ.

I didn't need to talk in order to communicate with him. I just had to accept this as a fact.

- Resentment is the fear that you will feel sorry for your actions while trying to accomplish what you really want. And in fact I will tell you from now that you will indeed feel sorry. You might need to apologize to yourself that you have got in trouble, that you have chosen a path that was not the best one. In fact you might have caused a lot of consequences for others too; your actions were not perfect. But this is natural, you are not meant to be perfect, but you are meant to head towards perfection. And in your path towards it, you will make many mistakes for which you will have to apologize. Unconditional apology is the tool that you have been given to combat resentment, to move forward. Once you truly apologize without any excuses, you stop suffering immediately. Suffering is growing the more you avoid apology, it is climaxing when you try to apologize, and it immediately vanishes after the act, along with your ego.

» And the fourth consequence is isolation, the fear of losing the compassion of others, which is created by your compassion to them. And I will tell you one important thing about that: If anyone cannot follow you to what you really are and gets negative feelings out of your pursuit of what you really want, then this person is not for you. You have to direct yourself away from these people, even from family, friends and societies, if they appraise you for what you are not. In fact appraisal is a jail: It subconsciously puts you in the state of trying to prove that you are worth it, even if this means sacrificing what you really want and who you really are. Thus this is my advice to you: Deny appraisals. Give those gifts back to their donors. You need no appraisals, the only thing you need is blessing, the blessing of God.

He was right. I was driven by appraisals, by the need to receive them on the one side, and on the other side by the need to prove that I am worthy of the ones I receive. How could I do what I really wanted? What I wanted was rarely followed by appraisal.

- Mikhaela, he said, you need to pay the price and accept the consequences. This is the only way to be what you really want, to find out who you really are. Many times people stay in front of the mountain, trying to imagine what it would feel like standing on its top. But this is not possible, for this would oppose the very meaning of the experience of life: To experience climbing it.

» You have to climb the mountain of Olympus to get the wisdom of Athena, the power of Zeus, the beauty of Aphrodite, the communication skills of Hermes. And these virtues will not be given to you at the top. They will come to you whilst climbing. The beauty of life lies in the journey.

But for me life was not beautiful, it was challenging and unfair. I knew he would guess my thoughts.

- Life is not beautiful at the bottom. At the bottom you are only dreaming of the top. To go for your dream, this makes life beautiful. And only at the top of the mountain will you be able to recognize if it is Olympus. If from the top you see any higher mountain in the horizon, then you are not standing on Olympus. Olympus is the highest mountain, always covered by the clouds of fear and it is the house of the twelve Gods, the virtues of Divinity.

» Once you reach what you think you want, only then will you be able to see the next step of what you really want. But you will gain virtues: The virtues are not gained only while climbing Olympus. All mountains are important. Olympus is the last mountain you will climb.

» Staying at the mountain's feet, you will only turn around it, trying to guess how it would feel at the top, without ever putting your foot on it. If you don't target only perfection, never will you reach it. You will be turning in time like the indicators of a clock, around and around, always trying to imagine what it would be like not to be inside the clock. You will manage to be the indicator when you are meant to be the clock. But this can happen only for a limited period. A helpless period of suffering. You don't have the ability to turn forever. The time will come for the clock to stop, for you are meant to be the Divine. You are meant to one day reach the top of Olympus and contemplate the skies. You can only delay it. No matter how many barriers you put inside a river, no matter if you divert it to pass through villages and lakes, the water will ultimately flow into the sea. You can only delay it.

I can only delay it, I was repeating inside myself. I can only delay it, here in front of my desk, thinking about his words, knowing that he is in Venice, away from me and next to me at the same time, I can only delay it, with my desk full of papers needed to be processed today and me incapable of doing anything.

And then I realized how I could only delay it: By accepting compromises. By being satisfied with anything less than perfection. By compromising, by faking that I am content with the imperfect, by not being willing to pay the price of the Divine, judging the price to be too high for something that I really wanted, but maybe was not my ultimate dream, without my knowing the answer, since I had never tried it. My ultimate dream could be seen only from the top of the mountain, not from its feet.

Thus by accepting compromises, by not striving for the absolute and the perfect, here I was again at the same point, the clock again showed twelve with me getting prepared to go into the next round, trying to fool myself that I would get something new, trying to fool myself that I have not yet understood that I am moving around, looking at God and asking Him where to go, what is my next step, watching Him yelling at me from the top of Olympus with all His power and all the air in His lungs, asking me for only one thing:

To come.

And Peter said: "If it is you my Lord, order me to come to you". And Jesus said: "Come". Then Peter stepped off the boat and started walking on the water. But the wind was strong and fear penetrated him. Suddenly he started sinking in the water, asking for His help. Jesus came closer and giving him His hand He asked: "Where is your faith Peter? What made you hesitate?"

I realized: I had gone too many times around the mountain. Until now compromise was my entire life. Until now I was the incarnation of fear not of Love. Until now I only gazed at the mountain, smelling its wonderful air, recognizing my distant dream at the top. Until now I was looking at the price first, and only then at the product. Until now I would try to walk around the consequence, without really facing it. Until now my head was bending down in front of the tall mountain. Until now I was weak.

But only until today.

This colorful, sunny first day of the spring of 1710 – seemingly just another normal day in office – would give inside me a birth. The birth of my Self. My birthday was shifted once and for all from the winter to the spring. Today I decided to devote my life to Him. I was calling Him Love, the priests' God, Alessio was calling Him the Truth. I also had a name for my dream. Just by standing alone in the office, staring at that endless pile of papers, I made the first step in my new life: I stopped the indicators of the clock. I stared at the mountain with my eyes wide open, ready to climb it and pay the price, combat the consequence with all my force, driven by His Force, accepting that I was nothing. I found the answer to my question posed only minutes ago:

What am I doing in life?

And that was the first answer I had found in a life where I had previously always only been seeking. In the divine combination of four, wisdom, concentration, faith and patience, I began finding. Concentration was the answer. Wisdom was hidden inside me, when I was only seeking for it outside, in the words of Alessio and the advice of my parents. Faith was the only thing left now to save me. And patience was what I could not avoid. At their junction, on the sacred number of four, today she died. And with her death, the death of the Other, the empty person I was until now, a new Self was born: Me. Devoted, mature, divine. The holy moment of the awakening. The resurrection of the dead. The sacred second coming that my church awaits from the skies. I finally lived it, in this life, on earth.

I was finally alive.

VI.2 The voice of Truth

The days that followed my awakening were anything other than tranquil. Questions were surfacing inside me and I was not trying to suppress them anymore. As if a cemetery full of questions was waking up, tomb by tomb, at an ever increasing speed, with the stones exploding from the soil that had kept my questions buried all this time. As if everything that was standing still suddenly wanted to move and to cheer, the gravestones, the crosses, the trees, everything in this graveyard wanted to stand up and join the uprising.

Instinctively I tried to find Alessio. Tears of happiness came to my eyes. The resurrection of the dead. A biblical promise, experienced. I was lucky; I was among the chosen ones. In an instant I was able to understand all his words. Words I remembered from time to time, knowing they were correct, but not knowing why. These words, their reasons and the reasons behind the reasons were being revealed to me, the book of Truth was now open, right in front of my eyes. The Egyptian key of life, the ankh, the key that could open all doors; I had it in my hands. Along with the questions I was recognizing the answers. His words, well buried in my mind, were starting to make absolute sense, I could understand their meaning, the reasoning behind them, I could even reproduce them, enhance them, derive my own words from them. I realized that the answers were buried in this same cemetery, just underneath my questions. I could not see that until now I had just not been digging deep enough beyond my questions. I could understand the answer to the philosophic question of Socrates: There is only one Truth.

Alessio's voice was often crossing my mind, making me wonder if this man had just been a voice in a dream, a spirit, or someone who really existed, someone who really came inside me to discover my most intimate substance. How could I ever run away from him? The moment of the Lucifer. I was once weak. But not anymore. I remembered the time he came from Venice to Malvasia only in order to see me. I was once blaming Elias for not allowing myself to take the opportunity and surrender. But now I was realizing that Elias was innocent. I was the only one to be blamed for everything that had ever happened to me, even for everything that would happen to me from now onwards and until I was resting beneath the earth; I was the only one responsible. Yes it was not Elias' fault, it was mine. Or to put it correctly: The Other's. Now I fully understood the meaning of the Other. A ghost inside me that was ruling my life. But now the Other had gone, along with its fears and indecisiveness. My life was now in my hands. Together with the realization of the Other, the Other had gone. Of course. The Other was never really there. How can a ghost be? I could feel that I was free, the Other had vanished.

And so had Elias from my heart. In fact, I had never let Elias penetrate my heart. My heart was like a labyrinth, well designed to prevent anyone from conquering it. The ones who had tried were lost inside it; they were kept inside it forever, inside a structure well built, they were unable to find the single way out. Even Elias was lost in this complex construction. Even myself. But not Alessio. Alessio was the only one able to walk through it using the divine thread of Ariadne, killing the Minotaur in its core. The Other. Yes the ancient Greeks were not writing fiction. With their myths they were describing true stories. And empty as it was, the labyrinth of my heart was now open and fearless.

I wanted to write to Alessio. Now that I was finally able to put my feelings on paper I did not even know if this paper would be read. I did not even know if he was still in Venice. I wanted him back. And now my heart was open, I was able to receive him. And as a flash I heard his voice inside my head:

"Mikhaela, there is no way back, the only possible way is forth."

How can it be? I started hearing voices. That was dangerous. In Venice the women who were hearing voices in their head were tried for witchcraft by the Inquisition and were sometimes burnt alive. Was I a witch?

"You are not a witch, Mikhaela. Hearing the voice of the Truth in your head is absolutely normal. It is a gift you receive with the awakening. Do you remember that I was able to hear your voice in my head too? Do you remember that I was able to hear your thoughts? Once you drink from the water of Truth, there is nothing hidden. The ankh reveals and opens all doors."

Of course I remember. With him I never needed to talk. He could do it better on my behalf, just grabbing the thoughts directly from my mind. It was his profession.

"Now this shall be your profession too."

I could not believe that I was talking to myself in my silent thoughts. But I was sure this was not me talking. I was sure it was his voice. Even though not coming through my ears, his words sounded the same. I realized what he was doing when he was silently looking into my eyes before starting to talk. He was tuning into my thoughts, he was carefully listening to what I had to say.

But now he was gone. He could not hear my thoughts anymore, guide me in my actions. After he had left from his short trip to Malvasia I had no news from him. He had escaped from the labyrinth, destroying it at the same time. The labyrinth was my heart. My heart was now empty.

"That was exactly my role in your life, Mikhaela. To kill the beast and leave your heart empty, empty from ghosts and preoccupations, empty from fear, a fertile ground for love to grow. You don't need me anymore. My mission is complete."

The emptiness was killing me. A whole cemetery was dancing in front of my eyes and I was feeling empty. Just looking at it, wondering how the gravestones could move, how the skeletons could seem alive.

"Let the graves go, Mikhaela. A beautiful garden will then flourish in this soil. And most important: Plants grow by themselves. You just need to wait and contemplate, exert faith and patience. It is your time of spring. Do nothing, just be. Isn't God magnificent?"

He is not. God left the garden empty, but He left me with a taste of him: Alessio. How would I stand the image of this empty yard? How would I wait for it to fill up with something? I did not want anything to grow. I only wanted the one with whom I was in love to come. I was in love with Alessio.

"You are in love, Mikhaela. You just are. It is a state of Being, it is who you really are. And the whole world is there to mirror your emotions, to create an illusionary subject and an illusionary object, to let you experience yourself through objects in front of you. You are in love. Nothing more and nothing less. You just are."

- I am in love with you.

"Who am I?"

- Who are you?

I was going crazy. Who was this voice in my head? Who was the object of my communication, the object of my love?

"You yourself. It always is, it only can be. Most people attach their state of being to an object, to somebody, another human, a pet, a tree. Being in love, being angry, being frustrated. But don't you see the meaning of the syntax? It's being. Then, if they are in love they follow their object and if they are frustrated they avoid it, hoping that their state of love would maintain or the state of frustration would vanish. Until they discover that they remain frustrated long after their object is gone or that they are still in love long after its departure. Like you now. How can you be in love with somebody after he is gone? He is a memory, he is not there now, but your memory and your thoughts are there now. You are in love. You are angry. You are frustrated. You may attach your being to anyone you want, but in this game it is only you. You are being reflected."

I wanted to cry even with his voice in my head. For sure this was him in my mind.

"It reminds me of the iconoclasts of Byzantium. They would discover God through an object, such as a holy icon or a cross, and then they would attach the Deity to it. They would literally start loving the object. Even in Venice the St Mark's Basilica was founded when Venetian merchants stole the relics of Mark the Evangelist from Alexandria and placed them inside the newly built church. The people tend to simply replace God with an object, an object reminding them of the Deity, bringing their minds closer to it. And it is true: This object really propagated their state of Being, it caused them to cry or see a vision or even heal. And then they worship the object. There are so many objects even now around the world, Mikhaela: Caves of saints and prophets, images found on mountains or the sea, holy places where the water that runs is considered holy."

"That is all so fictitious, Mikhaela. An object is just a representation, nothing more. The only object is the subject itself. You are mirroring your state of Being inside other objects. You are mirroring love to me."

I was not in love with myself. I was in love with him. And I missed him. I wanted him.

"You just are in love. And you just miss. You just want. All that you can be is this only: Be. When you pray to God, try to remove the objects, just leave the subjects in your words. How does it sound like?"

"I woke up the power of love inside you. You have experienced me and this experience was powerful enough to make you decide to enter and go through your labyrinth, thus destroying its fearful essence. In this process you destroyed the Other, hiding inside this labyrinth, making it seem impossible to enter. You were left with emptiness. Because this is what you really are. Inside nothing is everything. You have experienced me and ever since you have wanted me. But try replacing the objects in this sentence with the subject. In reality you have experienced yourself."

"You think I am gone and your mind tries to follow me. You think you have fallen from paradise and you want to go back, you want to return, you want to go home, you want to live what you now see as a dream, wondering if you ever lived it. Remember the vision of love, the vision of paradise. You did live it. You think that I am gone and you try to find me in the past, because in the past I was there. But I am not there anymore. Now the past is an illusion. It exists as much as a dream exists, both residing only in your mind. You are hunting the object, trying to reach me and you keep on hunting, realizing that in the object I do not exist anymore, not as I existed before. You are not willing to understand that the object is empty. If you stop hunting the object, you will see that I am here, right now, with you."

- You are in Venice.

"I am here."

- Who are you?

"I am the Divine."

- Alessio, are you God?

"I am you."

And that was my first conversation with God. An intimate conversation with myself in the voice of Alessio. I understood how the prophets were able to hear God's voice. I understood the difference between the object and the subject: Absolutely none. I understood why the world was said to be just a reflection, a reflection of one's self. I understood what was the difference between the material object and the Being, the empty and the whole, the meaning of the emptiness of everything in the material world.

I was in love. And this was a state of Being. And I knew that I had a choice: To either hunt the object like the iconoclasts or continue to be in love. The object was long gone, but the result was there. Everybody was saying that I had changed. But I had not. I was only born, not reborn.

The biblical resurrection of the dead. I could even understand the meaning of the bible now. Amazing.

I knew that I would never see Alessio again in my life. But his voice was in my head. In fact it was my own voice. The voice of God. Now I could write poems, paint, sing, play music, create using the only creating power there is: Love. The one that created me. The one creating my thoughts. Alessio. The one talking to me. God. Even Alessio was saying: "I am not saying anything on my own. I am just reading and reproducing your thoughts. You have created all this, not me. You are the author, I am the hand. I am nothing more than the bell tower of the cathedral. You are the one ringing the bells."

And even if I would never see Alessio again, He was inside me. He was my thoughts. He was me, my Being, not the object, not the man. Alessio was not Alessio.

But even so, I would be happy if my letters were to reach him one day. If only he knew that it was he who had given birth to what I am now.

"I know it, Mikhaela. I knew it right from the start, from the first time I looked into your eyes and you were instructing me of my mission. I even told that to you when you were unable to understand me, when you were only listening to me without understanding, when you were the Other."

- I love you.

"Now I know you do. I love you too."

VI.3 The boomerang revealed

The days that followed were revealing. I felt the need to escape, escape from my parents, from my sisters, from Elias, from everything and everybody in my social life. I felt the need to be alone. But this time I knew what I really wanted. I wanted to stay away from the Other. In my loneliness I wanted to discover myself, my real self, the one who had been waiting for such a long time, hidden behind an endless doing, a little child who had no time to grow up, overruled by a weird creature: The Other.

In my awakening a child woke up inside me and her only memories were in her childhood. She had stayed there, intact, as if put on ice, where everything is preserved and remains fresh after being unfrozen. I remembered the dreams of this lovely child. Lovely. It was the first time I had used this word when relating to myself, yes this child was lovely. Her dreams still the same. To travel, to experience, to love and be loved. And no, it was not a prince on a white horse. It was a common man, a man who could make her travel, travel in love, travel inside herself and around. Maybe a man like Alessio, but a man who would stay, in fact not a man at all, a boy, a childhood love, a boy who could watch with her the moon reflected in the sea and remain silent.

The child began talking to me. She was laughing, happy that she had opened her eyes again, loving me instead of hating me for covering her up for so long, replacing her with an ugly creature, the Other. She began talking to me about her dreams. Her wish was to travel to Sparta and stay for some time there with her grandmother. The child told me that her days were ending and I needed to tell her that I loved her and see her smiling, nothing else. This little girl, this child was wise. She could predict the future, sense the feelings of the people, know who was dangerous and who was to be trusted, take me hand in hand and lead me into the path of pleasure.

I asked for her name. Her name was Mikhaela. Of course, she was me. The forgotten me. She instructed me to go and sit by the sea. And so I did.

It was a magnificent night. The full moon was shining over Malvasia, reflected on the water, spreading a tranquil white light on the walls of the city. I sat at her favorite edge, near the lighthouse. It was at the same edge where I had shared my dreams with Alessio. I wondered how he was doing. I received the feeling that he was safe. Mikhaela was talking to me through feelings.

I felt happiness with this new presence in my life. I felt that with her I was safe, I had dreams and I could feel tranquil. Staying alone I would not feel lonely. My life had changed and the most important change was that my dreams had come back. My childhood dreams, remembered. But now I was not a child anymore. I knew that I could go for them. And even if I might not fully realize them, they would flow me into their journey, a journey where Mikhaela and me would walk hand in hand, laughing, in need of nobody, in fear of nothing. Alessio was describing this as the path of love, a path lead by a dream, a journey where striving was creating energy, the energy that keeps the whole universe in motion.

And my dream was not to copy documents, hoping for a better future. I decided to abandon what I had been doing since I finished school. My dream was not to be criticized for my wishes and actions. I decided to stay away from the friends of the Other, even if that meant staying alone. Because I knew that with little Mikhaela by my side, I would never feel lonely. In an instant I took the bravest decision of my life. To empty. To quit what I was doing, to destroy the castle in the sand that the Other had been building for so long, constantly being washed away by the waves, putting me in an effort of continuous reconstruction. I needed no castles. There was no need to maintain walls against the sea; my place was on the sea not on the shore.

With Mikhaela by my side I felt strong, with her I could travel the world. Mikhaela advised me to go away from Malvasia. Times would change and a sudden change would soon take place on this small piece of land. I realized how silly I had been all this time. It was so easy to go to Venice, so many boats were leaving for the empire's capital, even Alessio had arranged my trip there, the dream had always been hunting me, but I had been hiding from it, always refusing to accept it. The walls of the castle in the sand had no gates, they were keeping me and my sea apart. But the castle was now gone and I could see how beautiful I was feeling outside and how terrible I had been feeling inside.

I realized the importance of the school of sorrow. The result was there, Mikhaela awake, right by my side. I had just graduated and yes, Jeremias was right, only now I could understand its real value. I gained the ability to decide. To where did this fearful young lady go, the one who was never able to choose, who was always accepting what an unseen wise God was supposedly bringing to her? I needed to let Elias and my parents know about my decisions. I would go on a one way trip with an uncertain return, a journey inside myself, a trip inside a forgotten Mikhaela frozen inside a childhood. I knew that everybody would be sad, but one day I would come back, and they would need to face somebody else, a grown up Mikhaela, a mature child inside the body of a woman.

I did not want Elias to wait for me. I needed time alone and alone meant away from him as well. I wanted to devote myself to Mikhaela, I wanted to meet Alessio, but not in order to be with him. I only wanted to thank him. I wanted to thank him for colliding with me, making me discover that I was not a young lady in fear. That was the Other. I was a child, a mature child with dreams, inside the body of a woman, not a young lady any more.

With the boomerang in my hands, I realized its holy purpose. The boomerang is a lethal weapon. Its purpose is not to be thrown away in the air in order to renounce it.

From the air it will always return. Its purpose is to separate and kill, to challenge, to reveal and destroy the fake, uncover the covered on its return journey. The boomerang is the weapon of God against the Evil, of Love against the Fear, of Mikhaela against the Other. It is the lethal weapon of decision, the weapon of the final judgment of the Apocalypse, the weapon that separates the Truth from the Untruth. The weapon that killed the Other.

I decided to keep the boomerang with me. This bent piece of wood from now on would keep me safe, protect me from the fake, it was my weapon, a weapon that only the real can avoid. Because the real is a sphere, having an all-rounded vision and attentiveness. Because the unreal is a square, having only a directional vision. And because the boomerang always hits from the back, thus staying unnoticed by the unreal that is too busy looking only towards the front.

By now I had understood the purpose of Alessio in my life. He came to give me this lethal weapon, let me wound and kill myself with it, in fact killing the Other, revealing the true Mikhaela and making me devote my life to pay it forward, to help people fight against their untruths, go for their dreams, be children without shame. In my interaction with Alessio I understood what I had already read in the Bible: That the Truth always wins in the end, it is not a happy ending, it is the fate of every journey, the fate of humanity, the only thing that can happen, the predicted and natural result of the end of the world. In my interaction with Alessio, the Other collided with the Truth and it broke, the only possible result from the collision of the rock against the glass, of love against fear, God against the Evil, Truth against the Untruth, Mikhaela against the Other.

Yes, now I was sure. The end of the world would be the same as every other ending: Happy. Life was a big school, a school of sorrow, a dark tunnel and life would end once the lesson was learned or it would not end at all. I now understood why confused, seemingly bad people live longer, staying in the school of sorrow, unwilling to graduate. And with it, I did understand why another birth, another chance, a reincarnation is awaiting all the non-graduates, a non-forgotten karma awaiting the ones still not having incarnated the Truth.

Having made a decision to follow my dream, I got up to go home. A new journey was waiting for me, a journey for my dream, this time a path of pleasure, the only possible subsequent of the school of sorrow. I had decided to empty myself. I had decided to stay apart from the others in order to discover myself. I had decided to make a one way trip in my life, a trip that did not have a return because going back is never a choice. I had decided to move to Venice.

I had long lost Alessio, but in reality I had found him inside myself. He was there to accompany me for my entire life, love is indeed eternal and my other half, him, was residing inside me.

As I got up to go, Mikhaela was smiling. This little lovely child was confirming with a smile that my thoughts were true.

VI.4 The End

- Today I will convey to you the most precious experience of my journey, I said to my curious listeners.

The classroom was full of eyes, wide open, as if they wanted to hear the voice of Mikhaela using their retina as a tympanic membrane. Even the parents of the children had come, curious to see why this new teacher was so beloved among the school kids. The sun was rising over the sunken city.

- Avoid the noise.

» The noise resides in your ears, in your eyes, in your hands, in your mind, a gift coming from your surroundings, ending up inside your own body. In the walk of life keep yourself clean and select the quiet place for your residence.

» The world was quiet when it was given to you. Anything breaking the silence of earth is singing. Listen to the birds and the cicadas, look at the flowers and the clouds; everything around you is either singing or remaining silent. When you open your mouth, do it only to sing.

» Avoid the busy harbor, because the noise encloses the meaning of the Lucifer. The Lucifer does not reside underneath the earth, neither does God reside in the skies. The Lucifer resides in the noise and God resides in silence. And the noise is there to blind you, to confuse you, to delay you, to prevent you from hearing the song of silence.

» And in the silence listen to your feelings. It is God speaking through feelings. Listen to your pain, because pain tells you to stop, to empty, to cease, to let die, to not be, to accept becoming as the only alternative. And listen to your happiness. It is God telling you to continue. God talking through pain and joy, both to be heard and respected, both arising only in the moment of silence.

Silence followed. Mikhaela kept the smile on her face. The eyes of the audience were still wide open, as if those eyes had just woken up from a deep sleep. The silence continued. One by one people started rising from their chairs. With their eyes still wet they were hugging

Mikhaela tightly and then heading for the exit. But not a single word was said to obstruct this silence.

I left the school last, together with a young boy who didn't want to let me go. A sunny Sunday was beginning and I decided to take a walk around the canals. Hand in hand with the boy I started walking, thinking of my romantic dream to walk these canals together with Alessio, feeling complete. I was feeling complete now. A gondola cruised by our side. What a beautiful and silent day!

I thought about my days in Malvasia. Through the dark tunnel comes the light, I thought. I had heard about the dark tunnel from Alessio. But I was now in the light, the light coming from inside, lighting not only myself but all those people who had sacrificed their early Sunday sleep to come and listen to me. The boy turned his head towards me and gave me a look that was innocently questioning. Was he guessing my thoughts?

By now I had understood Alessio saying: "I am not telling you anything on my own. I am just reproducing what your thoughts are telling to my mind. The creator of whatever I am saying is you". I blessed this young man for coming into my life and mirroring myself in front of me, waking up the love inside me, the love that was springing out of the silence.

I gave a smile back to the boy. Yes, communication is not verbal. When God divided the language in Babylonia, He did it because we were misusing the words, using them only to create noise. He thus directed us to seek and find the universal language of love, the non-verbal language that goes beyond the words and can convey all meanings with melody and silence.

Heading towards the Grand Canal, I saw two gondolas crossing in the distance. Approaching each other, the gondoliers held their singing and passing by each other, they made a gesture of greeting before continuing in opposite direction. What a gentle form of communication, I thought.

Even singing can produce noise if not performed in harmony.

Crossing the Rialto bridge, I stopped in front of a sign. It read: "One way". I remembered my dream. Just as Jeremias had foretold, it had all come true. I wondered if he was keeping well. By the end of 1715 Malvasia along with the entire region of Morea was reconquered by the Ottomans. The Orthodox religion was banned and many monks were forced to leave from their monasteries and chapels. Many houses in Malvasia were destroyed by the war and I was among the lucky ones to have already left the town.

I figured out what Malvasia was for me: It was my driver, my initiative to discover myself and my virtues, discover that I was not destined to be copying government documents forever; this was just a step in the long ladder I was climbing. Because there is really no forever. We really do not have the choice to be, to remain on one single step, denying to move on. I figured out that Venice was bound as well to be only a single step for me, that it too one day might be destroyed. Whatever comes, goes and since I came to Venice, I would have to go too. But what remains is silence. What remained in my mind was the singing voice of Alessio speaking out the singing voice of my revealing self, transmitted through the attractive lips of a handsome body, making me fall in love with him, and finally with myself.

And thus I realized the importance of Alessio for me. He came to Malvasia to kill me. He came to indulge me to follow him into the dark tunnel and lock the door behind me, make me experience that the past is not a choice and then leave me in the darkness, standing on a passage of my labyrinth of life, looking not for a mansion but for the light.

And after my desperation, after I stopped seeking, I started finding and the light came from within. My body started growing, expanding more and more, the outer shell stretching, until one day it exploded and the soul residing in it, me, came to see the light, wide awake.

I remembered the picture of the Archangel in the chapel of Jeremias. The head of all angels had not killed the body of the greedy in a fight against him. The Greedy had killed himself, unable to bear his untrue existence, thus revealing the light to his innermost holy soul. And the Archangel was holding the soul in his left hand, standing on the dead body.

I realized: For me, Alessio was an angel.

And just as Jeremias had said, I was protected by the Archangel himself, such a significant value, revealed subconsciously by my name.

After the war in Malvasia, I decided to stay in Venice and become a teacher. I loved children and teaching quickly became my passion. I thought that even if one misses a hundred opportunities, there are a million ways for the river to flow into the sea.

And here I was in Venice, forced out of Malvasia, walking together with a wonderful child, my child, on the streets of Venice, looking at the gondolas, listening to the songs of gondoliers, feeling happy. Happy that I had died, happy that I was born, happy that I followed my dream, happy that I myself found the courage to be transmitting now, with these very words, to you as my audience the silence of the light and happy to be teaching from my own experience the universal truth that I had once heard:

That every ending can only be happy.

THE END

Printed in Great Britain
by Amazon